THE CHAMPION

GLEN ROBINSON

Prevail Publications
www.prevailpublications.com

Cover design by Matthew B. Robinson

Cover photography by Mindy Robinson

ISBN: 1484841891
ISBN-13: 978-1484841891

ACKNOWLEDGMENTS

A project as large and complex as this series doesn't happen in a vacuum. The six years it took to write this series would have been wasted without the valuable input from myriad readers and editors. My profuse thanks go to:

My fellow editors and colleagues Tim Lale and David Jarnes.

The many readers who added their comments through the short story and novel phases.

The tireless input from The Rough Writers, especially Edward Cheever II and Kathy Douglas. Thanks, guys.

My loving wife, Shelly, who after all these years remains an inspiration to me.

And finally, as always, I thank my Lord and Savior Jesus Christ for his infinite wisdom, patience and love. I never want to lose sight of what's important.

CONTENTS

"The greatest trick the Devil ever did
was convincing the world that he didn't exist."
—Keyser Soze, *The Usual Suspects*

Be sober, be watchful: your adversary the devil,
as a roaring lion, walketh about,
seeking whom he may devour.
—I Peter 5:8

PROLOGUE: THE DEVIL'S PLAN

It might have been the boardroom of any modern high rise, complete with a walnut table, swivel chairs, and an impressive view of the cityscape. But it wasn't located in any city on earth, there were no doors to enter the room, and the view was of a historical event that many would consider the turning point in earth's history.

This room was located in the spiritual realm, a dimension that exists parallel to the physical plane that mortals call The Universe. And even though the one at the end of the table looked like he would be at home in front of any modern board meeting, he was not human. When one looked at the other three beings in the room, that became obvious.

"Impressive," a woman/being said, as she stood by the large windows looking down on the spectacle before them. "No, that's not the word. Flawless. His plan was flawless." The four of them watched as four Roman soldiers collapsed beneath the crush of light flowing from two beings that descended from the sky. One stood surveying the scene, while the other walked quickly over to a large boulder that covered the entrance to a cave. The angel rolled away the boulder and entered the cave. A moment later, the angel reappeared. With him was a man—no, a God—who reflected the light that the other two beings put off.

"Shut it," the Chairman at the end of the table said. "I've seen enough. We've all seen enough." In response, the panorama disappeared and the wall became just another wall.

The woman turned away and faced the other three. "You know, it's just not fair. He took on mortal form, He became a man, and He died as all men do. They why didn't He stay dead?"

"Yes," a dark, formless shape said, who sat next to the Chairman. "I've said from the beginning that God didn't play fair. He let His Son intervene, become a man. You would think we could pervert Him the same way we did everyone else on earth, but…"

"But we lost," the fourth being said, who took the form of a hulking, scaled creature with green skin and red eyes on the opposite end of the table. The Chairman looked up with those words, and the demon flinched. Then the Chairman smiled slightly.

"Relax," he said. "You're not saying anything than what we are all thinking. I brought you three here because in all of Damnation I trust you to speak your minds." The Chairman stared at each of the three beings in turn—the formless shape, the woman, the lizard-like demon—before he spoke again.

"I realize that we have lost the war," he said. "God has come up with a way out for man. There is nothing we can do about that. The question is, what do we do now? Do we sit on our hands and wait for Jesus to return and for it all to be over? I think not."

He paused and waited for the others to respond. Finally, the demon spoke.

"We have an advantage that God doesn't have. Numbers. A few believe in Him, but many millions don't."

"Or at least they don't follow Him," the woman said. "Remember the days when we had as many people worshipping us as He did?"

"So we make them worship us again," the formless shape said. "We offer them the same thing we did the first time. I can offer them power beyond imagination. There are few men who will turn away from that kind of power."

"And I have lust on my side," the woman said. "Lust always works."

"And I will feed their hatred and revenge," the demon said.

The Chairman stared at his lieutenants thoughtfully, before finally nodding.

"Then it's decided. In the end, we are just as mortal as man. But while God will save a few, we will corrupt and destroy the rest of them. That is the best way to hurt Him. While many worship what you represent, most will come to believe that the existence of God is a myth."

The woman spoke up. "But if they think He is a myth, won't they think that you don't exist either?"

The Chairman smiled broadly this time.

"Exactly."

1 WISHES GRANTED

The crystal water flowing from the tap ran over Harris Borden's shaking hands. He scooped it up and splashed it into his sweating face, its peaceful coolness contrasting with his throbbing temples and the muted shouting from the other room. The broken air conditioner put everyone's nerves on edge, the angry shouting made him want to run, and Harris' head felt like it was in a vise. A day in the life of a pastor, he thought.

Life as a pastor sucked. Or maybe he just sucked as a pastor.

He felt like one of those caged tigers at the zoo, not necessarily wanting to kill someone or something, just pacing. Pacing. *He didn't belong here.* His temples throbbed.

His eyes were drawn by the darkness of the Nevada night through the open window, cranked open to let a little air into the cinder-block multi-purpose building. Tonight it was the church board meeting room; tomorrow morning it would once again serve its usual purpose as the elementary school. He could hear the small voices of Pathfinders down the hall as he stared out across the parking lot toward the small A-frame chapel of the Round Rock Community Christian Church.

"Eight years," he sighed. "Not what you expected," Harris muttered to himself. *What* did *he expect?* he thought, arguing with himself. As in response, the shouting in the next room went up again.

"Duty calls," he whispered, sighing. He reached into his pocket for the small packet of Excedrin he had brought with him for tonight and tore it open. He popped the pills into his open mouth, then leaned forward and sucked up some water from the bathroom faucet. He dried his face on a paper towel, pasted a smile on his face, and pushed through the restroom doors into the room where church board continued. He paused and scanned the small group. *Sigh.*

The rebellious part of him suddenly took over and decided to play a game. If board members were dogs, what would they be?

He looked at the end of the folding table, and a slight smile played across his lips. There was Gregory Phipps, the retired missionary, who had served as head elder for 13 years until his heart had started acting up. He was a widower in his 70s who had been everywhere, done everything and always had an opinion. Phipps would be a bloodhound, always seeking the truth, with a capital T. Lately he had been quieting down on his own opinion, though, because of the bigger dog in town.

Across from Phipps was the rottweiler—Frank Hollis; Dr. Hollis to friends and enemies alike. The Hollises could be traced back to the beginning of this church, founded with money from their original clinic, now the Hollis Memorial Hospital. Money talked—here as it did everywhere—and if you forgot it, Dr. Hollis would remind you.

Harris watched while the rottweiler tore into a beagle—their church treasurer.

"I just don't understand what the problem is," Dr. Hollis said. "The catalog says it costs $599. Just pay the $599."

Sweat beading on his forehead, Jules Russell shook his head. "It's not that simple. Not only do we have to get an estimate for the fountain itself, we have to run the water pipe to the site. And we have to get a permit from the city before we do anything."

"So get the permit."

"It's summer. The city council won't meet for another two months," Russell explained. "We have to go through proper channels. These things take time."

"Horse puckey," Dr. Hollis said. "I know the mayor personally. I'll get him on the phone right now." He pulled out his cell phone and began pressing buttons.

"Frank, Frank…please let me do my job," Russell pleaded. "It has to be done right." He reached up and unbuttoned his top shirt button, then loosened his tie. Harris could see a cornered look of desperation appearing in Jules' eyes, and knew that was his cue to intervene.

"It has to be done *now!*" Dr. Hollis roared.

Harris took a deep breath and spoke up. "Gentlemen, please quiet down. After all, the Pathfinders are meeting down the hall." He stared down Dr. Hollis, who was used to getting his way, and surprisingly, Dr. Hollis relented.

Change the subject, Harris told himself, and his mind scrambled. "You know, the Community Services room looks really nice since the new coat of paint was put on it," he said. "We had tons of complements at the last community pastor's meeting." There was a pause, as if the three of them were trying to comprehend the switch of topics. Then Jules smiled broadly, Greg winked at him and he even got a wisp of a smile from Dr. Hollis.

After that, the rest of the church board meeting was a lot less eventful. The group dealt with the monthly balance sheet, a request for the Pathfinders to take a weekend campout, and voted two outgoing transfers of membership.

"Thank you for being patient, Frank, uh, Dr. Hollis," Harris told him as they pushed back the chairs after benediction.

"I just don't understand the holdup," he said, shaking his head. "I wanted the drinking fountain installed in time for my grandson's baby dedication in two weeks. This isn't the way my hospital is run, you know."

"I understand," Harris responded. "Just be patient with us. We're only human." Harris' voice trailed off as he realized that Dr. Hollis hadn't heard the last part of the comment. He was already headed out the door. Harris looked up at Greg Phipps, who stared at him for a brief moment, then shook his head.

"I know you're young," he said, and Harris immediately knew he was in for another lecture. "But you can't let a board meeting get out of control like that. You've got to pull in the reins once in a while." Greg took his right fist and clenched it in front of his eyes.

Harris shrugged. "I thought I pulled things together there at the end. The paint comment, after all."

Greg nodded curtly. "Good, but after the fact. You've got to make sure they know you're in control."

Harris stared at him blankly for a second. "I thought God was in control."

Greg tightened his lip. "Not from what I saw in here tonight." He turned and sighed. "Ah well, you're young. You still have a lot to learn about being a pastor."

He turned, and Harris hesitated; then decided to ask him something he had wondered about for a while.

"Greg," Harris called after him, and he turned expectantly. "Do you ever miss it?"

His bushy grey eyebrows narrowed for an instant as if he didn't quite know where the question came from or where it was headed. Then his face relaxed.

"Mission work?" he asked, suddenly amused.

Harris shrugged. "Not just mission work. Being on the front lines, I guess."

Greg turned dramatically and looked around the room, sweeping the empty building with his wrinkled hand as well as his steel grey eyes.

"What do you call this?" he responded sharply.

"This is the ministry, yes I know," Harris said, not sure if he should be so honest with him. "But I have a feeling I'm here because the Powers That Be don't want me to change too much. Round Rock is the kind of pastorate where things'll never change. They won't let you change."

He stared into Harris' eyes. "We go where God calls us. We do what we're told."

He turned to leave, then paused for a long moment before adding a final word.

"I've seen miracles in my life, and I've seen true evil." He stood staring at the door as he talked, his bent body hunched over. "And you don't have to be in the mission field to see either one."

Harris watched his bent form move slowly out the doorway into the dark parking lot beyond. A car door slammed. An engine turned over and started. He stared at the streetlight outside for a long time in a stupor. Finally Harris realized that he had been staring at the light for more than ten minutes. He was alone in the building, except for a lone cricket that decided to serenade him in the desert night. The clock ticked on the wall, and he just stood there.

His reverie was interrupted by his cell phone chirping. The tone told him that it was Katya, and his depression instantly vanished. She was the bright star in his life.

"Hello, Chickpea," he answered.

"*Zdravstvuj!*" she replied. Her silk voice took him back to that night in college when he had heard her sing a solo and had fallen in love with her. He

8

still couldn't believe how much he had been blessed; to meet and fall in love with someone who by all rights should be singing with the St. Petersburg Opera instead of living as a pastor's wife in a backwater desert town. He thought about her tall, slender form, thick, straight black hair and full mouth and face and wished he was with her.

"Are you ready to come home to your loving wife?" she asked. "I thought we could work some more on The Project." Harris blushed and grinned.

"Almost," he said. "I want to spend a few minutes with God before I come home. Is that OK?"

He heard her make a little throaty whine, and knew that she hated these times apart. The Project was her code name for their attempts to get Katya pregnant. After two months, they were still unsuccessful, but he was glad they kept on trying.

"All right," she said finally. "I know that I am second in your life, but I don't mind playing second cello to God."

"That's second fiddle," he corrected her.

"I prefer the cello," she quipped. "See you in a little while."

"I love you, Sweetheart," he responded, then put the cell phone away.

With the cell phone disconnected, the shrouds of gloom once again fell on him like dark, sticky cobwebs. The depression had haunted him on and off for weeks. He knew he was healthy, and so he believed that the cause was something spiritual.

And that was the reason for his nightly visits to the darkened church sanctuary where he lay his soul bare before God's eternal throne. He left the room dark because it gave him a greater sense of privacy, realistic or not. The dark room also allowed the streetlights to brighten up the room through the one stained-glass window in front of the small chapel. Harris left the metal folding chairs of the fellowship hall that spoke to him of business. He entered

9

the realm of polished oak pews that whispered strong suggestions of worship. Harris felt he was leaving the workshop and entering the throne room of God.

He quietly strode forward in the room and sat in the front pew without saying anything. He knew that God read his heart. He knew that the words that wanted to leap from his mouth had been said time and time again. He sat in the silence, savoring the knowledge that God loved him and cared about his gloom.

"Master," he finally whispered. "I am truly, truly grateful that you granted my wish. I love being a pastor. I love being able to speak in Your name, to recite the sacred scriptures that You left for us. I love the pulpit…even though I don't think I'm very good at preaching. But it's such a great honor to serve in Your name."

Harris paused, a mixture of gloom and guilt swirling through his soul like grey and black clouds.

"But I feel—I *know*—that there's more out there. Somewhere deep inside me there's a voice that tells me that this isn't what You intended for me. I don't have the disposition, the patience, to spend my days dealing with budgets and school board meetings, with disputes between angry church members, with mowing the lawn and cleaning out the gutters for the church because no one else will do it before the rains come."

A tide of anger rolled inside of him. "Is this what You called us to do? Maintain the church plant so the same 50 people can do nothing their entire lives but come to church each weekend? And if their children choose to leave the church, then oh well, they just want to be like the rest of the world so let's pray for them." He realized that his voice was rising, and he was thankful that the Pathfinders had left.

"Didn't You call us to baptize people in Your name? The only baptism I've scheduled around here was called off because the church board voted that the three children wanting to be baptized hadn't demonstrated that they could live a Christian life."

He realized he was still upset at what happened, and wondered if that was the beginning of his despondency. Three sixth graders had asked to be baptized. The church board had seen it otherwise. They weren't serious enough, according to the adults. They needed more "maturity" to "appreciate the sober responsibility" that came with being a Christian. It had been a terrible battle, and Harris had fought hard, and lost. Even now he could see the anger on the faces in the church board meeting. It had been only six months before, but Harris felt like he had aged ten years since then.

He took a deep breath and tried to calm down. Harris' heart thumped in his chest. He looked out the open doorway behind him and heard a siren in the distance. *Evil was roaming the streets of Round Rock, Nevada*, he thought. *And what was I doing about it?*

Out of words, he let his thoughts wander back to the stories of church pioneers he had studied in college. The prophets of old had dedicated their entire lives. Many had died to champion God's cause. The same happened in the New Testament. Stephen had been stoned; Peter had been crucified upside down; Paul had been imprisoned and finally executed. Christians had died throughout thousands of years for refusing to deny their beliefs. *So what were we doing here?*

"God," Harris whispered harshly and hastily, almost afraid he might change his mind. "I believe that You're waiting for someone among your faithful to step forward and volunteer to champion Your cause. I think nothing is happening here because we're waiting for something to happen rather than making it happen. Therefore I call for You to make it happen. And make it happen, beginning with me."

He looked out the door and heard a second ambulance join the first. "Scripture says that the Devil is going about as a roaring lion seeking those whom he may devour. Someone has to stop him." His heart thudded in his chest.

"*I volunteer.*" The words blurted from his mouth. "I volunteer to fight evil in all its shapes and forms. I volunteer to follow You into battle—*real* battle—and stand if You tell me to stand, and charge if You tell me to charge." Harris paused to catch his breath.

"Lord, I know that You have greater things planned for us than we can ever imagine, and if we just lift our eyes we can catch a glimpse of those plans. But we can never really understand how vast and glorious those plans go, because we don't have Your vision. I ask for a little bit of that vision right now.

"And if there are greater things out there..." He listened as several more sirens went by, "then I commit to doing Your will. I commit to being your champion through hell and high water, through persecution and death, until my last breath."

Harris paused to catch his breath again, and was startled to see a movement in the shadows to his left. And then he heard it. Clapping.

An athletic young man dressed in jeans and a T shirt stepped from the shadows. He looked about sixteen. He clapped slowly and deliberately as he took a couple of steps toward Harris. The sanctuary was dark enough that he had a difficult time making out much detail in the young man's face. A chill went down Harris' back.

"Well said, well said," the stranger told him in a soft, yet strong voice. "God loves to hear words of commitment."

A moment of anger hit him. "You're mocking me," Harris said.

"Not at all," he said. "I'm here as a messenger. He has decided to grant your request." He stepped forward again, and moonlight from a side window slashed across his face. He was handsome, but not to the point of standing out in a crowd.

Harris looked at him sharply. *Some joker had been walking by and had heard my prayer*, he thought. "Who are you?"

"I'm not a joker, if that's what you think," he said. "I'm a messenger of the Most High God. I've gone by a lot of names over the years, and throughout the Realm. But maybe it would be easiest to just call me...The Messenger."

Yeah, right, Harris thought. *Some nutcase kid is now professing to be a prophet, just like that fellow in college who stood up in vespers and told us that God didn't want us to keep pets.*

"I'm not a prophet, and I don't really mind if you have a pet," The Messenger said. "In fact, I'm partial to cats." His voice had a melodic quality that was stronger even that Katya's. Still not sure what was going on, Harris decided to let him talk. In the meantime, he decided to get between the young man and the door.

"OK, Messenger," Harris said. "What's the message you have from God for me?" He leaned back and cocked an eyebrow.

"What did you pray for?" the stranger asked. "No, I'll tell you what you prayed for. You asked God to be used in a bigger way. That request has been granted. But let me ask out of curiosity: haven't you heard that those who are faithful in small things will be granted mastery over larger things?"

Harris nodded. "Yeah, so?"

"Don't you believe that these little things that frustrate you so much are important in the plan of God?"

"Important? We argued for an hour over a drinking fountain! A stupid drinking fountain in the church lobby! Tell me how that's important in the plan of God."

Harris saw now that the Messenger's hair was a sandy brown, and he had the build of someone involved in sports, probably baseball or track. His face

13

was unlined, but carried a seriousness that a normal 16 year old wouldn't carry. He shook his head.

"Sometimes it isn't the decision that's important, but how the decision is reached," The Messenger replied. "In that sense, you have a long way to go. You could do a lot in this congregation if you wanted."

"Tell me how I could do a lot here," Harris responded, annoyed. "This church hasn't changed membership in 30 years, except as children grow up and leave the church."

"It isn't my task to set your pastoral duties straight. I'm just a messenger."

"OK, OK," Harris stammered. "This is ridiculous. You're just some kid who came in off the street and is jerking my chain. You've had your fun, now go ahead and leave."

"I'll leave," The Messenger agreed. "But you need to understand that God chooses whoever He wants, and the quality of the messenger isn't always a measurement of the message itself. God has decided to appoint you as His Champion. You'll find that with great responsibility sometimes comes great pain and sorrow. Are you ready for that? I'll visit you soon to make sure you understand and agree to the responsibilities God has given you."

Harris' curiosity piqued. Maybe this guy did really have a message for him.

"If God has a mission for me to do, how'll I know what it is?"

"You'll know."

"When?"

"Tomorrow."

Harris expected him to say something cryptic, like *In due time* or *When God wills*. Instead he was getting specific...and making Harris nervous.

He stood up and turned away from the stranger. The room was still dark, but somehow Harris could see more details than ever before. He turned and looked at the Messenger again.

"One more thing," he said on a whim.

"What is it?" The Messenger responded.

"Show me what you *really* look like."

He nodded slowly. The Messenger raised his hand and the blast of a hundred searchlights hit Harris like a slap in the face. The room was bathed in brilliant white light, all spilling from his figure.

"I'll be back in a few days," Harris heard his voice say, but he couldn't see anything. He was blind. He fell back onto the carpeted floor and lay like a dead man. His eyes were closed, but the brilliant light crept through his eyelids. After a long while Harris realized that the room was darker, and knew he was alone.

2 DEAL WITH THE DEVIL

Harris didn't know how long he lay on the carpeted floor of the sanctuary. It seemed like hours, but was probably only a few minutes. He'd never been so scared in his life. He suspected that The Messenger had been an angel; heaven knows he had in essence told Harris as much. He believed in angels, just as strongly as he believed in God. But this experience taught him the difference between believing something—and experiencing it first-hand.

Slowly he got brave enough to open his eyes and sit up. His eyes played tricks on him. The retinas were apparently still burned with the image of The Messenger as he had raised his hand and blasted Harris with the brilliance that was a part of his face, and apparently part of his nature.

He sat there on the carpet in the sanctuary for a long time, not sure what to do. Harris believed that he was a faithful Christian. He believed that his prayers were sincere and heartfelt. Now he felt that all he was, all that he had said in every prayer he had ever prayed, was a sham. It was easy to talk about being a Christian; surrendering your life to God, opening yourself up to Him, and yielding to His will. Now Harris was faced with earth-shaking evidence of His will…and it scared him down to his bones.

And yet he'd asked for this. He'd been disillusioned by the pathetic anemia of his Christian life, and had asked God to use him in new ways. God had heard that request and answered him. The question was: now that he had his request answered, was that what he really wanted? And was he beyond the point of saying no? If he turned his back on God's mission for him, was he lost forever to salvation? On the other hand, did he have the courage to accept God's mission? And what was that mission anyway?

Harris was grateful that it was late at night and he was alone, sitting in the dark of the empty sanctuary. He thought long and hard, and only succeeded in thinking of more questions. He realized he had to go home. He had lingered in God's presence long enough. And still he sensed that this wouldn't be the last time he'd be exposed to God or His heavenly messengers.

So he got up from the carpet, brushed himself off and walked back to his office. A lone light bulb burned in the hall outside the office door. He unlocked the door and looked inside. The newspaper lay on his desk where he'd left it. His tennis shoes and sports clothes from jogging this morning lay folded in the corner behind his desk. Through the tall, thin window on the far side of the office he saw his Toyota Corolla parked in the pastor's space outside. All of these things were familiar, yet seemed strange somehow. He was a changed man. How could he go back to the way things were?

Harris looked in his office and wondered why he had wanted to go in there in the first place. He stood in the hallway, a man torn by indecision and faced by the Eternal. He sighed and closed the door, locking it.

He went out to his Corolla and got in it, heading for home. He decided not to say anything to Katya; at least not at this point. What would he say? What could he say? The Messenger had said that he would get more information tomorrow. He had no idea in what form that message would come, but as the Bible instructed, "Don't worry about tomorrow; for it has enough worries of its own."

So in the end, he simply pulled into his garage at home, went into a darkened house with a sleeping wife, undressed, climbed into bed and went to sleep.

* * *

As handguns go, the weapon was pretty basic, but Harvey Weinstein considered it the prized possession in his collection because of the important part it played in an event in November, 1963. He carefully lifted its display case and the revolver from his wall safe and placed it on the desk. Pulling the red satin covering back, he gazed at the Colt Cobra .38 Special, serial number 2774 LW.

He had had it verified four times by independent brokers. After spending close to $100,000 for this relic, had had to be sure. But he knew that there was no doubt that this was the very handgun Jack Ruby used to shoot and kill Lee Harvey Oswald, assassin of John F. Kennedy in Dallas on November 22, 1963.

He stared at it longingly for a long moment before replacing the red satin and Plexiglas cover and returning it to the safe.

* * *

The next morning he awoke, refreshed. Katya had already left for her secretarial job downtown. Harris noted that she left a message on the refrigerator, stating that she would be home early, most likely to do the "project work" that they didn't get to last night. Monday was his usual day off, so he had nothing on his to-do list. He sensed, however, that it was likely to be an eventful day.

Harris got up, showered and dressed and fixed breakfast. Not knowing from where or in what form his information would come, he felt a bit paranoid. He sat at the kitchen table and turned the TV on, watching the local morning news. There was a news report about a three-alarm fire near the church last night, and he assumed that was why he had heard the sirens. But beyond that, there was nothing of significance that he could see on TV. He switched it off and wandered into the living room.

He'd been reading an autobiography of Benjamin Franklin, and the book lay on the arm of his reading chair. But somehow the book that had intrigued Harris yesterday now seemed irrelevant and uninteresting. He picked up his Bible, opened it randomly and began to read:

1   For, behold, the day cometh, it burneth as a furnace; and all the proud, and all that work wickedness, shall be stubble; and the day that cometh shall burn them up, saith Jehovah of hosts, that it shall leave them neither root nor branch.

Harris realized that he'd opened to the book of Malachi. He was partial to Psalms, and needed some comfort in all this confusion. So he closed the Bible, and tried again. This time it opened in I Peter 5:

8   Be sober, be watchful: your adversary the devil, as a roaring lion, walketh about, seeking whom he may devour,

"Well, that's not too comforting," he muttered to himself. Harris closed his eyes, and prayed.

"Lord, I know we're in a war here, and that I volunteered for the front lines. You're not telling me anything I don't already know. What I'd like at this time is a little guidance, please?"

Harris decided to try it one more time, and let the Bible fall open. This time it found Matthew 21. He read, and a felt a chill come into the room:

12 But before all these things, they shall lay their hands on you, and shall persecute you, delivering you up to the synagogues and prisons, bringing you before kings and governors for my name`s sake.

13 It shall turn out unto you for a testimony.

14 Settle it therefore in your hearts, not to meditate beforehand how to answer:

15 for I will give you a mouth and wisdom, which all your adversaries shall not be able to withstand or to gainsay.

16 But ye shall be delivered up even by parents, and brethren, and kinsfolk, and friends; and *some* of you shall they cause to be put to death.

17 And ye shall be hated of all men for my name`s sake.

18 And not a hair of your head shall perish.

Harris looked up from the text and thoughts swirled in his head. "OK, Lord, you've got my attention," he muttered, and stopped his experiment. He deliberately flipped through the pages to Psalm 23.

After an hour of reading, Harris decided to drive downtown and get their mail. He and Katya had had problems with vandals smashing their mailbox on the street, so they agreed to get a post office box for mail. Harris rented one for them and one for the church, so it was relatively easy to take care of both at the same time.

It took him all of six minutes to get downtown and park his car outside the post office. He saw Jules Russell a few doors down going into the hardware store, and waved at him. Jules smiled faintly and waved back. Harris knew that Jules felt that he wasn't respected as church treasurer, but Harris wasn't sure what to do about it.

Harris took his keys and opened the church mailbox, unloading a few magazines and a couple of bills. Then he went down to Katya's and his box.

Harris unlocked it and got out a solitary letter. He looked at it. It was a personal letter, written in longhand from someone named I. P. Kratchnow in St. Paul, Minnesota. But it wasn't addressed to Harris. The address read: Attention: Collections, Universal Finance, San Francisco. The P.O. Box for Universal Finance and for Katya and Harris were the same, but everything else was different. San Francisco was even in a different state; they were in Nevada.

"Hmm," he said to himself, scratching his head, feeling a mixture of annoyance and curiosity. Staring at the envelope, he carried it back to the front desk and gave it to the postal worker, an attractive, middle-aged black woman.

"Box 35 is the right box, but that's the wrong city and state," Harris said to her, chuckling. "And I'm not Universal Finance."

The woman looked at the letter and her eyes opened wide. "That's strange," she said. "OK, I'll take care of it." She turned to place it in a bin behind her, then looked at a message board a few feet away.

"Looks like we have some more mail for you," she said, stepping back behind one of the shelves. She reached down and pulled a plastic box from one of the lower shelves. It was full of mail. She plopped it onto the counter in front of him.

Harris pulled back in surprise. He reached out and picked up one of the envelopes. It was addressed to Universal Finance.

"These are all for Universal Finance," he said, looking up at the woman in shock and surprise. "And I know I'm not them."

'Hmmm," she muttered, apparently not sure what to do. "Let me check the computer." She turned to the computer and began typing in information. After a long pause, she turned back to him, but her eyes never left the monitor.

"It says someone put a request in last Thursday to forward all mail to your address," she said.

Harris stared at her blankly for a long moment. "But…but…but why?"

She shrugged. "It could be a mistake, but not likely. It's too much bother to fill one of these things out.

"I can hold onto this mail if you want, or you can take it. It's legally yours."

Harris opened his mouth to tell her to keep it, but then a tickling in the back of his mind made him hesitate. He reached out and grabbed the plastic container, and pulled it to him. "Thanks," he muttered, and left for the street outside.

He wasn't sure what he was going to do with the mail, but he felt that what happened last night followed by this was unlikely to be a coincidence. Harris was loading the box into the front door on the passenger side of the Corolla when he heard a voice behind him.

"Pastor Borden," the soft voice said. He shut the door and turned to face Jules Russell.

"Hey Jules, how're you doing?" Harris held out his hand and shook Jules', placing his weak, clammy skin in the folds of his fingers.

"I…I think I have a way to expedite the drinking fountain situation," Jules began. He then went on in lengthy detail to explain how he could get the permits processed and approved early. He seemed happy with himself, proud that he was accomplishing something "outside the box"—at least from his perspective—and Harris smiled and encouraged him. But Harris' mind was not on drinking fountains at the moment. It was obsessed with a night visitor and a plastic carton full of letters in his car.

"Well, keep on it, Jules," he told him. "We definitely made the right choice when we made you church treasurer." The comment had the intended effect; Jules left with a wide grin on his face.

Harris did his best thinking when he jogged, and as he was driving home, suddenly the desire to hit the road came over him. Then he realized that his exercise clothes and Nikes were left in his office. He dropped by the office and grabbed them and headed home.

He was lacing up his Nikes at home when the phone rang. For a Monday, the phone had been exceptionally quiet, and Harris picked up the phone after the first ring.

"Hello."

"Oh, thank goodness I caught a human being," said a woman's voice. "I'm sick and tired of talking to recordings.

"My name is Leticia Williams. I'm calling from Harrisburg, Pennsylvania. I need to talk to someone about my credit card bill."

Puzzled, Harris grinned to himself. "OK, I'm happy to talk to you, Ms. Williams, but I'm a pastor and don't have anything to do with your credit card bill."

Pause. "Isn't this 1 (800) 555-1782?"

He chuckled aloud this time. "Nope. Not even close. I'm sorry I can't help you."

"Sorry to bother you, pastor," she said. "I'll try again."

Harris hung up and smiled to himself. Then he stopped smiling. This was too weird.

A moment later the phone rang again.

"This is Pastor Borden," he answered it this time.

"Pastor, this is Leticia Williams. I'm sorry to bother you again, but I know I dialed the right number. Somehow the call got forwarded to you."

Harris felt lightheaded and sat down. He wasn't sure what to say at this point, but stammered out a few words.

"Uh...I, uh...well, I can try to help you. What's your problem?"

"It's just that, we borrowed money against our credit card to complete our deck on our new house. Right after that, my husband broke his leg. Now he can't work and we can't make the payments on the credit card."

"Ouch," he said. "I'm sure someone at the company would be willing to work with you on that."

"That's what I told my husband," she said. "But I've tried and tried to call someone at the company. We've written letters, e-mailed them, even posted comments at their website. But the only response we get from them are threatening letters telling us that if we don't pay our bills they'll take us to court."

"Surely they must have other phone numbers to call," he volunteered.

"I tried them," she said. "All of them. I got recording after recording. This is the only one where I got a live person to talk to. And you're that live person. Do you think God led me to you?"

Harris knew the answer to that, but hesitated. "I'll do what I can, Ms. Williams. Let me get your phone number and I'll see what I can do."

He hung up the phone and stared at it for a long while. Suddenly it rang again. Before he could say hello, an angry man's voice blasted him through the receiver.

"You idiots better quit threatening me," he said. "I've paid my bills faithfully for the past year. It's not my fault I got sick to begin with. Three hundred dollars a month for a year, and I'm more in debt now than I was when I started!"

"Sir, I...uh..."

"No excuses!" he said to Harris. "Get off my back, or I'm personally driving down there to your office and rip your face off!" The receiver slammed down in his ear.

Harris hung the receiver up carefully. Immediately it rang again. He picked it up and heard the sound of a woman crying.

"My husband took on two jobs to get us out of debt, and then he had a heart attack," the voice said. "He's gone! I hope all you credit card people rot in hell!" Click.

He hung up, and the phone began to ring again. This time he didn't answer it. Instead he decided to head out the door and jog, as Harris had originally intended.

What was going on? he wondered. Obviously there was a problem, apparently with credit cards. After a brief disaster with a credit card right out of college, Katya and Harris had sworn off them. They had a debit card they used when they had to, but found it increasingly difficult to operate in modern society without a credit card. Especially on vacation—or on a business trip. It was often hard to find a rental car agency or a hotel that would accept them using only a debit card. The temptation had been strong to get a credit card again. Now Harris was glad they hadn't.

He turned off of their short street, crossed the railroad tracks, and jogged down Chieftain Avenue, the main street that ran through their town. It was clear as always this time of year, and he could see all four stoplights that marked the official downtown area. For late morning, traffic was light. A sheen of sweat broke out across his body, reminding him that it was summer in Nevada. But he had become used to sweating, and welcomed it. Harris kicked himself into second gear and fell back into his reverie.

The whole situation seemed odd to Harris. What do credit card bills, an angelic visitor and a burned-out pastor have to do with each other? He hadn't opened the letters, and now he wondered if he should have.

25

And if the matter had to do with bad credit, or even with a corrupt finance company, what could Harris do about it? He had no credentials, and other than a class in personal accounting he took ten years ago in college, he had no background in business. He even got a C in the class.

And yet the angel had said that God had called Harris to do something important. This is not what he had in mind, but he knew God well enough that He rarely did things in predictable ways. It all seemed like some great cosmic joke to him. At some point, Harris expected the skies to pull back and see God and the angels laughing at the confused pastor running down the road in dusty Nevada.

Well, the Messenger had told him that he would return within a couple of days. In the meantime, Harris decided to find out everything he could about the situation.

His jogging went into overtime that day, and it was late afternoon by the time he got back to his house, dusty, sweaty, tired and still confused. Harris noticed Katya's Tercel in the driveway, and felt a mixture of warmth and bewilderment. What was he going to tell her?

He came into the living room and immediately heard her voice rattling off in rapid Russian. She was on the phone, and Harris knew that she was angry. He knew just a little of that complicated language, but he recognized one or two words that he had only heard her say when she was boiling mad.

"OK…you do that, Mister!" She replied harshly into the phone and hung up. Harris heard her mumble something to herself in Russian that he knew he wasn't supposed to hear, especially since he was her pastor as well as her husband. Finally she looked up at him, and her eyes screamed *help*.

"Harris, what is going on here? I have been home 15 minutes and the phone hasn't stopped ringing. And all the calls have been for some company in San Francisco!" As if on cue, the phone began to ring again.

"*Nevozmozhnoe*," she muttered again.

"Uh, don't pick that up," Harris advised her, but she had already lifted the receiver.

"Hello," she said gruffly. Pause. "No, this is not Universal Finance." Pause. "No, we are not trying to avoid your calls." She looked at me and shook her head. "Sir, this is a home in Nevada. *Neh-vah-dah*. I am sorry for what is happening to you, but I cannot help...." She paused and put the receiver down. "He hanged up."

Harris held his hands out in front of him, as if to ward off the phone calls. "Let the phone ring. Let's go out and sit on the back porch where we can talk." Katya smoothed her skirt and strode out the back door. Harris grabbed the plastic post office box full of letters he had left at the end of the couch and followed her. He knew she was still mad, and wondered what she'd feel after he told her what had happened to him last night.

Surprisingly, she took it all in stride. They sat in two folding chairs under the shade of the small pepper tree that was the only living thing to survive in their small back yard. He could hear the muffled sound of the phone continuing to ring in their living room, but ignored it. Katya folded her elegant, tall, thin body into the patio chair and listened intently to him, her eyes never leaving his face. She had the utmost confidence in Harris' abilities, confidence that he wished he felt in himself.

"And then there was this flash of light and he was gone," Harris told her. "I lay there for a long time, not sure what to do. But nothing else happened, so I got up and came home."

Harris expected her to doubt his story, or at least have him explain it more than once. But he had never understood his wife's logic, and her profound faith. "*Zaebis*," she said in amazement. "And then what happened today?"

Harris told her of his visit to the post office and showed her the letters in the plastic box. "The postal worker said the letters were legally mine, but I haven't had the courage to open them."

Katya reached into the box and grabbed the nearest letter. Harris followed her example and took one himself. It read:

Dear Universal Credit:

I have tried to contact you by phone and hope that you will respond to this letter. It was a mistake for me to take out that credit card from you. Because of that account, my credit has been ruined. Promptly after we began using it, a virus made my husband so sick he had to quit his job. I have a young son who has just graduated from high school. Now I wonder if he will be able to go to college. I have contacted my attorney, who has said that even though ethically you have done awful things, legally you cannot be touched. I know that I am just another customer to you, but you need to know that I am a human being with a life of my own. I beg for your mercy. Please let me know how I might get out of this impossible situation.

It was signed by a woman in San Diego. Harris put it down and read three others. They were all similar. Some were angry, some argued with logic, some seemed to be weeping through the pages of their letters. All of them were desperately seeking a way to get out of the spiral of debt that somehow followed the opening of a credit card account with this company.

Harris looked up at Katya, who was crying. "What are you going to do, beloved?" she said.

His first reaction was to tell her, *I have no idea.* Instead he said, "The Messenger said he would be back. I'll know what to do then. But for now, I'm going to take you into our bedroom and try to give you the child you want."

Harris entered the living room and disconnected the ringing phone, then followed Katya into the bedroom.

3 BATTLE PLAN

Their interlude in the bedroom was apparently the right choice. Not only did they continue to make efforts toward "The Project," it gave both of them time to think. And the ringing phone had stopped, mainly because they had unplugged it. Harris never appreciated silence more in his life.

The couple got up and had a late dinner, and then Katya proceeded to open the rest of the letters while Harris washed dishes. He turned the TV to a Reno station and the evening news to see what was going on in the world. As Harris continued with dishes, he began to feel guilty after a while, so he plugged the phone back in. It immediately began ringing. He picked it up.

"I'd like to speak to your supervisor," a man's voice began, even before Harris said hello.

He grinned and held the phone out to Katya. "It's for you."

"I am not at home," she threw back at Harris, and stuck out her tongue.

"If this call is for Universal Finance, this is a wrong number," Harris said into the phone.

The obviously frustrated voice on the other end of the line huffed and puffed for a long second.

"I have men at my door right now wanting to repossess my big-screen TV because Universal Finance says I still owe money," he said finally. "I paid that off months ago."

"Sir," Harris answered. "I wish I had an answer for you. Universal Finance sounds like bad news. We're swamped with calls and letters here, and we have nothing to do with them."

The man sighed. "Well, I don't think this is going to end well, for them or for us. Pray for us all." *Click.*

Harris started to hang the phone up, then thought better of it and lay the receiver down beside the phone. As he did so, something caught his eye. A commercial for the Pay Later Visa card was on the TV, sponsored by Universal Finance. The ad showed an attractive young family in the manicured front yard of a very nice white two-story home, with a new Lexus in the driveway. The slogan at the end read, "You can have it all…with the Pay Later Plan." The last panel showed a screen full of small print which was too small and passed by too rapidly for anyone to read.

"Would you look at that," Katya said, and all Harris could do was shake his head.

It all smacked of fraud to Harris, and he wondered if anyone had ever investigated the company. He saw all those investigative reports on TV, where they find out that the meat sold to the public is contaminated, or that gas prices are being artificially jacked up. This company sounded like prime territory for this kind of study. Surely someone, somewhere had heard a complaint and looked into it.

"I'm going online," Harris announced to Katya. "Someone has got to know more about this than we do." The trick was getting the phone to stop ringing long enough to use the dial-up service to go online. Harris hung up the phone and it immediately rang. He lifted the receiver, apologized and hung it up again. Before it could ring again, he pushed the dial-up number on the computer in the corner of our living room, and it began calling out.

Harris immediately Googled the Pay Later Visa Card. He was rewarded with 17,550 hits; most were people complaining on their personal websites, a few were promotional websites for the card. He didn't see any information of substance, so he entered the words Universal Finance. This time Harris got 102,320 hits. Again, the first few were promotional websites and the main site for the bank. A few followed that were less than complementary but were based on personal opinion and not hard research.

On the third page of Google, Harris came across an article written last year in the *San Francisco Herald*. The headline read: Deke Assumes Head Post at Universal. The article was written by Michelle Kinkaid. The story told how 28-year-old Kenneth Deke surprisingly became the CEO of Universal Finance, the fastest growing bank in the world. The article was short, and did not give a lot of information about either Deke or Universal, although it did say that Universal was not a public company but was owned and operated by a special regency board.

Regents? Harris wondered. He'd only heard that term used in relation to a university or college. He reached for the dictionary on the shelf above the computer monitor. He read: *Regent: one who rules during the absence of a sovereign.* A cold chill ran down his back and he didn't know why.

The article had a link where comments could be sent. Harris typed out a quick e-mail asking Michelle Kinkaid to call him on his cell and sent it off.

Nothing more happened that night. Harris kept the phone off the hook so they could get some sleep. He checked it again in the morning and the calls started up right away. Tuesday was Harris' morning to visit the church's elementary school, and he always looked forward to it. With summer vacation coming, he only had a couple of weeks left to spend with them. He was up and ready to go by 8.

Harris led out in worship with the teachers at the small school, then paused before beginning prayer. "I hope you can remember me in your prayers this week," he said. "I have some major things going on, and need your spiritual support." The teachers looked at each other, and immediately Harris knew what they were thinking.

"No, I don't have a job offer somewhere else," he said smiling, although Harris wondered if the church might be better off if that happened.

"We also want to remember Douglas Washington," Haddie Brenton, the school principal said. "His mom stopped me this morning and said that he's scheduled to go to Reno for lab tests tomorrow. She's frightened—the whole family is. This visit will determine whether he needs more intensive chemotherapy or whether his remission is holding up."

Harris nodded silently. Dougie, as he called the little guy, was a valiant eight year old in the congregation. Harris drew courage from him and his continuing battle. He bowed his head and led the teachers in morning prayer.

At 9 a.m. the kids came to the gymnasium and they had worship together as a school. The principal introduced him and Harris had a short devotional talk. For some reason, he always seemed to have a special bond with these kids. Where the adults seemed to reject Harris, the little ones accepted and appreciated him. And life, friendship and even God's love was a lot simpler in the eyes of these children. That's why Harris lingered as long as he could at the elementary school.

Harris was sitting on the bench in the school's playground when his cell chirped. He didn't recognize the number, and then realized that the prefix was 415, the San Francisco area code.

"This is Harris Borden," he answered.

"Mr. Borden, this is Michelle Kinkaid at the San Francisco *Herald*. You left a message for me to call you." He could hear the bustle of a newsroom behind her voice.

"Hi there, Ms. Kinkaid," Harris told her. "Thanks for returning my call. I'm calling from Round Rock, Nevada. Something very strange has happened here. I'm receiving phone calls and letters from literally hundreds of upset people who are customers of Universal Finance."

She paused for a long time. "I see," she said flatly. "And this involves me, how?"

"Well, I and a lot of other people have been trying to reach anyone at that corporation, and having no success. The level of trauma I'm hearing from these people is pretty serious."

Silence.

"Ms. Kinkaid, are you there?"

"Yeah, I'm here," she answered. "I'm just waiting for you to tell me why you called me. What does this have to do with me?"

Harris was becoming frustrated.

"You wrote the article about Kenneth Deke taking over as CEO of Universal Finance," he said. "In fact, it was the only article of substance I've been able to find on the Internet about the company. Everything is either a sales pitch from their marketing division or complaints from people on their personal websites. All I'm looking for is a little information about these people so I can try to resolve this problem."

"Mr. Borden...."

"Actually, it's Pastor Borden," Harris corrected her.

"*Pastor* Borden, I really advise you to steer clear of these people," she said, and he could hear a tenseness enter her voice. "It took me six months of solid foot-to-the-pavement research to come up with the article that you saw there. I wrote several pages of information on this corporation, little of it flattering, none of it safe, and then had my editor cut the story down to a few paragraphs.

"You won't find out any more than you see there for two big reasons. First, the company is not public owned. They don't sell stocks; therefore they're not obligated to release any information they don't want to."

"The article said they were run by a regency board," Harris said, interrupting her.

"It's not a regency board," she hissed. "It's a *cabal*. Do you know what that is? It's a secret society that takes care of business with new members only being voted in as old members die."

He felt his heart pounding in his chest.

"That's the first reason you won't find out anything. Here's the second."

"They have connections at the Department of Homeland Security. They've passed all their vital information over to them. As part of the Critical Information Infrastructure Act, they don't have to tell us anything, even stuff that would ordinarily be available to the press and the public through the Freedom of Information Act. You can look it up."

Harris sighed, and Kinkaid heard it. "Yeah, my sentiments exactly."

"Look," she said after a long pause, while they both searched for the next words. "These guys put up a great front. Their commercials are cute, their website is flashy, but they are cutthroat killers. And I mean that literally. I was ready to take them and their whole corporation down for the crooks that they are until word came down from my publishers that the paper would be doing no more stories on Universal Finance."

Harris sighed again and looked down at the ground. "Well, thank you, Ms. Kinkaid. I hope I didn't get you into any more trouble."

"Naah," she said, her voice trying to sound casual. "Don't worry about it. I'd just about forgotten about the whole mess. Just take care of yourself. These guys'll do bad things to you."

Harris hung up his cell and put it in his coat pocket. What was he going to do now? The task before him was growing from a crack to a pothole to a cavernous pit. The web of despair that had enveloped him for months had been gone for two days. Now it came back, ready to cover him again.

* * *

Michelle hung up the phone and exhaled sharply. Despite the usual frantic pace that swirled around the newsroom as they neared deadline, her world had come once again to a screeching halt. The specter of Kenneth Deke and Universal Finance was something she had finally put behind her, and now when she had forgotten it, it was back in her head.

She shook her short blonde mane and tried to get back to the article she was writing about the National Dog Show being held in town that weekend. Every hotel room in San Francisco was booked, she was sure of that. It was a story she'd looked forward to doing for a couple of months, now that she was off the investigative beat for good.

She wrote a couple of lines on her computer, and then found herself staring into space, once again thinking about the research she had done on Universal the year before. She could see the young, extremely handsome, charismatic Kenneth Deke as she had seen him from a distance. She had tried to ask him a question in a restaurant once, but had been waylaid by security officers and whisked out of his presence within seconds.

The whole situation was highly suspicious, and her "spidey sense," as she called it, had gone into overdrive, tingling with excitement. And then the hammer had fallen. By the time she had written the rough draft of her exposé, she had been called into a meeting with her news editor, the editor-in-chief, the publisher and two attorneys. She was flattered at first, surprised that her research had resulted in such attention. But within a half an hour, she knew that her career was at stake. She agreed to compromise, turning over all her files—electronic and paper—on Deke and Universal in exchange for the small article that Pastor Borden had seen. And they agreed not to fire her.

Her eyes roamed from the blinking curser on the unfinished article in front of her, down to the drawer on her lower right. In the bottom drawer, beneath a false bottom that she had discovered when she inherited the desk, lay a CD with a second copy of all the files she had turned over. When the time was right, she was prepared to put it all on the line and complete her exposé. Something told her that the time was rapidly approaching.

* * *

"Hey Pastor B, look at me!" Harris looked up at Dougie, the black, bald-headed second-grader who stood on the top of the slide. Harris admired him greatly. Dougie had been fighting cancer for two years. He was now officially in remission, but even when he was bedbound he refused to be anything but a little, animated boy. He had more courage than the entire adult membership of his church.

"You go get 'em, Dougie!" Harris shouted back at him. Dougie slid down the slide and reached the bottom just as a larger kid ran over and shoved him off the side of the slide. Harris instinctively jumped up to help Dougie. But before he could stand, Dougie was up and grabbing and wrestling with the larger boy.

Harris watched Dougie and the other boy wrestle in the tanned bark that covered the playground area. Dougie picked up a small piece and put it in his mouth, then blew it out at the boy. Both were grinning the whole time.

Dougie was determined to live his life to the fullest, and had the courage to back that determination up.

"God, give me some of Dougie's courage," Harris whispered.

* * *

That night Harris couldn't sleep, so after Katya was pleasantly snoring, he got up, got dressed and drove down to the church. He felt like Alice in Wonderland. The more he investigated, the more he looked for hard facts, the more surreal the whole situation became.

Harris entered the darkened sanctuary and immediately felt like turning some lights on. He knew that God was very close, yet now he knew that evil was close as well. And he had a hunch that he'd receive another visit tonight.

Harris waited for about fifteen minutes; for what, he wasn't sure. But when his visitor did come, he was totally caught off-guard. The locked metal double doors leading from the church lobby to the parking lot began to rattle, as if someone were trying to open them, or were trying to get his attention. Considering how easily the Messenger had arrived before, Harris doubted that this was him.

He pushed the crash bar and opened the left side. At the edge of the darkness outside stood an elderly man dressed in some stained, torn coveralls. The man held a floppy hat between two hands and looked up at Harris from a grizzled, weather-beaten face.

The church had seen its share of panhandlers, homeless, and families just down on their luck. They weren't far from Reno, and casinos and other gambling spots scattered throughout the desert did their best to destroy the finances of a lot of families. Harris was used to taking needy people to breakfast, lunch or dinner, and stocking their waiting automobiles up with either gasoline or canned food from their Community Services stores.

At first glance, this guy looked to Harris like more of the same. Then he looked into his clear, grey eyes and recognized the first look of ageless maturity that he'd seen in the 16 year old's eyes two nights before. It was him.

Harris paused, then peered skeptically at the visitor.

"You're him. Aren't you? The Messenger, I mean?" The old man stared back with a faint smile, then nodded quickly.

"I know it takes some getting used to," he said to Harris. "Over the years I've appeared to countless humans in countless situations. And each time I have had to take on a form appropriate to the occasion. When you do that so much, you get used to changing your appearance just as a human would change clothes."

Harris continued to stare.

"Oh, come on, Harris," he chuckled. "Most people never get a visit from heaven—at least that they're aware of—and you've had two. Plus you got a glimpse of the real me. If you can't get past changing physical form—which is highly overrated—how will you deal with the rest of it?"

Harris blinked, and shook himself.

"Right."

"I see you've been doing some research. What have you learned?" The Messenger asked through perfect white teeth.

"That hundreds of families—maybe thousands—are being financially destroyed by this company called Universal Finance. That no one can contact them or even find out anything about them. And that they're dangerous."

The Messenger smiled thinly. "Oh, you have no idea how dangerous." He shook his head slowly. "You've seen the tip of the iceberg. And if you know anything about icebergs, you know that ten percent is above the water, but 90 percent is below the surface. Want to see what lies beneath those waves?"

Harris looked at The Messenger seriously. "I don't know. Do I?"

The Messenger stared at him beneath bushy eyebrows as if trying to read something written on his soul. "Have you changed your mind? Perhaps you've learned that when you ask God for something, He takes your request seriously?"

Harris suddenly felt at a loss for words. "What if…what if I don't…can't…."

"What if you decide you can't do the task that God has given you? Will He love you any less?" The Messenger reached out his hand and held his open palm against the side of Harris' head. "I think you know the answer to that." And he did. God couldn't love him any more than He did right then. But Harris also knew that he would be losing out on something special if he refused to be used by God.

"You need to decide right now if you want to continue with this," The Messenger said to Harris, his hand still resting against his face. "If you don't, things will go back to the way they were. If you do continue, don't be surprised if things get worse than you could ever imagine."

As they stood together in the foyer of the church, Harris took a deep breath and let it out. He realized that his involvement with this involved Katya as well. And yet, she knew what was going on. He made his decision.

"God has opened the door for me," Harris said. "I can't do anything but go in."

"Very well," The Messenger said. "You've made your choice, but other choices will need to be made too." The grizzled stranger walked up the center aisle of the sanctuary and climbed the steps onto the church platform, and Harris was amazed at how natural it seemed for him to be up there.

"What do you know of the story of Elijah?" The Messenger asked.

"You kidding? I'm a pastor," Harris said. "His story starts with his arrival before Ahab, king of Israel, to tell him there would be a drought until he said otherwise."

"And why did he do this?"

"Because Ahab led the country in worship of the false-god Baal."

The Messenger nodded. "And how did the confrontation end?"

"Elijah invited the priests of Baal to the top of Mount Carmel where he challenged them to a test...sort of a barbeque. The first side that could get their god to light their sacrifice on the altar would win. It would show that their god had the power. Elijah won because our God exists, whereas Baal doesn't."

"Wrong," The Messenger said. "I should know. I was there." He strode swiftly forward and grabbed Harris' wrist, his eyes wide with energy. "Watch and learn!"

Harris felt a moment of disorientation, when he felt that the universe had been turned on its side. Then he looked down on a bleak landscape. He could see figures, humans, gathered on a mountaintop far below. The terrain was barren like the moon, and the sky around him was deep blue without the hint of a cloud.

The sky was cloudless, yet Harris was tempted to rub his eyes, for there were strange shapes floating, swirling, here and there. Brilliant points of light hung above the ground at different altitudes. The lights rolled through the sky like fireflies, some touching near the earth, other soaring high over his head.

Then Harris noticed the lights contrasted with dark patches; places in the sky that reminded him of how he imagined a black hole might look. When he looked into the darkest patch, he felt a pang of depression and failure.

Although he was high above the earth, he felt no motion. He turned and saw that The Messenger, brilliantly shining, still held his wrist.

"What is this I am seeing?" he asked.

The Messenger's face shone. "This is Elijah on Mount Carmel, as I remember it. You are seeing good and evil as they are, more or less. But perhaps you prefer a more traditional view of the conflict." He waved his hand and the scene changed.

Suddenly Harris felt the motion of flying through the air. Around him, wisps of black and white swirled like feathers caught in a whirlpool. And suddenly he realized that they were not feathers. They were angels. And the wisps were massive in size.

And there were a lot of them. Thousands, in fact. The sky was full, and there seemed to be some sort of conflict going on.

"Incredible," Harris said, relaxing a little bit, but not too much. "Is every angel's memory this vivid?"

"Yours would be too, but thousands of years of sin have corrupted your minds," he said. "Look over there." Harris looked where he pointed at a giant red figure, struggling against countless white angels who held him back. Harris looked back at The Messenger.

"That is Baal," he explained. "His name in heaven was different. Baal means 'Lord'. He's chosen the path of rebellion. He's a mighty power to be dealt with, for he's one of Satan's chief lieutenants. He has sixty-six legions at his command."

"Sixty-six legions," Harris repeated, adding in his head. "That's more than 360,000 angels."

"Evil angels," The Messenger corrected him. "Or demons, if you prefer." He looked up at the massive demon that it took hundreds of angels to hold back. "They gain their strength and status when they can convince humans to worship them. That's why this conflict is so important."

Harris looked below him and saw that the priests of Baal had been cutting themselves and calling upon the restrained demon to set flame to their sacrifice. As Harris watched, a lone figure told them to clear out of the way. He suspected that the simply dressed man must be Elijah, and he longed to get a closer look at him.

As if in response, The Messenger bolted out of the sky and carried him to within a few yards of the long-haired, bearded Elijah. Harris watched as servants carried water and poured it over the dead animal that Elijah had laid on his altar. Then he knelt simply and prayed silently to God.

Except from the perspective of angels, the prayer was not silent. It ripped through the atmosphere like a sonic boom and made the demons around them scream and clutch their ears. They began to fly higher and higher in a spiral, as if to escape the prayer words that blasted against their ears like a gong. Then a cry went up, which turned into a blood-curdling scream.

Above Harris the sky opened, and he saw what must have been the gates of heaven. Harris knew that no words can ever describe it. But before he could even get a conscious fix on it, something brilliant began to pour through those gates. It was fire.

A stream of fire fell from the sky, and his hair stood on the back of his neck.

"Behold the glory of the Lord!" The Messenger shouted, and he was joined by a thousand others. The fire roared through the atmosphere like a comet, and boomed into the old stone altar and sacrifice below them. It devoured everything it touched.

As one, those who had worshipped Baal fell to the ground and proclaimed God as Lord and Master of all. And as Harris watched them begin to worship the True God, the strength of the demon called Baal visibly diminished until he vanished from sight.

"Is he gone? Dead?" Harris wondered aloud.

"No, not dead," said The Messenger. "Not until the Lake of Fire at the end. But he has lost power for now." The angel looked at the place that had been occupied by the monster demon. "He gains strength when he's worshipped."

The Messenger looked at Harris seriously. "Remember what you've seen here."

Harris looked back at him, dumbfounded. *How could I ever forget what I've seen?"*

"I'm grateful to you for showing me what you have," Harris said to The Messenger. "But what does this have to do with the task God has for me?"

The Messenger carried Harris high above the earth, and Harris watched as God's angels chased random demons from the sky.

"This man you investigated, this Kenneth Deke," the angel said slowly.

"Yes?" Harris responded curiously. "He's the man in charge of Universal Finance."

"He is not in charge," The Messenger said. "Baal is."

4 MOMENT OF TRUTH

Maybe he understood that Harris wouldn't absorb much after that bombshell. But after letting him know who the enemy really was, The Messenger pretty much left Harris alone. Before he knew it, Harris and the angel were back in the church sanctuary. Harris stared at him, dumbfounded, as he quietly slipped through the double metal doors and disappeared into the night.

After the usual slack-jawed interlude—Harris was making a bad habit of that—he shook his head and tried to make himself useful. What did he know? One, that he had volunteered for Spiritual Special Forces and been accepted; two, that the battle orbited around the credit card company Universal Finance, which was somehow making a lot of people desperately miserable; and three, that this was no ordinary Fortune 500 company. How the demon Baal was behind all of this—or more importantly, why—was not evident yet. But he was sure that soon enough it would be.

The Messenger had said that Baal gained strength from those who worshipped him—or her, or it. What was worship, but putting another being before yourself? Could it be that making someone indebted to an evil angel could constitute worship? Harris didn't know; this was all new ground.

Fact is, he didn't know many people who were specialists in this area. Harris pondered it a moment, and then realized he knew one person who might be able to help. It was late, but because of the special circumstances, he went ahead and speed dialed Greg Phipps. After half a dozen rings, Harris heard his sleepy voice on the other end of the phone.

"This is Greg Phipps," he said.

"Hi, Greg, this is Harris," he replied. "Sorry to wake you, but I needed to talk about something important." Harris paused to catch his breath, and suddenly realized how idiotic he would sound. *Have you talked to any angels lately?* Or perhaps *The Old Testament god Baal is alive and living in San Francisco.* Suddenly he lost his courage.

"Yes, Harris, what it is?" Greg asked patiently.

"I…uh…." The words escaped him, and he prayed to find them.

"Uh, look Greg, this is hard for me to say, but it's important, so just give me a second, okay?" Harris began to break out in a sweat.

"Sure, Harris, take your time," Greg said, his voice uncommonly calm and patient. The clock ticked on the wall, and Harris prayed silently. This was either going to be the right thing to do, or going to be really, really hard on his credibility as a pastor.

In the end Harris decided to tell him the whole story. He started with his frustration as a pastor, and how he had asked God to use him in a big way. He told of both visits from The Messenger—going light on describing the special effects—and how he and Katya had received the hundreds of letters and phone calls addressed to Universal Finance. Harris ended by telling Greg of his conclusions about how he needed to do something to stop what was going on, and possibly stop Baal from gaining a foothold in people's lives.

"And right now you're probably wondering if this young and inept pastor has completely lost all of his marbles," he said to Greg.

There was a long pause. "Well, Harris, you can imagine how your story sounds to someone hearing it for the first time," he said. He chuckled, and Harris relaxed a little bit.

"The truth is," he continued. "In my years of mission work I've experienced things I was hesitant to share even with our brethren. I've seen things so profound, so miraculous, that it seemed like blasphemy to even repeat them to someone who might try to rationalize them with our Western way of thinking. And I have seen the Devil work in ways that would make the common church member cringe in fear.

"I'm not the one to decide if what you described is from God or not," he continued. "But I can tell you that Satan and his demons are real. The only advice I can give you is to do what the Bible says. If God is calling you to confront evil, follow the examples of others who've had the same task as you. Is it going to be an Elijah situation? A John the Baptist situation? Or are you going to upset the tables of the moneychangers like the Original Troublemaker Himself?"

Harris smiled to himself, which turned into a grimace.

"To tell you the truth, I was hoping you'd tell me," he replied. "Guess that would be too easy."

"You know where the answer lies," Greg said. "On your knees, my son, on your knees."

Harris knew Greg was right, and hung up. But sometimes you want someone—a human, even—to tell you what you already know deep down. Harris gained some confidence in knowing Greg didn't think he was a lunatic. Or at least he didn't act as if he thought so.

Harris prayed for another hour in the sanctuary, and the late hour became later. Emotionally drained, he finally decided to head home. To his surprise, Katya was awake and up, waiting for him. She sat in her red bathrobe on the beat-up couch in their tiny living room, her right hand nervously flicking through the TV channels with the remote. Her eyes switched from the bored, vacant stare of watching late night TV to one of recognition, joy and relief when he walked through the door.

"*Zdravstvuj!*" she said as she sprung from the couch and ran into his arms. Even after eight years, her reaction caused Harris' heart to race and adrenaline to pump through his body. Is it possible to be excited around someone, while at the same time feel at peace with them? That's exactly how he felt around Katya. To Harris, she was the most remarkable person in the world.

Somewhere along the line, she had decided to put her career aspirations on the back burner to support him and the hope of having a family of her own. Harris knew how important family was to her; both from her talk of life as a child in Leningrad and her continued wish for a child of her own.

One of the most inspirational moments anyone had around them, one that allowed her true feelings about family—and about her music—to show, was when she and Harris performed a duet. He accompanied her on guitar while she sang the traditional Russian lullaby:

"Bai, bai, bai, bai,

Báyu, Detusku mayú!

Bai, bai, bai, bai,

Báyu, Detusku, mayú!

Shta na górki, na goryé,

O visyénnei, o poryé.

Ptíchki Bozhiye payút,

F tyómnam lyési gnyózda vyut."

Harris would usually translate the words into English for the audience:

Bai, bai, bai, bai,

Bayu, orchid, little dear.

Bai, bai, bai, bai,

Bayu, orchid, little dear.

    On the hillside in the spring,

Birds of heaven sweetly sing,

Seeking for their young what's best

    In the forest dark they nest.

It was a simple, traditional Russian lullaby. It was also a window into Katya's soul, and an intimate glimpse into the life of a complicated, highly intelligent, compassionate, self-sacrificing woman. Performing the song usually brought her to the verge of tears, as it did her audience, and Harris cherished it as an intimate moment they shared. He knew she missed her family, and missed the land of her birth. She had given it all up to be his wife and go with him wherever God called him to be.

"We need to talk," Harris said, holding her at arms length and coming back to the present. They sat back down on the couch, and he told her first what had happened at the church that night, and then of his phone call to Greg. Her eyebrows raised, but once again, to his surprise she didn't act as disbelieving as Harris thought she would.

"You know, Chickpea, I don't know how it is in Russia, but most wives here in the United States would have a lot more time believing the stories I've been telling you."

A smile crept across Katya's face, and then she looked down at her hands. They began to tremble.

"My father had a lot of trouble in the old Soviet Union," she said. "He was a man who would not play the political games. He was too honest, and he made a lot of enemies." She looked up and Harris could see tears forming in her eyes.

"When I was nine, I remember Pappa being taken away. We all knew we would never see him again. The chief of police hated him and hated Christianity. We knew he would do whatever he could to stop Pappa. He had already said in public that my father would be killed sooner or later. So we knew that if there was not a miracle, he would die." The tears ran freely down her face. Harris reached out and put his hand on hers, but she pulled away and stood up, looking out the picture window into their blackened front yard.

"We got on the telephone and called every church member that had a phone. For the next three days and nights we held a prayer vigil. By the time we were done, hundreds, if not thousands, prayed for my father's release."

She turned and looked at him, a wild look in her eyes.

"The next morning, Pappa came home." Her voice broke with the last word, and she began to sob. "They had told him he would never live to see the outside world again. They told him that he was going to die. Then suddenly, they just let him go."

Harris stood and walked over to his sobbing wife, holding her against him.

"I saw a miracle that morning. There are a lot of miracles that happen in a lot of places to a lot of people. But this one happened to my Pappa. It happened to me." The tears flowed freely, and his joined hers. Soon Harris pulled free enough to reach for the tissue box for both of them.

She sniffed, then pulled away from him and pounded his chest with her fist.

"So don't tell me that miracles don't happen, that angels don't exist, that God doesn't care," she said, bawling again. "I know better." Tears smeared across her face and her nose ran freely, but to Harris she looked as beautiful as the day he married her.

They sat on the couch and he held her for a long time. When she was composed again—when they both were composed—they talked about what would happen next.

"You must confront the company," she said matter-of-factly. "You must tell them that what they are doing is an aboni—abdono—what you say in English *zlo*."

"Abomination, evil," he told her.

"Yes, what you said," she said, smiling shyly. "It is wrong what they are doing."

"Pull an Elijah," Harris said, more to himself than to her.

"Yes, exactly. Like Elijah," she said, still sniffing.

Harris didn't want to tell her, but his mind went to all the troubles that Elijah had after he condemned King Ahab's court. Living in the wilderness with nothing but ravens to feed him, running for his life, and the confrontation on Mount Carmel. Is that what he wanted? He stopped himself. It wasn't what he wanted, of course, it was what God wanted. What was it The Messenger had said? "With great responsibility sometimes comes great pain and sorrow." Harris looked at Katya, and suddenly the prospect of being called by God didn't seem so appealing.

"But I don't know where or when to address this company," he stammered. "They seem to be as hard to catch as a six-legged racehorse."

"Then we will pray for direction for you," she responded. "We will pray for God to tell us exactly where you need to be."

In the end, they decided to pray for direction, as well as one more demonstration that God was behind this plan. Harris remembered Dougie and his visit to the doctor. They both prayed that he'd show an improvement.

Wednesday was always a busy day for Harris. So after they agreed to the plan, Katya and he went off to bed. They took a little time for the Project— there was always time for that—but he was able to get a few hours of sound sleep for the next day.

Harris had Bible studies with two young people, met with the local ministerial association for lunch, took an hour for his daily run, and then got called over to the school to meet with two students and the principal. Apparently there was a difference of opinion between the two sixth graders that had resulted in a fist fight. Harris talked with them for about a half hour and finally had them shaking hands and going back to their class as friends. At the end of the afternoon, Harris got over to his office for a couple of hours of paperwork.

That evening, he'd just kissed Katya after dinner and was headed out the door to prayer meeting when his cell phone chirped. Text message. He never used text messaging because his cell phone service charged extra for it. Harris looked at the number that sent it and didn't recognize the number—or even the area code. He switched to the message and read:

Universal Finance Cabal Meeting

Pan-Pacific 360

Thursday, 1 p.m.

Harris stared at the message, then showed it to Katya. They looked at each other in disbelief.

"One prayer answered, one to go," she whispered, then smiled and looked up at him. "Who sent the message?"

He shook his head. There was no name associated with the phone number. Harris hit callback and waited for the other phone to ring. It rang ten times without an answer, so finally he hung up.

One more to go, Harris breathed to himself as he headed off to prayer meeting.

* * *

"Flip" Ledger had been watching the old man for a long while. He had followed him from the Gun Collector's show, knowing that the man had money, and was a serious collector. Well, Flip was a serious collector as well. Trouble was, he didn't have cash, and he needed bread for life more than he needed something to decorate his trashy apartment. So it was that the items the old man cherished as pieces of history, Flip would see as just another paycheck. How Marty, his fence, viewed them was up to him.

He watched the man enter his San Francisco townhouse. The doorman helped him carry his packages to the second floor. That made it easier for Flip to get in the front door and watch them go up the elevator. Flip hid while the doorman came back downstairs and went outside, then he took the elevator as well.

He waited until he thought the old man was probably asleep—Flip could handle himself, but preferred heists without any trouble—and then picked the lock on the front door. He used bolt cutters on the door chain, and he was in. He scanned the palatial townhouse, and quickly concluded that the old man lived alone. He listened, and could finally hear the man snoring in the bedroom. Two other doors opened off the hallway: the restroom and a second bedroom, or study. He decided to try the study before the bedroom.

He had just recently decided to focus on gun collectors, and been pretty successful in picking out ones that were profitable. As in any area of collection, one had to know what was valuable. The guns he was attracted to weren't necessarily worth that much, because he thought of functionality rather than history or craftsmanship. But he knew that if he kept with it long enough, he would learn to distinguish the gold from the lead.

As soon as he picked the room lock and took a look around, he realized that he had hit the jackpot. The walls were covered with guns—muskets and blunderbusses from centuries ago, as well as pistols, derringers and revolvers in a variety of display cases. He knew from experience that one gun weighed a few pounds; several guns weighed quite a bit. He had learned to pick smaller guns, which often were more valuable than the larger ones.

He also knew that the most valuable would be in the safe. He went to the only painting in the room and pulled it away from the wall safe. He took a few minutes to crack the lock, and it was open.

Inside was one revolver in a Plexiglas case. It didn't look that spectacular, but Flip had learned that appearances could be deceiving. He carefully stuck the revolver and its case into his backpack.

* * *

When Harris got to prayer meeting, he didn't have to wait long to get the other response he was looking for. He could hear the commotion as soon as he stepped through the double doors to the sanctuary lobby. A crowd of about a dozen people huddled around one person he couldn't see. They were cheering and crying. Finally the crowd parted and Harris saw that it was Moira Washington, Dougie's mom. They were back from Reno.

"Oh, Pastor," she said, tears falling freely. "The doctor said he usually didn't give results from the lab right away, but he was so astonished with the results that he had to tell me. He did three tests and they all said the same thing: the tumors—all of them—are gone! I had hoped that we would show some sign of slowing the disease, but this is just…just." She burst into tears and fell on his shoulder.

Prayer number two answered, Harris thought to himself. *At least you are being straightforward, God.* And he knew what was coming next.

Tomorrow Harris was headed to San Francisco.

5 CLOSE ENCOUNTER

The mysterious text message had said the cabal meeting would happen at Pan Pacific 360 at 1 p.m. on Thursday. After prayer meeting, Katya and Harris got on Mapquest and figured out how far the drive would be. It turned out the whole trip there would take about five hours and a tank of gas. So about 7:30 the next morning Harris got in his trusty 2002 Corolla and headed west.

It didn't take long to get to I-80, and that led him through Reno, Sacramento and on to San Francisco. He was left with his thoughts, as morbid and frightening as they might be. Eventually he thought he would try to find some music to lighten his mood. He switched on the stereo.

"*Ain't no time to wonder why. Whoopie, we're all going to die,*" crooned the first song, and he quickly switched channels.

"*Soy un perdedor, I'm a loser baby, so why don't you kill me?*
Soy un perdedor, I'm a loser baby, so why don't you kill me?"

"Well, that's uplifting," Harris muttered to himself. "Let's give it one more try." He switched the radio again and recognized the Eagles, a favorite old group.

"We are all just prisoners here, Of our own device, And in the master's chambers They gather for the feast, They stab it with their steely knives, But they just can't kill the beast."

The Hotel California didn't make much sense to him before this, but now it made too much sense. Harris reached for the knob before they came to the chorus, and switched it off.

"Lord, I guess it's going to be just you and me," Harris prayed aloud as he drove.

The morning was clear, and traffic behaved pretty well for a Thursday. He got to the Bay Bridge right on schedule and headed from Oakland into San Francisco. He once again marveled at how God worked things out. Both Katya and Harris had recognized the name Pan-Pacific 360 from the text message. The Pan-Pacific Hotel was an art deco style hotel in the Nob Hill section of San Francisco. Eight years before, Katya and he had spent their wedding night at that hotel. Pan Pacific 360 referred to the rotating restaurant at the top of the hotel. Though it was a little pricey for them (ok, a lot pricey), they took advantage of their honeymoon to splurge on one meal and ate in the restaurant that featured one of the best views of San Francisco and the Bay. It was atop a 19-story hotel. From a table in the rotating restaurant one could see pretty much all of San Francisco, Oakland, and on a clear day, the Sierras in the east and the Farallon Islands in the west.

Harris knew exactly where the Pan Pacific was, or at least he did eight years ago. Katya insisted that they get a little navigational help from Yahoo, and so he brought directions with him. He crossed the Bay Bridge, and exited I-80 at the Harrison Street exit as the slip on his lap instructed him to. Then he turned right onto 6th Street, which quickly turned into Taylor Street and reintroduced him to San Francisco bumper-to-bumper traffic. They went up one hill and down the other side. He was dodging an electric streetcar and a couple of cabs when California Street came up, where he was supposed to turn right. Problem was, he was in the left lane passing the taxis. The buildings seemed to get taller and taller around him, the streets more narrow, the traffic more dense, and every time he wanted to turn right, the street was one way in the other direction.

Harris tried to cut back to California on the next street and found it was going left instead of right. After another block, he gunned the engine and cut in front of a cab to make a right turn. This was definitely not Nevada traffic. In Round Rock, three cars in a row was a traffic jam.

He could see signs in Chinese a few blocks away and knew that he wasn't far from Nob Hill. Chinatown and Little Italy were within a few blocks of the hotel, as he knew from their honeymoon. Finally he crossed Mason Street and saw the 60s-style architecture of Pan Pacific with the round rotating restaurant on top. He was within walking distance.

Harris had found the place, but had come to his second worry. Parking was notoriously bad in San Francisco, especially this part of town. He breathed a prayer as he jockeyed through the narrow streets. His hope was to find a place that would be easy to get in and out of, especially since he had no idea what kind of reception he'd find at the meeting.

He turned down a side street and saw two young boys, one black and one Asian, holding up a piece of cardboard that said, "Parking: $5." Harris smiled at these two young entrepreneurs, and made a right into their alley.

"Hey fellas," he said, standing at the doorway of his car. "Is parking legal here?"

The black kid looked at the other, and then back at him. "This is Mikey's father's shop." He gestured to the brick building that they stood behind. "We get to use this space to make money. We're going to buy a Playstation."

"Well, I'll tell you what," Harris said, reaching into his pocket. "Leave this space behind me free so I can get out quickly, and I'll pay you $10."

"Deal, Mister," Mikey said, and quickly took the money.

It was a good place to park. Harris was two easy blocks away from the hotel, and yet was not obvious. And, if his business partners kept the other space free, he'd be able to get out in a hurry if he needed to.

As he got his suitcoat out of the passenger seat and straightened his tie and white shirt, Harris realized his hands were trembling. It was nothing new. Every time he preached, not only did his hands shake, but sometimes his knees did, too. This was a bit different, however. Harris wasn't a person who took a lot of risks. Today he was taking a big one.

He left the alley and walked out onto Mason Street. The day was typical of San Francisco, cool and clear, even in summer. It reminded Harris of that day eight years before when Katya and he had first come here. They had just sat down and placed their order at the restaurant when the fire alarm went off. Their server had escorted them out of the spacious dining area and into the back preparation area. There he'd taken them into a service elevator and down to the street level.

"I'm really not supposed to do this," he said apologetically. "But you two look like nice people and I didn't want to make you walk down 19 flights of stairs." The service elevator had opened into the parking garage in the basement of the hotel. From there it was a quick walk to the street.

That trip was on Harris' mind as he stepped through the revolving door and entered the lobby of the Pan Pacific Hotel. The spacious room looked just the way he remembered it. Gold leaf decorated everything, including the pillars at the entrance. A thick red wall-to-wall carpet shouted luxury. A wide staircase faced him, with alabaster elephants on the right and check-in agents to the left. And then Harris noticed something else that was different.

Spaced about every ten feet around the room were burly young men with blue sports coats on. Each had a radio on his belt, and Harris was pretty sure that each was armed as well. One especially big guy scanned the room until he saw Harris standing in the doorway, and his eyes fixed on him as if he were trying to will Harris to go away—or memorizing what he looked like. Harris suddenly felt naked.

"Where to now, Lord?" he whispered. He looked over at an easel that advertised the Pan Pacific 360 and saw that a special notice was emblazoned across the front of it: "Closed for private event." Harris knew which event they referred to.

"No, I'm sorry, Sir, but all suites on floors 16 through 19 have been reserved," the agent to his left was saying. "Yes, I understand, but there are no exceptions." His attention went from the agent to a couple of teenagers who attempted to board the express elevator that went to the top floors. One of the burly guards held up his hand and told them in no uncertain terms that they had to take a different elevator.

Then Harris saw something that made his mind up for him. He looked at the ceiling and realized that a security camera was pointed right at him. He stood staring for a long second, and realized that he was giving the hotel and the finance company a permanent record of who he was and what he looked like. Harris turned and walked back out the revolving door.

"Looks like Plan B, Lord," he whispered, and rounded the corner to the entrance to the hotel's garage. People were driving in and out of the entrance, and the attendant was busy paying attention to them, but he noticed that the attendant didn't even look up. He walked down the first long aisle of cars, rounded a corner, and stood before the big metal door of the service elevator.

There were no buttons on the outside of the doors, but he knew there had to be another way in: a key perhaps. Deliveries came to the restaurant all the time and they had to get them up there. Harris saw an intercom on the right and a button. He pressed it and waited to see what would happen.

"Yes?" came a metallic voice.

"It's me," he said on impulse. In response, Harris heard a ding, and the service elevator doors opened. He took a deep breath and stepped inside.

There were no buttons on the inside either, and the ride to the restaurant took just a few seconds. The doors dinged open and the familiar sounds, smells and sights of Pan-Pacific 360 wafted toward him. Harris stood there for a long second, then someone walked by, and shoved a white coat into his hands.

"It's about time you showed up," the man said, not bothering to look fully at him. "Punch in, then you have tables three, four and five. Hurry up. These guys are demanding."

So this is the way it is going to happen, Harris prayed silently. *OK, I can play along.* He took off his suit coat and hung it with others in the back, then put on the white server's jacket. Fortunately, he'd spent one summer in college working as a server at the local Italian restaurant. He found an electronic chart on the wall by the time clock that showed which tables were which, grabbed an order form, and headed over to table three.

"Good day, gentlemen," he said to the table filled with white-haired men. "My name is Harris and I'll be your server today. Would you care to start off with something to drink?"

"Yeah, what wines do you recommend?" one old guy with a red, bulbous nose said to him, reaching up and clutching his arm.

"Well, the restaurant has a lot of good wines, I'm sure, but you'll want to keep you mind clear for such an important meeting," he said. "Can I interest you in a sparkling non-alcoholic beverage?" He don't know why he had resisted selling them alcohol—ingrained personal values, he guessed—but to his relief, it seemed to be the right thing to do.

"The young fellow's right, Bob," another at the table said. "I want to be sharp for this presentation." Harris took down their order, stumbling through the abbreviation he thought a server would use for that menu, and stepped back into the shadows to survey the room.

About a hundred people—mostly men in their 60s and 70s—filled the restaurant serving area. He didn't know what he expected the cabal to look like, but more than anything it looked like a meeting of the local Rotary club. The room was full of laughing customers, busy servers in white coats buzzing between the tables, and the occasional clink of a wine glass or dinnerware on plates.

The only exception was a small table set over in the corner. As Harris watched, a small line of men—and a few women—stepped up to a basin in the center of the table. They took a knife laying there and slashed over the inside of their forearm. Harris saw the elderly man in front pull back his sleeve, slash the knife across his skin, and drip his crimson blood into the basin. He picked up a napkin and covered the cut while another took his place. Harris turned to look elsewhere, but the image stayed in his mind.

The cityscape was spectacular. To his right, Harris could see the afternoon sun glinting off the Golden Gate Bridge, and further to the right was the Coit Tower, a pale white in the sunlight. To the far left, sailboats dotted the Bay. The view was awe-inspiring, but waiters and customers alike hardly glanced up to see what he saw.

Across the room from him, Harris saw the stage that had been set up in the center of the rotating room. On it sat two men, both about his age. One he recognized as Kenneth Deke, the CEO of Universal Finance, from his picture in the *San Francisco Herald*. Muscular and fit, with close-cropped dark brown hair and a sharp-chiseled face, Deke exuded calmness and poise. His suit looked like it would have cost Harris a month's salary. But he also had something that went beyond good looks. The expression on his face exuded a confidence and control that Harris had never seen before in his life.

If there could be a polar opposite for Deke, it was expressed in the second guy. About the same age as Deke, the second man was about 60 pounds overweight, with pasty skin and red, disheveled hair. He looked like he slept in his clothes, and the tie that he had around his neck looked like it had been borrowed at the last minute. He reminded Harris of the computer majors in college who spent 14-hour days in the computer lab, only to come out and eat and sleep.

Deke stood and tapped the microphone. Smiling, he scanned the audience.

"Thank you for all being here," he said. "As you know, and as it says in the quarterly report you received when you checked in, the past three months have shown phenomenal growth for Universal. We've been blessed with unprecedented profits, and we've stabilized our earlier precarious financial position.

"But this is just the beginning. We're going to change the world. Always remember that the plan for Universal is projected as a diversified corporation, and that compound interest loans are just the first step on our road to global success."

Did he just say global? Harris asked himself silently.

"We're more than just a corporation," he continued. "If you want profits, we can help you in that department. It might say 'In God We Trust' on the dollar bill, but we all know where our trust lies. *The true glory comes in serving The One.*"

"We live to serve," the audience said in unison, and Harris felt a chill come across him. They broke into applause.

"With our success comes power, not only for us, but more importantly for him," Deke continued after the applause. "You've seen the success of Phase One. Very soon we will be moving on to Phases Two and Three. His glory will become apparent to everyone."

"We live to serve," the audience repeated.

Now is the time, Harris heard a voice inside his head say. *Do it.*

His heart was pounding in his chest. Harris stood a dozen steps from the platform, and without thinking he reacted. He stepped forward quickly and raced to the platform, pulling the microphone from Deke's hands.

By the time he'd turned around and faced the audience again, two guards were racing across the room toward him. Deke held up his hand for them to stop, and allowed Harris to speak.

"Who are you? The IRS?" someone at the first table slurred drunkenly.

"Who I am isn't important," Harris said. "But I've come with a message from the Most High God." His hands were trembling, but as he began to speak, a new courage came into him. Rage at the injustice this company had committed both gave him energy and calmed him.

"And what does your God have to say?" Deke said behind him, his voice slippery smooth.

"Simply this: you've ruined enough people's lives in your search for profits and power. God won't stand for it anymore. If this company continues on the path it's chosen, it'll be destroyed. And anyone who continues to invest in it will be destroyed as well."

A couple of hoots of laughter came from the tables. Deke snorted behind him in glee and started to take the microphone from him. Harris jerked it away.

"There's more," Harris said, an edge coming into his voice. "I know who the real leader of this company is. I know who you worship."

The laughter became silent, and after a pause, Deke gestured for the guards to come forward. Harris knew he had just a moment more to speak.

"Baal has fallen before, and he'll do so again," he said, and the microphone was jerked from his hands. "Idolatry leads to death!" he shouted without the benefit of the microphone. A big fist came flying out of nowhere and caught Harris on the side of the jaw. He saw stars and collapsed to the floor below the platform.

"Make sure he doesn't come back," Harris heard Deke quietly tell one of the guards. "Make it an accident."

A metal-toed boot caught Harris in the ribs, and the stars turned to waves of pain. Strong arms grabbed him on either side, and dragged him to a stairwell a few feet away. Harris shook his head and tried to get his senses back together as they dragged him up a short set of stairs to a metal door marked, "To Roof." He looked to his left and right and saw that the guards were built like NFL linebackers. They each outweighed Harris by close to a hundred pounds, and he somehow knew that it was sheer muscle. No overpowering these two.

The one on his left, a six-foot beast with a blonde crewcut, pushed the crashbar on the door and popped it open. He checked it.

"You got a key?" he said to the other one, a taller, black mastodon. "We don't want to get locked up here when it's over." The black one shook his head.

The blonde one shrugged. "I don't think it'll take more than one of us to do this," he said. "You hold the door. I'll take care of it."

His head a lot clearer now, Harris suddenly realized what the It was that he referred to. They were going to throw Harris from the roof of the hotel, and make it look like a suicide. Not much would be left after falling 20 stories to the pavement below. He dragged Harris clear of the door and continued toward the side of the slowly revolving rooftop.

"Think I'll find my own way out," Harris muttered, and twisted suddenly in his grasp. Caught off guard, the blonde giant loosened his grip, and Harris almost got away, but then he regained it, clutching Harris' arm and the collar of his coat. He popped Harris in the face again, and his head jerked back.

"Hehe, slippery little guy," he said to Harris quietly. "Well, I've dealt with a lot of guys more slippery than you."

"I'm sure you have," Harris responded, suddenly straightening up and turning around. Harris kneed him in the groin as hard as he could. Although he didn't go down in a heap as Harris had hoped, the big man loosened his grip on Harris' arm. Harris leaped forward and slipped out of the white server's coat that the giant still held onto.

Harris looked back at the door and realized that in the few seconds that it had taken for him to free myself from Blondie, the black guard had left his post holding the door open and was bolting toward them. Harris knew he could not take him in a fair fight. The guard was already reaching into his coat for the weapon that Harris knew he kept there. So Harris reacted instinctively. He stopped his run away from the guard and kicked sideways behind him. His black dress shoes caught the black man on the side of the knee and he went down in a heap.

The door was locked behind him. Harris had nowhere else to go. And he knew that the next round with the two guards wouldn't go in his favor.

Jump, he heard a voice inside his head say. *Jump*.

Jump, he thought, and ran for the edge of the rooftop. But rational thought kicked in just as he came to the edge. *Are you crazy?* he asked the voice inside him, and came to a screeching halt. Teetering on the edge, he turned to look at the men behind him. One was running his direction, the other was raising his gun to fire.

It was at that moment that he lost his balance and toppled forward, over the edge.

6 ESCAPE

Max Heinrich picked himself up and dusted off his grey pants and blue sports coat. His groin ached where he'd gotten kneed, but he'd been hit there plenty when he was playing college football, and more recently in security training. He walked casually over to Willis Greer and reached out to help him up from the gravel-strewn rooftop.

Greer flinched when he put weight on his bad knee, but like Heinrich, he was a professional and didn't let the pain slow him down.

"Think he's gone?" Greer asked, stepping toward the rooftop edge and peering over.

"Gone?" Heinrich snorted. "Man, he's paste. Twenty stories'll do that to anybody." Heinrich joined Greer at the edge and looked down to the concrete pavement below. "Deke wanted an accident, and the guy obliged him. Game over, man, game over."

"So, where's the body?" Greer asked.

"What?"

"His body," Greer asked again. "Where is it?"

* * *

The instant that Harris lost his balance and fell off the rooftop, he was sure it would be the last thing he did. Survival instinct had caused him to fight the two guards on the roof. Then the words came, and while he sensed that God had a plan, common sense overruled and caused him to hesitate. A lack of balance overruled common sense in the end, however.

Since both eyes were closed, Harris didn't see what happened. But he felt it. He felt a sharp pain jam both knees when he hit something solid below him, and then sharp rocks pricked him as he rolled. Harris opened his eyes and he was on another gravel rooftop, quickly rolling toward the edge. He flung his hands out at his sides, and stopped rolling just inches from open air. He lay there for a long second, both hands bleeding, his suit shredded at the knees and his white shirt red with his own blood.

And then Harris understood what had happened. The two guards hadn't considered that the round, rotating restaurant stood on a square pedestal of the hotel roof. Harris fell as the restaurant rotated, just in time to be caught by one of the corners of the square base 20 feet below. Both knees aches, his ribs shot pain through his side, his face was already beginning to swell, but Harris was alive.

He turned and looked toward the restaurant—and stared directly at the four men sitting at the table he'd served earlier. The elderly man who had gone with the sparkling non-alcoholic drink Harris had recommended held it up to him in salute. All of them had a dumbfounded look on their faces. Harris suddenly realized that if they saw him, others would as well. And he remembered the guards above him.

Harris quickly rolled back to the edge of the restaurant rotating a few feet away. Fortunately, the restaurant window started about a foot above the rooftop he lay on, with a gap beneath that window that he quickly rolled under. His quickly thrown-together plan was to stay out of sight of the guards and anyone inside until he found a way out of his predicament.

He didn't have to wait long. An access door rotated above him. He noted with relief that someone had locked it, but hadn't pulled it completely closed. Harris rolled out from beneath the gap and grabbed the doorknob. As he stood, the pain in his side grew sharper, and he knew something was seriously wrong. But his biggest priority was just getting out of the building and back to his car.

Harris opened the door and saw with relief that he was in the kitchen. Directly across from him, about 20 feet away, was the freight elevator he had ridden up. He quickly walked across the busy work area and was totally ignored. He pushed the button by the elevator and was rewarded by an immediate ding. The doors opened, he stepped in, they closed, and Harris breathed a sigh of relief.

* * *

Kenneth Deke was used to hearing thunderous applause, and his final gesture, a toast to the wonders of compound interest, brought the house down. Every cabal member was rich because of Universal, they all knew it, and they also knew that Deke and his leadership had a large part to play in their newfound riches.

The Brotherhood of the Altar had been around for many years, thousands of years if his father's stories were accurate. They'd made money and held power in years past. But Kenneth Deke had plans to multiply their riches beyond their wildest dreams, and to help them gain power that few men in the modern world would ever see. And all of this would be in the public eye, under the protection of the most powerful nation on earth.

Deke stepped from the podium, waved to the crowd, reached out and shook the hand of Ed Whiting, his invaluable, yet plain and unassuming assistant, and stepped from the stage. The two massive guards from the rooftop were waiting for him.

"Job done?" he asked them quietly, still smiling to the audience.

Greer nodded, and Heinrich added, "He did us a favor and made like Louganis on his own. He's dead for sure."

"Did you see his body?" Deke asked. The two guards looked at each other, then looked back at Deke blankly.

"Did you see his body?" Deke hissed. A couple at the nearest table looked up as Deke's voice got louder.

"We…uh…didn't actually see the body," Heinrich said. "But there's no way…."

"No body," Deke said. "No death." He watched the waiters coming and going. "The serving staff was all carefully screened. Somehow he got in here. That shouldn't have happened." He grabbed Greer and shoved the big black man toward the kitchen.

"You go talk to the server supervisor and find out what happened," Deke said. "You," he gestured at Heinrich, "go downstairs and find a body for me. And don't come back until you have one."

Deke watched the two men go, and looked around the room. This was totally unacceptable. Security was a disaster, and he knew that as time went on, it would be a bigger and bigger issue.

"Hey Kenny, look at this." Deke turned to see the frumpy figure of Ed Whiting approaching, a suitcoat in his hands. "I found this hanging up over by the elevator." He reached into the inside coat pocket and pulled out a wallet.

Deke took the wallet and flipped it open. A driver's license with the unwelcome visitor's picture on it stared back at him from a plastic window.

"Harris Borden," Deke read. "Round Rock, Nevada. Hmm."

"What's this?" Whiting said, reaching into a space where credit cards usually went. A green laminated card read: "Ministerial License."

"We've got ourselves an ordained minister," Deke muttered.

* * *

The pain in Harris' ribs went from bad to worse. He limped the two blocks to his Corolla and got into it, collapsing into the driver's seat. He toyed with the idea of heading for an emergency room, but he wanted to put as much distance as he could between him and his attackers.

Harris started up the car and drove out of San Francisco and across the Bay Bridge. Fortunately he'd thought to fill up the gas tank before he parked, so he didn't stop at all for the five hours to home. His cell phone rang several times, but he ignored it. The pain kept him from taking a full breath, and eventually he had a hard time reaching up with his hands.

Sacramento passed eventually, then the long drive up the incline to the state line, Reno, and then he got off I-80. It was night by the time Harris got back to Round Rock. His whole body was throbbing as he pulled into their driveway. He turned off the key, pulled the parking brake, and realized that he didn't have the strength to get out of his seat. He released his seat belt and let it slide back into the holder, and then just sat there.

Katya was home. Fortunately, she saw him drive up. She opened the front door and ran out to his car. She took one look and realized that Harris was in trouble.

"Let me help you out," she said. She opened the car door and put herself under his left arm. She lifted and he gasped in pain. Harris tried to walk and took about six steps before his feet collapsed beneath him.

Somehow she had the strength to get Harris around to the other side of the car and back into the passenger's seat. He fell into the seat and let her strap the seat belt on him. Then she drove him to the Hollis Memorial Hospital Emergency Room. Harris was barely aware of the trip there. She took the cell phone off his belt and dialed them on the way, and they met the two of them at curbside with a wheelchair.

* * *

"A broken rib, facial contusions, and a few stitches on those hands of his," Dr. Frank Hollis said to Katya and Harris in the ER examination room. "Where did you say this happened to you?" Katya started to open her mouth to speak, but caught Harris' eye and realized that for now he wanted to keep the whole thing quiet.

"I didn't," he said weakly. "I just ran into the wrong people while on church business."

"Well, I wish you'd let me call the police," Dr. Hollis said. "There was no gunshot wound, so legally I'm not required to, but you've definitely seen the wrong side of someone's anger."

"Yeah," Harris muttered, slowly attempting to sit up. "I guess so." The white tape around his ribs held them tight. It helped a lot with the pain, but made it impossible to take a deep breath.

"I take it that my daily runs are out of the question for a while?" Harris quipped weakly. Hollis chuckled and shook his head.

"Give it about a month before you try anything like that," he said. "And try to keep your bar fights to a minimum as well." He stepped out of the room and left Katya and Harris alone.

She looked at him expectantly, her patience once again impressing Harris. He hadn't said a word about what had happened—he hadn't had a chance to say anything—and yet she knew that when the time came, Harris would open up to her.

"So..." he began, looking up at her sheepishly.

"So," she repeated. "Was it worth it? Did you make a difference?"

Harris shook his head slowly. "I really don't know, Katya. I don't think so."

He didn't feel like Elijah, or any messenger of God for that matter. Harris had said what he thought God had wanted, but it had not turned out as he had expected. In his heart, he felt that something had gone wrong.

* * *

A knock came on the doorjamb of the office of Paul Meddows, news editor of the *San Francisco Herald*.

"It's open," he said, without looking up from the monitor.

"Hi, boss," Michelle Kinkaid said as she breezed into his office. He looked up.

"Hey," he said, smiling and leaning back in his old wooden chair. "Good job on that Dog Show piece. Made me want to go out a buy a dachshund."

"Yeah, right," she said, shaking her head at his bad joke. She threw a press release onto the desk in front of him. "Seen this?"

Meddows picked it up and scanned it quickly. "Radical minister attacks CEO of Universal Finance at private stockholders meeting," he read. "Yeah, I read it already. Guy broke up the meeting, slugged the CEO, then climbed up to the roof and jumped off.

"I'll have Sandy over in rewrite putting something together for tomorrow's evening edition. Not a biggie. Probably bury it inside somewhere." He started to turn back to his computer.

"But I bet you haven't seen this," Michelle said, thrusting another release in front of him.

Meddows took a breath and shook his head. "Michelle, we've been through this already. I thought you were done obsessing about this company. It'll bring you nothing but grief——."

"Just read it, will you?" Michelle said.

Meddows took the second release and glanced at it. "What the——." He furrowed his brow, as if he didn't understand what he was reading, then looked at the time of the release and back at the original.

A faint smile played across Michelle's lips. "The second release tells us to completely disregard what was in the first release. Says they were mistaken about details of the event."

"How do you mix up the details of a reported assault and suicide?" Meddows leaned back in his chair and scratched his head. "Something stinks here."

"Want to hear the best part?" Michelle said, suddenly cheerful. "I think I know this pastor they're talking about."

.

7 TELLING THE TRUTH

The elevator doors opened and Ed Whiting strode into the brightly lit hallway, clad in his usual wrinkled sweatshirt and jeans. He'd expected the offices to be empty this late in the afternoon, but many were still occupied as people tried to get last-minute items done. The big day was coming up within a couple of weeks, and as Whiting knew, if you weren't sharp around here, you got whittled on until you were.

As if in response to that thought, Debbie Estevito, the public relations officer for Universal, burst from the big double doors at the end of the hall, the ones Whiting knew led to the Big Guy's office. Or, in this case, from his office.

"Debbie, Debbie, you ok?" Ed said to the crying young woman. Her mascara was running down her otherwise attractive cheeks as she sobbed her way into his arms.

"He…he fired me for that press release," she said, her voice choking emotionally. "I just did what he told me to do."

"Now, now, don't worry about it, girl." Whiting ran his hand over her head, smoothing her hair. He grabbed her shoulders and smiled at her, who still sobbed. He pulled a wadded-up tissue from his wrinkled coat and gave it to her. She took it and smiled weakly, holding it up to her nose.

"I…I just don't know where I can go from here," she said.

"You're a smart kid, Debbie. If you need a reference, just have them give me a call."

She looked up at Whiting, a flicker of hope in her eyes. "Really? You'd do that for me?"

"Sure. You're my girl!" He patted her on the shoulder. "Now go get you stuff packed up and get out there. There's a better job just waiting for you."

She smiled, sincerely this time. "Thanks Ed. You were always a good friend."

Ed smiled at her and patted her again on the shoulder. He continued down the hall to the big oak double doors. Pushing them open, he saw Barbara, Deke's secretary, just getting her personal items together to go home for the day.

"Night, Barbara," Whiting said. "Say hello to Tom for me."

"Mr. Deke's in there, meditating as usual," Barbara said. "Night, Ed."

Ed pushed the second set of doors open to enter the private office of Kenneth Deke. The previous occupants of these offices had used it as a spacious board room. The windows showed a cityscape that was intended to take the breath away. The floor was made of polished marble, the walls were made of mahogany, set off with ancient tapestries. Deke's massive desk, set on one end of the room, was custom made of teak and alabaster. Several displays around the spacious room featured antique artifacts one would expect to see in the British Museum. Behind Deke's desk the wall was covered with displays from one of the largest and most expensive historic handgun collections in the world. But Deke knelt on the other side of the room, before the most unusual feature one could see in an executive office anywhere.

The entire wall that Deke faced was made of ancient stone, imported, Whiting knew, from the Middle East. Etched into the stone was ancient script decipherable only by those who specialized in dead languages thousands of years old. In addition, a golden table about three feet wide stood in the center of the wall. On it was a single golden cup. Whiting knew that it held blood. Human blood.

Jacketless, Deke did not move from his kneeling position as Whiting came in, but Ed knew that Deke was aware of him.

Whiting stood staring at the collection of handguns on Deke's wall, some dating from the 1600s. He squinted and pointed at a flintlock pistol in the far corner.

"That flintlock in the corner new?" he asked.

"The Dutch one," Deke said quietly. "No, it's been there all along. Heidi bought it for me more than a year ago." Heidi was Deke's assistant who specialized in finding and purchasing artifacts, including Deke's handgun collection.

"I guess I just overlooked it. It's just not too pretentious," Whiting said, shrugging and moving over to the other side of the desk. He watched Deke for a few more minutes in silence.

"You're not yourself today, Kenny," Whiting said, leaning against the front of Deke's desk. "I expected to see Debbie's head on the altar when I came in here."

Deke waved his arms to either side of him, swirling clouds of incense into his nostrils. He muttered a few words to himself; his eyes closed, then opened them and stood up. He turned to face Whiting, a faint smile on his lips.

"What can I say? I'm a soft touch."

"Yeah, right," Whiting said. "You've never been soft about anything in your life." He picked up a curved, silver letter opener on Deke's desk that looked like it had been used against flesh once or twice before, and touched the tip against his finger. A drop of blood welled where he'd touched it. Frowning, he put it back down.

"Knowing you, Kenny, you have it fixed that she'll get run over by a cable car thirty minutes from now. Something that can't be traced back here."

Deke walked over to a coat rack and picked up his Armani suit coat to put back on. "Well, you're right, Ed. You know me pretty well. You've known me for close to ten years. Probably know me better than anyone else alive. What can I say? We do have plans for Debbie. Just can't tell you what they are at this point."

"That another secret between you and You-Know-Who?"

Deke's face went from casual humor to somber stone with Whiting's words. "I wouldn't speak so lightly about him if I were you."

Whiting flinched. "Right. You wanted to see me?"

Deke walked across the room to a small bar and poured himself a drink. "I heard he didn't die. So what can you tell me about our friend Reverend Borden?"

Whiting shrugged. "Not much more to report there. Harris Borden, age 30, born in Boise, Idaho, parents both dead, graduate of a small college in Washington state. He's an ordained minister. Married to Ekaterina Dubrovika, born in Leningrad, Soviet Union, now called St. Petersburg. No kids."

"Was he alone in all this? I have a hard time believing he isn't part of some conspiracy."

Whiting shook his head. "As far as I can tell, he has no ties to anyone inside the organization. But we'll check it out again. As far as anyone else involved…."

"You don't know," Deke finished his thought. "Well, he's getting his information from someone, somewhere." Deke put his half-empty tumbler down on the bar. "I feel uneasy about this. Let's make sure we know everything about him. We could send out a wet work team to take him down, no problem. But I want to make sure that we tie up all the loose ends before we take that step. He could be working alone, but let's make sure."

"So 24-hour surveillance? You got it." Whiting winked at Deke and turned to go, but Deke held up his hand.

"One more thing. You ever get that glitch taken care of?"

"You mean that software bug that transferred our calls elsewhere? Yeah, we got it. As far as I can tell, it was some virus that the Cray picked up. I took care of it as soon as we isolated it."

"Everything else on schedule?"

Whiting nodded. "Everything's under control. Our assets continue to grow daily, thanks to the accounting software, and of course that special mojo that comes with the package." He nodded to the altar on the other side of the room.

"Our brothers in the cabal seem happy. The homage they pay to our lord is a small price to pay for the obvious rewards."

"And our customers?"

Whiting snorted. "Since when have you worried about our customers?"

* * *

Dr. Hollis prescribed some pretty strong painkillers, and Harris slept on and off on the ride home. He didn't even remember walking to the door, but he must have because he woke up the next morning in his own bed. He was one big bruise from head to foot, with an extra portion of soreness reserved for his midsection. It hurt to move. It hurt to turn his head. And it especially hurt to breathe. But Frank Hollis had told him that the more he tried to breathe, the quicker he'd recover. So Harris gritted his teeth and tried to take deep breaths.

Katya had taken the day off, he discovered, and she appeared a few minutes after he awoke with a tray of breakfast as well as more medication.

"Hello there," he told her. "You look good enough to eat."

She clucked her tongue, shook her head, then kissed Harris on the forehead. "We will have to hold off on the play time for a while, *petrushka*. You must be careful to take care of yourself."

Petrushka was Katya's pet name for Harris. Its literal translation was Pinocchio, but it referred more to someone who had a lot of passion—but little brain or brawn. He grinned and winked at her. "I don't need to worry. I have you to take care of me."

Katya stayed and talked with him while he ate breakfast. She would have cut the food and fed him if Harris had let her, but he already felt ridiculous. She sat as he ate and told her what had happened yesterday in San Francisco. After he finished both the food and the story, she added to it with information he hadn't known.

"Apparently, the story was in the news, but didn't make sense. Some said that you had attacked this Kenneth Deke, others said that you'd killed yourself. Still others said that the whole story was made up by the company for publicity." She shook her head. "All I know is that I'm glad it's over, and you're still alive."

Harris grinned at that. "Me too, but I have a feeling it's not completely over."

She brightened. "Nils Andrusen heard about what happened and your injury. He wants to come over and see you. I told him it depended on how you felt."

Harris' heart sank. Andrusen was the legal representative for his church association in Nevada. His visit could not be good news.

Andrusen drove in from Reno and came to their home with Frank Hollis and Greg Phipps that afternoon. By that time, his pain was less and

Harris had graduated to his sweats and a perch on the living room sofa. Their furnishings were meager, but Katya tried to make the conference president welcome.

Before they came, Harris struggled with how much to tell Andrusen—or anyone. He finally opted for an edited, simpler version of the story. He told the threesome that he had received the letters and phone calls. After hearing the tragic stories of the people caught in Universal's debt web, Harris decided that he should bring the problem to the attention of the company. He admitted he had crashed the private meeting and caused a scene. He told them that guards had roughed him up when they escorted him outside. Harris didn't say anything about angels or falling off of roofs.

"Well, that was pretty stupid," Dr. Hollis said at the end. "You could have gotten killed."

"Not likely," Andrusen said. "They wouldn't kill a pastor. But there are much better ways to address social issues like this. You should have called and gotten us involved."

"Probably," Harris agreed, although he knew secretly that he'd never have done that.

"Well, he still has a lot to learn," Phipps said to the others. "I think he learned a lesson yesterday."

"More than one," Harris agreed.

"Well, I'll need to draft a letter of censure, and put it in your file," Andrusen said. "But since they didn't identify you in the news, or tie you to your church in any way, I think we can let you off with a warning."

It's not the behavior that concerns him, Harris thought. *It's whether it embarrasses the organization.*

"In the meantime," Andrusen said, standing and walking to the door. "Don't go tilting after any more windmills without calling me first." He laughed at his own joke, and Phipps and Hollis laughed too. Harris smiled at them, but his heart wasn't in it.

Hollis and Andersen headed out the door, but Phipps stayed behind.

"I'd like to have a few words with the boy," he said to the other two. Normally Harris would have flinched at the word *boy*, but he was eager to tell Phipps the whole story, something he didn't feel he could do with the other two.

So after Andrusen and Dr. Hollis left, he told the truth—the whole truth—to Phipps. He wasn't sure how he would react, especially about how he'd interrupted the meeting in such a melodramatic way, and how he'd escaped from the two guards on the rooftop.

Phipps was quiet for a while, lost in thought. Finally he said, "Well, I've seen and heard of a lot of things, but this is unique. God works in mysterious ways, that's for sure."

He smiled at Harris, the first sign of approval Harris could remember receiving from him. He patted his leg and said, "God has plans for you, young pastor. I'd like to give you just one bit of advice."

"Yes, of course," Harris said to him.

"There'll be a strong temptation to do things your own way, to use your own worldly judgment as to what is reasonable to expect from God. If you expect God to use you, you have to be willing to sacrifice your own logic, your own strength, even your own survival instincts to Him. He doesn't do things the way we expect. That's what makes it obvious that it's from God. It's also what makes it such an honor to be used by Him."

"I've surrendered myself to His will," Harris responded.

"Have you?" Phipps asked, leaning forward and his eyes narrowing. "Have you, really?" He looked at him closely, and Harris began to get nervous.

"What about those guards?" Phipps asked. "Did God tell you to fight back?"

Harris stared at him blankly. "They would have killed me."

"Would they?" Phipps asked, a small smile breaking through. "You don't know that."

"They were going to throw me off the roof!"

Phipps shook his head. "That was their intention, but was that God's intent? If you're being used by God, you have to be willing to let Him save you—if it's His will—or not save you. When you step in and do your own thing, you're taking the glory away from God."

Phipps patted his knee and chuckled. "I know, I know, this is all new to you. But it's like peeling the layers of an onion. God's never done with us. I know I have a lifetime of growing in front of me—however long that may be."

"Anyway," he said, standing. "That's something to think about. In the meantime, you need to know that you have my support."

Harris watched Phipps go out the front door, grateful for the support he had shown, but concerned with the thoughts he had left for Harris to ponder.

* * *

Saturday morning dawned bright and fair, with an unexpected cool breeze blowing down from the Sierras. In the 36 hours since his incident in San Francisco, the rumor mill had been working overtime. Many of the church members had started to believe that Harris had been killed, hospitalized, arrested, or fired since Thursday. Only a couple had bothered to call and find out the truth.

The calls for Universal Finance had stopped just as suddenly as they'd started. It was a blessing to have some peace and quiet, but it made Harris wonder what relationship the change had to his God-appointed task. On the other hand, there were moments Harris wondered if he'd imagined the whole thing and had his own stupidity to blame for his broken rib and blackened, bruised face.

No one, not even Katya, had expected Harris to preach that morning. He had to confess that he had not put pen to paper or words to computer screen in anticipation of preaching. His antics at Universal and the other strange events of the week had cluttered his mind and kept him from thinking of preparing his sermon. But lying in bed and then on the couch in their home on Friday had given him quiet time to remember his responsibility, and he'd put a few thoughts together. Harris wasn't that good of a preacher to begin with, he'd already admitted that to himself, and he wondered if his problem was over-preparation. So, without telling anyone else, he planned on preaching, even when no one asked him one way or the other.

So it was that Harris found himself standing on the church platform, watching Katya lead the church in the opening song. As she sang with the small congregation, a wave of nostalgia surged over him, and he wondered why. *Was God finished with using him? Were more dangers ahead, and what would those tasks do to his pastorate here?* Finally the thought came to him, *Was this the last time he would preach here?* Normally, he wouldn't even entertain such thoughts. Although he didn't think he was very good, Harris loved preaching. For him, it was one of the most humbling experiences he'd ever had. To deliver messages in the name of God was to be honored beyond measure. The only experiences that surpassed it were officiating at communion service and baptizing someone.

Harris looked out at the congregation and was rewarded with a mixture of feelings. Greg Phipps sat in the second row on his right, where he always sat. He seemed surprised but approving that Harris had shown up today. Phipps stood with a slight smile on his weathered face, nodding at Harris as he looked at him.

Dougie Washington and his parents sat three rows behind him. They were all smiles, their arms wrapped around each other in joy at the positive news they'd recently received. There was nothing like almost losing a loved one, only to have them brought back to you.

Across the aisle from them sat the church treasurer, Jules Russell, and his pretty wife, Jana. Jules looked pretty composed after the debacle with the drinking fountain got put on the back burner. Jana, on the other hand, didn't look well. She was pale and her smile looked a little forced. Harris made a mental note to talk to them after church service.

And beside him stood Dr. Hollis. As head elder, he'd assumed that Harris' injury meant that he'd be preaching this morning. Harris could see Hollis' face fall when he showed up this morning. Harris had heard him preach a few times. No doubt the sermon Hollis had prepared for today once again talked about all the bad things the church members were doing.

Katya finished her singing and stepped off the platform to sit in the front row. Dr. Hollis stood and walked to the podium.

"Our scripture today," Dr. Hollis said without looking up, "is found in Ephesians chapter 6, verses 12 and 13: 'For our wrestling is not against flesh and blood, but against the principalities, against the powers, against the world-rulers of this darkness, against the spiritual hosts of wickedness in the heavenly places. Wherefore take up the whole armor of God, that ye may be able to withstand in the evil day, and, having done all, to stand.'"

Dr. Hollis closed his Bible and sat down beside Harris, a suspicious look creeping across his face as he looked at him. Harris smiled at him and stood up, a little stiff in the process, but successful in hobbling to the podium. He lay his Bible down and began to preach.

"Why are we here?" he asked the congregation, then paused. "As Christians, what are we here to do?"

"To preach the good news," Jules Russell said.

"To represent Jesus in our community," Moira Washington said.

"To speak out against evil," Hollis muttered behind him.

"How about, all of the above?" Harris answered them. "We want our words to tell of the good news. We want our actions to represent Christ to those around us. And we want to follow Christ's example in condemning the evil that exists around us.

"About a week ago, after our church board meeting, I was thinking about that very thing. I was pondering the evil that surrounds us in our community, in our state, in our country, in our world. I could hear the sirens of ambulances as someone was hurt or dying because of some tragedy.

"Evil comes in many forms. It can be as direct as a child abuser, rapist or murderer." Some of the more sensitive members drew back as he got to this passage. "Or it could be much more subtle—and in many ways much more deadly. But it all comes down to one thing: we are involved in a war, a war between good and evil, a war between the forces of God and the forces of Satan.

"And what is the reality of our foe?" Harris stabbed his finger into his Bible. "What kind of enemy are we dealing with? What does this passage say?" He let the words hang in the empty air, until silence captured them.

"They are not flesh and blood," Greg Phipps said, his voice ringing like a bell. "They are the powers of darkness."

"Exactly!" Harris pointed at Greg. "They're the powers of darkness." He took a deep breath and launched into the section that worried him, but Harris knew he had to address. And as he looked at Greg, Harris saw that Greg knew exactly where he was headed.

"Last Sunday night I realized that we were in that war, and asked God to send me to the front lines. I prayed that God would use me in a special way. And he answered my prayer." A few members began to whisper among themselves.

Harris paused before continuing, anticipating that the next words would have some sort of impact—positive or negative. "He answered in a way I could never anticipate," he said. "He sent a messenger—*an angel*—to tell me that He'd granted my request." The whispering grew louder, and he felt rather than saw Dr. Hollis begin to get restless behind him.

"Between the angel and unusual circumstances that affected Katya and me last week, we learned that a company—Universal Finance in San Francisco—is a front for demonic activity." Harris had anticipated a startled reaction to his words, but the response blew past him like a furnace. He tried to continue, but the room was in an uproar.

"Are you crazy?" said a man in the back Harris recognized as an off-again, on-again attendee at church. "Do you expect us to believe your fantasy as an excuse for the garbage you pulled in San Francisco?"

"What a crackpot," Mrs. Burgess, a 70ish member in the fifth row said out loud. She had always been a tough critic.

"Let him speak, let him speak," Greg said.

Harris felt arms grab him from behind and pull him aside. Frank Hollis hissed in his ear. *"Are you out of your mind?* This will be the last time you preach from this pulpit, I assure you!"

"I had to tell the truth," Harris said partly to Dr. Hollis and partly to the microphone. "I had to let my congregation know what I'd been through, and what's going on around them."

Dr. Hollis shoved him aside and took the microphone. "You have to understand that he's been traumatized lately, and delusions sometimes come with trauma. Let's close the service by singing song number 299." Hollis desperately tried to gain control of the members, who was talking animatedly among themselves, and ignoring what he was saying. Harris stood to Dr. Hollis' side, dismayed that he had been preempted so soon, yet satisfied that he had said what he had wanted. Harris knew that those who were curious would contact him. Those who condemned him had made up their minds a long time before this morning.

His eyes wandered to Greg Phipps, wondering what he thought of his presentation. He shrugged and winked. *It's OK*, Harris was sure he was saying. *Not ideal, but OK.*

He looked across the congregation as they continued talking and wondered which would be on his side, and which would be against him. Then he looked in the back row and saw him. It was the same blonde, crew-cut man who had attempted to throw him from the rooftop, dressed in a suit and tie. Harris didn't know how long he had been sitting in the sanctuary, but just seeing him sitting there made the hair stand up on the back of Harris' neck.

He looked at Harris for a long moment, then winked and pointed his index finger at Harris, pulling the thumb down like a gun. It was the universal signal that meant: *You're dead.*

Harris opened his mouth to speak, but the words caught in his throat. He watched the stranger walk out the back doors and disappear.

* * *

Michelle woke with a start from her sleep. It was early Sunday morning, the only morning that she got to sleep in. She was angry about waking up, but it was only a minor part of her anger.

Her mind was racing as it ran over the dream again and again. It had been so incredibly vivid that for a moment she almost thought it had really happened. But as she looked around at her darkened room, and looked down at the pajamas she wore, she realized with relief that it had, indeed, been only a dream.

You must tell him, a voice told her. *You must tell him.* The Voice was one she recognized as coming from her childhood, a Voice she had purposely left behind her.

Her mouth drew into a hard line and she pounded on her pillow, crunching it into a ball.

"It's not fair!" she said. "I don't want to do it! Why me?"

But she already knew the answer. There would be no more sleep for her that morning.

8 EYES AND EARS

It was gone.

Pastors can do without a lot of things, but in this day and age, a pastor can't do without his cell phone. At least, that's what Harris had come to believe. His phone usually rang constantly during the day, and a lot of the discussion he would have needed to scurry here and there to take care of was resolved electronically. Now it was gone, and he was at a loss.

Well, actually, he knew it would show up eventually. Harris had a bad habit of misplacing stuff, which Katya was relatively insensitive about. Today was no exception. She'd been all caring and supportive the week before when he had a broken rib and bruises. His rib was still sore, but manageable, and the bruises were turning yellow and disappearing, and so was Katya's sympathy.

"Honey, have you seen my cell phone?"

"*Udivitelnyi.* It is your phone. I do not have a phone. How should I know where you put your phone?"

"I'll take that as a no, then," Harris said, turning the corner into the kitchen. As usual, Katya was doing three things at once; loading the sink with dishes and turning on the hot water, making herself a sack lunch, and applying her makeup.

"I am late for work, and you are old enough to take care of yourself," she said matter-of-factly.

In response, Harris wrapped his arms around her and held her against himself. "Yes I can, but it is so much more fun when you do it."

She kissed him quickly, then pulled away. "I love you, *petrushka*, but I must go. Bye." She grabbed her sack lunch and rushed out the door to the living room. A second later, she popped back into the kitchen.

"They are here," she said.

"Who's here?"

"Termite inspectors," she said, waving and running back out the front door.

Harris looked out the front picture window and saw a white van with the words "County Termite Inspection" on the door. Two men in white coveralls approached the house. One was carrying a ladder; the other had a large toolbox. He met them at the front door.

"Termite inspection?" Harris said. "I've never heard of termite problems here in the desert. Don't they need a wet climate?"

The burly man in front looked at him and then at his partner. "There's a new strain infiltrating the area from Mexico. Dry termites. We want to make sure that area houses are clear, so we are testing houses on a random basis."

It sounded very fishy, and Harris stood his ground.

"Sir, if you don't want us to do the inspection, we can choose another home," the man said in the front. "But those who participate are getting a 20 percent discount on their property taxes this year."

Harris was still skeptical, but he let them in finally. While they were working in the crawl space beneath the house and in the attic, Harris tried to concentrate on his sermon notes for the next week. He didn't know what the week would bring, and Hollis had threatened to force him out of the pulpit, so Harris decided to continue working on the next sermon and see what happened.

The congregation had been drawing up sides for the past three days, with half supporting Hollis in calling for Harris' dismissal, and the other half supporting the pastor and his version of the story. He didn't know how it would all pan out, and hated the idea of splitting the church like this, but Harris wasn't sure what else could be done. He'd decided that his stand against Universal Finance had a good chance of affecting those around him, and it was their right to know exactly what they were facing. At least, that was his rationalization.

About an hour after Katya left for work, the termite inspectors finished up and left as well. Harris was alone with his thoughts. That is, until the phone rang. Harris half expected it to be more people complaining about their credit account with Universal. Instead it was a voice he was totally unprepared for.

"Pastor Borden, do you know who this is?"

Harris paused for a second, and realized the woman on the other end didn't want her name used.

"Maybe this will help," the voice continued. "You sent me an e-mail about some letters?"

Harris realized he was talking to Michelle Kinkaid, the reporter in San Francisco.

"Yes." He cleared his throat. "How are you?"

"Fine, thank you. I know this is sudden, but I am wondering if I can meet with you. It's important." <click>

"Hello, are you there?" Harris asked.

"Yes, I'm here," she said. "I think the clicking is on your end of the line." <click>

"Well, yes, I can meet you. How soon?"

"Tonight, if possible," she said. "And at a public location."

Public location? "Oh-kay, there's an International House of Pancakes in Reno just west of town on I-80. That way you won't have as far to drive."

"Fine. I'll meet you there at 8 o'clock. I'm the blonde wearing a red dress. Is that ok?"

"Eight it is," he said. Just as Harris started to hang up, he looked at the number on caller ID. It was the one that had text messaged him about the cabal meeting.

* * *

"So you sent the message about the cabal meeting?" Harris asked Michelle, as Katya and he slid into the booth where she sat. For a Tuesday night, the place was pretty crowded.

Michelle nodded. "Let me show you something." She reached into her purse and pulled out a cell phone. It was black, and a lot less fancy than Harris'. She got up from the booth and walked over to the trash can and dropped it in.

"Doing investigative journalism teaches you a lot of tricks," she said, returning. "One of them is to make sure your target doesn't make you a target. I buy those disposable cell phones at a local electronics store. You have a limited number of minutes that come with the phone, so there's no paper trail. When you use the minutes up, or when you think someone might trace your call, you just toss it."

"Neyzeli," Katya said. "Incredible."

"Michelle, this is my wife, Katya," Harris said, embarrassed that he hadn't introduced her before this.

"Pleased to meet you," Michelle said, shaking Katya's hand.

92

"So I suppose you heard about my adventure in San Francisco last week," Harris told Michelle.

She nodded. "I'm amazed you're still alive. I notice they got in a few licks." She gestured at his still-bruised face.

"Well, they also left a pretty good impression on my ribs, but yes, I'm still alive. God took care of me."

"You better hope God continues to take care of you, because it's not over." Michelle said. "In fact, it's just beginning."

"What are you talking about?" Katya asked.

"Why do you think I wanted to meet here? In a public place?" Michelle said quietly. "That I'm just paranoid?"

"Well…yeah," he said sheepishly.

"Well, maybe that's true, but you have to remember that I've got a history of dealing with these guys. And I know that they won't just forget you. There's a good chance that you're being watched. And that your house, cell phone and office are probably bugged as well."

"Bugged?" he asked incredulously.

"I didn't want to say anything on the phone, but you know that clicking sound we heard on the phone?"

"Yeah?"

She didn't answer, but looked at him expectantly. Realization hit him, and Katya and Harris looked at each other. *The termite inspectors.*

"Harris did what God asked him to," Katya said. "He is finished. When they realize this, they will leave us alone. Yes?"

"This isn't over," Michelle said, shaking her head.

"It is for me," Harris said. "It is if I'm putting Katya in danger."

"You can't stop now," Michelle said. "You drew public attention to the company. That's good. A few news people are aware that something's fishy, but that's not enough. You have to pursue it."

"That's your job," Harris said to her. "You're the investigative reporter."

"Not any more," she said. "I go out on assignments like dog shows. I don't do investigative journalism." Her words slowed down, and then she paused.

"Look, it's *your* job," she said. "And the reason I know that is because God told me so." Silence. She dropped her head in her hand, then shook her head.

"I didn't want this to happen," she said. "I told him no, but He wouldn't take no for an answer."

Harris saw that Michelle was struggling to find the right words, that she was overcome emotionally, and reached his hand across the table for her.

"What are you trying to say, Michelle?"

She looked at the table for a long time, still shaking her head. Finally she looked up, tears threatening to appear in her eyes.

"I grew up going to the Presbyterian Church, and was baptized when I was young. I told God that I would do whatever He wanted me to do. Then, there were some problems in my family. I...I don't want to go into it...but I stopped going to church and I gave up on God. I haven't prayed in almost twenty years. I'd forgotten God."

Harris looked at her tenderly. "But apparently He hasn't forgotten you."

She took a deep breath and blew it out forcefully, regaining her composure.

"No, I guess not. This person, or alien, or angel, or something—he called himself The Messenger—came to me in a dream early Sunday morning and told me that I was supposed to bring you a message."

Harris looked at Katya. *Why hadn't he come directly to me? Was it because I defended myself on that rooftop?*

"What was the message?" Katya asked.

"That the battle was just beginning. That you must tell Universal to stop ruining people's lives or they'll be destroyed."

Harris sat back in his chair and was stunned. *I have to go back?*

"No…no," Katya said. "He is through."

"Look, I didn't make up this message," Michelle said. "I delivered it, just as I was asked to do."

"How…where?" he asked weakly.

"There's a public event scheduled for next week, on the fourth," Michelle said. "They're announcing they're going public with their stock. The millionaires on their cabal are going to be billionaires overnight. They're also starting work on their new headquarters.

"I'll work it so that I cover the event for the paper. You show up and rip off their smiley faces for the public and expose them as the monsters they really are."

"Deke had said that there were three phases. This must be phase two," Harris said carefully, more to himself than to Michelle or Katya.

"Very likely," Michelle said. "Going public will make them more vulnerable to public scrutiny, but it'll make some major alliances possible. They'll be able to bribe their way into the hearts and minds of every corrupt government official in the U.S."

"In the world," Harris whispered. "Deke said their aspirations were global."

"That's why we need to stop them."

* * *

Kenneth Deke looked on from behind Ed Whiting's chair as Whiting manipulated the controls on the large screen. A dozen monitors covered the wall in Whiting's office, termed "The Batcave" by his many assistants. Right now, Whiting was switching the view from one security camera to another in a Reno restaurant. The view popped from the kitchen, to the waiting area, to one service area, and then to another.

"There," Deke said, pointing at the screen. "Zoom in." Deke and Whiting saw Harris and Katya Borden speaking intensely to a young blonde woman in a booth.

"She looks familiar, but this is a bad angle," Deke said.

"Let's try this," Whiting said, pressing a button. Whiting switched to a security camera over the teller in the lobby. A reverse view of the threesome appeared in the distance, and Ed zoomed in on the young woman talking to the Bordens. Whiting pressed another button and the camera froze frame, instantly turning the video image into a digital print.

"We need to find out who this new conspirator is," Deke said.

"Your wish is my command, boss," Whiting said. "I'll have a file on her delivered to you with tomorrow's breakfast and *Wall Street Journal*."

"I think it's time to turn it up a notch," Deke said. "We have a lot of firepower at our fingertips. Let's use it."

* * *

"Things are not going as you would like."

"No, my Lord," Deke said to the darkness, as he sat on his office floor facing the stone wall and altar. "The traditional methods have been unsuccessful with this Reverend Borden. We've tried to kill him and make it look like an accident. We've tried scaring him. And it seems that the harder that we try, the more his strength grows."

"And so you come to me for help."

"Yes, my Lord. You've helped many times in the past. Were it not for you, our company would not be as successful as it is."

"Were it not for me, you would not exist."

"That's true, my Lord. We're helpless without your great power."

Silence. Deke closed his eyes and meditated, the incense filling the air with sweet fragrance.

"Very well. It is in my interest for your plans to succeed. I will therefore loose my minions on the forces that oppose you. We will see if spiritual forces can succeed where man's forces apparently cannot."

Deke face broke into a slight smile. "Thank you, my Lord."

"It will, of course, require a blood sacrifice."

"I have anticipated as much, my Lord. It will be done."

Deke bowed before the altar, then stood. He walked over to his desk and picked up the phone, speed dialing a number.

"Hello, Debbie? This is Kenneth Deke. How would you like another chance with Universal? I have something special in mind for you."

* * *

The mood was somber at prayer meeting that Wednesday night. It seems that everyone had prayer requests. And when people are hurting, it seems that prayer meeting attendance goes up.

The Washington family was there—all of them. They were grateful for Dougie's apparent miraculous recovery, but a new problem plagued them. Medical bills had overwhelmed them, and they were having difficulty getting insurance to pay their part, or even be sympathetic to their plight. Right now, the hospitals, doctors and laboratories were threatening to take them to court to get their money. The Washington family was afraid they were going to lose their home. Deservedly, they asked for everyone's prayers.

Jules Russell was there. He raised his hand after Moira Washington spoke. "Jana collapsed at work this morning. They took her to the hospital and have been doing tests all day. They have her in isolation. They don't know what's wrong with her."

Harris looked at Jules and saw a man at the end of his rope. "I can't lose her...I can't. We need your prayers, my brothers and sisters." Jules dropped his head in his hands.

Harris stepped forward and put his hands on Jules' shoulder. "We'll certainly remember Jana. She's an important part of this church family."

"Anyone else?"

Harris saw a hand go up in the back row. It was Donna Hollis, Frank's wife. Harris admired her courage in coming, considering that he was still *persona non grata* to her husband.

"Many of you remember our daughter Kelly," Donna said. "She lived here for many years before she went off to college and got married. She had her wedding in this church six years ago."

"Sure," Harris said. "We all remember her."

"I got a call from her last night. Her husband, Bob, has decided to leave her for another woman, and has asked for a divorce." At this point, Donna's voice broke, and she pulled out a handkerchief. "There was no advance warning at all. It just happened. Kelly's devastated, as are we all. Bob was a part of the family. We just want to pray that they can work it out."

"Certainly," Harris said, grimacing to himself at the accumulating bad news. He sighed.

"Well, as you can all see, the Devil is busy. Apparently, he's targeted this church for attack. We need to put on the armor of God and pull together if we're to survive all of this. Let's pray."

They knelt on the sanctuary floor and brought the prayer requests before God.

* * *

"I got your message," Katya said, walking over to the bench where Harris sat. A small patch of dried Bermuda grass and two trees made up the Round Rock city park.

"It's nice of you to suggest that we meet for lunch. I have not been in this park before."

"Neither have I, such as it is," he told Katya. "But you understand why I suggested this, don't you?"

"The wiretap you found on our phone at home?"

Harris nodded. "Chances are that's not the only bug they put in our house. They're probably in your office and mine as well. I had to think of a place where they wouldn't consider us going. We've never been here before, so it seemed likely." As Harris spoke, he watched a white van circle the park slowly.

"I found my cell phone. Or more accurately, it found me."

"Really? Where was it?"

"O'Reilly's Liquor Store. They called this morning."

Katya looked at him blankly. "Say that again?"

"They suggest that either I left it there, or someone who had stolen it dropped it there."

Katya grinned. "Well, unless you have taken up habits you haven't told me about, I would think it was left by someone who stole it."

Harris shook his head. "I think it's been bugged as well. I'm afraid to use it."

Katya and Harris sat on the park bench, staring straight ahead. Both of them felt caught in a cloud of confusion.

"What has happened to our lives?" she asked.

What will happen to our lives tomorrow? Harris said inwardly.

9 HARBINGERS

"Whoever thought up the idea of doctors pulling 24-hour shifts should be shot," Frank Hollis muttered to himself for the ninth time that evening. The only consolation he had was that he was close to the end of his shift, and his own bed in his own house beckoned to him.

Even as medical director of the small hospital, Dr. Hollis made it a practice to do what he expected all of his physicians to do. That's why he did rotations just as all other staff physicians did here, regardless of how tired he was or how much his back ached or how much he would rather be home. *Discipline was the key*, he reminded himself.

Just as discipline is what's lacking in our church, he thought. *I've been very patient with Pastor Borden for all these years. It is time to get someone who is a true leader—and who can follow direction.*

He finished adding his notes to the patient chart and put it back in its holder. *Four more to go for this unit. Maybe there* is *an end in sight.*

His thought was interrupted by the sound of someone crying. A child. He looked around and didn't see anyone. He walked over to the nurses' station.

"Did anyone else hear that?" he said. "Sounded like a child crying. Visitors' hours were over a long time ago. Find out who it is and tell them to leave."

"Yes, Dr. Hollis," the nurse said.

Hollis went back to the hallway and picked up the next chart. He flipped it open—and heard the voice again. This time it spoke.

"Help me," said the voice. "Help me."

"Nurse?" he said. "Nurse?" But no one was at the station.

He looked around and realized that he was all alone in the ward.

"Help me, please." The voice continued. He realized it was coming from down the hall.

"Guess I have to deal with it myself—as usual," he muttered, and walked quickly down the hall. He followed it past some double doors, past the laboratory, to a dead end. The voice stopped when he came to the door marked "Morgue."

He hesitated. The door was locked.

The crying resumed, and it was obvious it came from the morgue. Dr. Hollis had a key to the door—he had a key to every door in the hospital—but something told him to get help.

He unclipped his cell phone from his belt and dialed security. "Can you have someone come down to the morgue?" he asked. "Apparently some teenagers are playing a prank."

Five minutes later, two security guards appeared.

"Unlock the door," Dr. Hollis told them. He wanted witnesses to whatever was behind the door.

A crisp, cold wind blew from the opened door. Hollis remembered that the morgue was kept extra cold, considering the nature of the work being done there.

"Well, whoever's in there is probably a popsicle by now," Dr. Hollis said, as he waited outside the doors.

"There's no one in there," the first security guard said, coming back out. "Nothing but cadavers."

Dr. Hollis looked inside. Beneath a filmy plastic sheet lay a young girl who had been opened for autopsy. No one alive was in there.

* * *

Hailey Rasmussen had served as church treasurer for 22 years, up until three years ago. At that time, there'd been a discrepancy in the church budget of $14.32. Meanwhile, she had come down with a vicious case of the flu. When she returned to the church board a month later, she'd been replaced by the present treasurer, Jules Russell.

Actually, she got along with Jules quite well. Years ago, he'd been a student of hers when she taught fifth grade here. And since she had recently marked her 80th birthday—privately and quietly—she had convinced herself that having someone take over may not be the worst thing in the world.

That was until Jana Russell got sick, and Jules called for Hailey's help. Suddenly she remembered why she enjoyed bookkeeping so much. The view of the overall picture, the feeling of control, the mastery of something that mystified so many people—they all turned her on. All these things were coming back to her as she went through the monthly expenses and income in Jules' office at the church. She had no one to answer to at home, except her cat Rufus, so she stayed on the job late into the evening hours. She really didn't know what time it was until someone rapped on the large double doors by the foyer.

She glanced up at the clock. 12:15. She grinned to herself. She hadn't stayed up this late since "Matlock" was taken off the air. She stood slowly and hobbled out to the doors. She unlatched the deadbolt and pulled the door open. No one was there.

"Hello?" she said out the door. "Is anyone there?" She was greeted by the sound of crickets.

"Mmm," she grunted. "Kids." She closed the door and bolted it, then turned to go back to the office. She had taken three steps when the pounding returned to the doors, this time louder.

"Ah," she said, smiling to herself. "Gotcha." She whipped around and unbolted the door, hurling the door open unbelievably fast.

"What do you want?" she barked as she opened the door. She was surprised as she saw that again no one was outside. She stuck her head outside, then stepped a few feet out the door, looking in both directions.

"I'm not afraid of you!" she croaked to the darkness. "I ran earliteens for 22 years. I'm not afraid of anything!" Again, all she heard was crickets.

"What the—double digit—mmm," she mumbled to herself, going back inside the church. She relocked the door and walked back to the office. As she approached the office door, she noticed light flickering from the entrance. She looked inside and saw flames leaping up from a metal trashcan. Smoke began to roll outside the door into the foyer.

She knew exactly what to do. She calmly stepped over to the cabinet that held the visitor's book and bulletins when they came in. On the backside of it, on the wall, hung a red fire extinguisher. She pulled the safety ring off and turned it over, spraying flame-retardant fog over the fire and quickly putting it out.

"Thought you'd scare me, did you," Hailey said. "You messed with the wrong girl." Acrid smoke hung in the air, and Hailey coughed. She turned on the fan and opened the window to blow the smoke out. Still coughing, she went out to the phone in the foyer and called 911.

"I'm sure it's just some ratty kids," she told the dispatcher. "But you probably need to send a patrol car by to make sure." She knew that church insurance would require her to make a report to the police, even though she knew she could handle it.

After making the phone call, she looked down and realized that somewhere she had gotten soot on her hands, and probably elsewhere on her.

"That won't do," she told herself. "You never know who will show up." She wondered if that cute police officer with the cleft chin that had given her the speeding ticket would come.

She hurried to the women's restroom to wash up. She pushed the doors open and started toward the sinks, when she saw something that stopped her in her tracks.

"Someone's getting on my nerves," she whispered, frowning.

Written in red on the wall facing her was one word.

Submit.

* * *

Greg Phipps had had trouble sleeping since his wife Martha had died ten years ago. After forty years of marriage, it was hard to get used to sleeping alone. He had eventually come up with the system of watching the 11 o'clock news in the living room, then heading off to bed and reading his Bible until he fell asleep in bed.

Tonight he hadn't made it into bed, but had fallen asleep during the news. He awoke with the grandfather clock in the hall chiming three. He stirred and stretched, then switched off the TV.

"Hello, dear," he heard a familiar voice say. He turned toward the hallway and saw Martha standing there. She looked the way he remembered she always did when it was time to go to bed. Her robin's-egg blue floor-length nightgown shimmered in the light of the living room. He looked at her and had an initial reaction of longing. It was her.

"I've missed you so much," Martha said. "Have you missed me?"

Greg rubbed his eyes with the back of his arm, then looked again. She still stood there. His eyes told him that it was his wife. Her voice was the same too. But he knew it was not her.

"Get thee behind me, Satan," he breathed.

Martha held out her hand to him. "Greg, don't be silly. Come on to bed."

Greg shook his head. It was not her.

"I'm sorry," he said quietly to no one in particular.

Then he raised himself up and took on his preaching voice.

"In the name of Jesus Christ, Lord of the universe and Savior of mankind, I command you to leave this place, demon!" He spat the words out, and conviction grew with each syllable that he spoke.

With the word *demon*, the apparition vanished.

* * *

Harris Borden was dreaming, and he knew it. He remembered going to bed that evening, worried about the events that had transpired, and how they would affect his wife, his church, and his community. Now he was sitting on the side of his bed, awake but asleep.

He got up from his bed, leaving Katya still sleeping, and walked out the front door of his house. Wisps of white, red and black that looked strangely familiar floated through the sky and between rocks and buildings. And then he remembered that they were angels. As he remembered it, detail came into focus and he could see that a terrific battle was going on throughout the town. Angels not only flew through the air and in all directions, flashes of impact occurred here and there as a red or black image came in contact with one of the white ones. Harris remembered what The Messenger had said about the angels' appearance, and wondered if what he was seeing was the way they really were. The whole thing, which made sense when The Messenger explained it, confused him now.

Harris got into his car and, without the use of a key or turning the ignition on, began to drive. He drove over to the church and saw a narrow band of white surrounding the building. A small, brave band of angels protected the church from a greatly superior number of red and black angels who continued to pummel them, constantly looking for an opening. He could see that unless the white angels received reinforcements soon, they would lose the battle.

He drove through the town from one side to the other, and realized that the white angels were outnumbered by the red and black ones. He passed by the houses of members, such as the Washingtons, the Hollises and the Russells, and saw that all their homes were under siege. Only at Greg Phipps' house did he see the white forces in control, with the demons in full retreat.

Discouraged and concerned, he decided to drive home. He saw that angels were in vigorous combat there, but the battle was still undecided. He carefully entered the front door, trying to avoid the gaze of two massive red angels who were perched just above the entrance, glowering. He entered the bedroom again, and caught his breath.

Just above Katya was the most hideous creature he'd ever seen. It was a demon, he knew, but it had none of the physical attributes of an angel, such as some of the other demons had. This one was shaped more like a giant gorilla-type creature, but with scales, and dripping with venom. Somehow he knew the demon intended to kill his wife at the first opportunity. And he was hideous, regardless of what he really, truly looked like.

Protecting her were three white angels with fiery swords, much smaller than the large demon, but with a brilliant aura around them. They stood their ground on three sides of Katya. She slept at peace beneath them, oblivious to the danger that threatened her so close by.

The war is being fought no matter what I do, Harris thought. *All I can do is choose sides*. He carefully lay down next to his wife, his eyes watching the three protective angels that circled his wife tirelessly.

The last thing he remembered in the dream was looking into the eyes of one of the good angels and seeing a look of resolve. *They know what is at stake*, he thought.

Harris woke up a few hours later, realizing that he could not back down.

* * *

Flip Ledger was hurting, and he knew it. He sold about a dozen guns he had lifted from the old man's house as soon as he could, and gotten only about $200. With prices as low as they were, he decided to hold onto the one he had taken from the safe. He suspected it was worth a lot more than that.

After that, he had had nothing but bad luck. The police hassled him twice about the burglary, but could never pin anything on him. He picked up a severe case of the flu—vomiting and everything—and had been bedbound for close to a week. As soon as he got out of bed, he got rolled by a couple of thugs outside his apartment building, who took the $200 he had just gotten from the fence.

Now he was broke, no leads on a new heist, with only the gun in the Plexiglas trophy case to his name. He decided to stop thinking about tomorrow and take care of today. He had rent due soon, and would like to get some groceries as well. Trouble was, Marty had skipped town right after he had sold the guns to him. He would have to resort to selling at the local pawn shop.

He tried to keep pawn shops out of the loop, simply because so many of them worked closely with the police. But he'd pretty much run out of options.

A-1 Pawn had taken some stuff from him before, so that's where he headed this morning. He hoped he could get enough for his rent and at least one steak dinner. Maybe his luck would change. Maybe.

10 INTO THE LION'S JAWS

Horatio "Pudge" Nelson sat at the control panel in the Fox News truck busy eating a bag of Doritos while getting ready for The Big Show when he heard a sharp rap on the door.

"Go away," he barked without looking. "You're not supposed to be in here." He was answered by another series of banging noises. *Someone thought they should have access to the truck,* he thought. *They were wrong.* Frustrated, he finally got up from his chair and went to the door.

"Look, I don't know who you are or what you are selling, but....Michelle!" His tone changed dramatically when he saw Michelle Kinkaid standing outside, as perky and sexy as ever, he thought. He had been trying without success to get her alone in this truck for three years. Now she stood at the doorway, asking permission to enter. Far be it from him to say no.

"Hey, Pudge," she said with a soft voice and a smile. "Can I come in?

Pudge looked down at the crumbs on his Star Wars Episode III T-shirt and quickly wiped it clean. He took his other hand and pushed the door open wider.

"Come on in, Babe," he said. "It's about time you came and visited me. Ready for The Big Show?"

"Sure," she said. "I thought I'd get a better view from in here." She climbed the metal stairs and stood behind him as he took his seat at the control board. "Wow, this is a lot more complicated that writing for the newspaper. And you're in charge of all this by yourself?" She tried to look innocent.

"What can I tell you, Babe," Pudge said, leaning back in his chair. "I'm the man with the power." His words were followed sharply by a tinny voice coming from his headphones.

"Pudge! Get your finger out of your nose and get ready for sound check!"

Pudge sat up suddenly and grabbed his headphones.

"Sorry, Babe," he said hastily. "Duty calls."

Michelle took a deep breath and rolled her eyes as Pudge ran the cameramen, producer and sound engineers through their sound check. After a minute, things slowed down just a bit, and Michelle cleared her throat.

"Pudge, I didn't really come in here to watch you work. I came in to ask you a favor—a big one." Her voice reverted to its usual, businesslike tone.

Pudge looked up from the board and pulled his headphones off slowly.

"A big one, eh? Big enough to be worth a date with me?"

Michelle hesitated, cringed, then nodded. "Big enough for a date...anywhere you want to go."

Pudge's mouth dropped open. It was Christmas, his birthday and Fourth of July rolled into one.

"Name the favor, Sweetheart," he said. "I'm your humble slave."

"Two things," Michelle said. "First, you saw that they're using wireless mikes. Know the frequency?"

Pudge nodded. "Low band FM mikes. Why?"

"I need you to block their signal temporarily, when I tell you. Can you do that?"

Pudge grinned. "Babe, it's all a matter of power, and I got...."

"Yes, I know. You have the power. Now here's the second thing."

She held up a CD-R.

Pudge's eyebrows shot up. "Sounds like fun. Could lose us both our jobs, but extremely fun. I'm in."

* * *

"OK, we're all set," Michelle said to Harris and Katya on the street outside the enclosed area. March music from a local high school band was playing from the enclosure. The street was crowded with people curious about what was happening inside. But security was tight, and only those with proper ID were able to go inside.

"I wondered why they chose the Fourth of July for this event, but it makes sense now," Harris said. "If they'd planned this for a regular workday, traffic would be so bad no one could get near this place." He looked down California Street toward Chinatown, then turned and looked down Sansome toward the heart of the Financial District. The street was crowded for about three blocks in all directions, but the Financial District emptied out further on. Chinatown was always crowded; today the streets were filled with tourists.

"Well, at least it's a beautiful day," Katya added. "Maybe we can go to Ghirardelli Square afterward."

Harris and Michelle threw each other a sober glance. *If we live that long.* "Yeah, sure, Chickpea. Anything you want," Harris said.

"Got your mic?" Michelle asked. Harris held the stubby black rod up and nodded.

"OK, it'll feed through the system, but only after their mics have been blocked," she said. "Here are your hat and camera." She gave Harris a floppy Stetson that not only kept the sun out of his face, but partly covered it. The camera was an antique medium-format camera. It was a bulky relic that also helped Harris keep his profile to a minimum.

"These should help with the security cameras," Michelle said. "The big problem is going to be getting in." She looked over at the metal detector at the gate, and the crowd of blue-coated security guards who stood there.

Harris exhaled sharply. "Well, if as you say, God wants me there, then He'll take care of it. Ready?"

Michelle nodded. Katya grabbed Harris hand and squeezed it, tears threatening to come to her eyes.

"*Ya tebya lublu*," she whispered. "I love you, *petrushka*."

* * *

Kenneth Deke was in a foul mood. The date for this event—the beginning of construction of Universal Tower and the official date of public offering of Universal stock—had been set in stone weeks before by the Brotherhood of the Altar. And it seems just as soon as it had been committed to, everything conceivable had started to go wrong.

First had come the appearance of the minister that embarrassed Universal and Deke in particular during the important cabal meeting. Then his security agents had failed to get rid of this pesky Borden guy. Both those items had prompted Deke to take the time to interview for a director of security that would take this worry off his hands. After 100 possible names and a few interviews, Deke had decided that at this important juncture, he couldn't afford to put this in the hands of someone new. So, once again, the president of a billion-dollar corporation that would be the leading financial institution in the world within a few years was forced to do the dirty work himself. He wasn't happy, but he knew the work would get done. His way.

And of course, Deke knew he wasn't totally alone. Ed Whiting, despite his slovenly appearance, was invaluable with electronic communications and all things computer-wise. The sloppy genius had been a key player in getting them to where they were now. And of course, He Who Remained Nameless would turn circumstances in their favor as always.

Deke stepped onto the red, white and blue decorated platform, his suit impeccable, his shoes spotless, and the audience applauded. He was followed onto the platform by two security guards, who stood on either side and just behind him. Deke looked out at the crowd of reporters and cameramen standing on the grassy knoll overlooking the junction of California and Sansome streets. It was indeed fortunate that the corner where the Universal Tower would be built was across the street from a small park. That was where they had built an enclosure so the media could watch the demolition of the old building that stood there. It played well on TV, and the enclosure kept the media safe—and under his control.

"Welcome, ladies and gentlemen," Deke said into the microphone. He held up his hands as questions were shouted from the reporters. "There'll be plenty of time for questions later."

He gestured to the band set up beside the platform. "Did you enjoy the music? Let's give a hand to the San Francisco High School band." He led the audience in applause.

"But now you're probably waiting for the Big Show, as it's being called," he said, chuckling. "We were hoping to have a groundbreaking ceremony by this date, but we'll have to settle for letting you see the strategic implosion and demolition of the building that we'll be replacing." He gestured to the old, empty office building across the wide street. It had once been an important part of San Francisco's Financial District, but now looked quite lonely.

"Before I give the go-ahead, I would like to officially—." Deke's voice stopped when he realized that the microphone no longer worked. Puzzled, he tapped on it and got no sound. He looked to the trailer on his left where

Ed Whiting was working. Ed looked up and shrugged. Something was wrong, very wrong.

"My name is Elizabeth Katzburg, and I live in Salem, Oregon," he heard a voice say over the loudspeaker. "Universal has ruined my life. I started a credit account with them and immediately was overwhelmed by a series of unfortunate incidents. I was in an auto accident, I lost my job and my husband left me."

Deke grabbed the radio from the belt of one of the security guards. "Where is that coming from?" he hissed at Whiting. "Find the source and stop it!"

"I have no idea where it's coming from," Whiting's voice said. "I'll do my best."

"Just stop it, will you? This is a major embarrassment," he hissed into the radio, then gave it back to the security guard.

"I know it sounds strange, but I think that Universal had something to do with my situation," the disembodied voice went on. "It can't be coincidence that when I borrowed money from them, I suddenly developed many reasons why I couldn't pay them back."

Deke smiled at the audience, but they had stopped paying attention to him, and were looking around to find the source of the voice. Deke waited another 20 seconds, trying to give Whiting enough time to stop the signal from wherever it was coming from. But when another testimony started up though, telling how Universal had ruined his life, Deke lost it.

He jumped down from the platform and ran to the trailer where Whiting was working. He threw the door open and shouted, "Shut it down! Shut it all down!" Whiting obliged by reaching behind him and throwing the main power switch. The sound system shut down, as well as the mysterious voice, disconnected in mid-sentence. Deke took a deep breath, and exhaled it. Then he heard a familiar voice, and dread crept through him.

"These were just two testimonies from people whose lives were ruined by Universal Finance," he heard the voice say. "I have recordings from at least 20 of them, but you get the idea."

"Borden," breathed Deke.

"It's coming from an independent power source," Whiting said, looking at his dead control board. "I'll have to power back up to find out where."

"Do it," Deke said. "But find him."

Deke scanned the audience of several hundred reporters, but couldn't see the face of the preacher. Then a hand shot up from the middle of the crowd. It held letter envelopes. Deke saw Borden holding a microphone, and looking straight at him.

"I have here about two dozen other letters from people complaining about Universal Finance," Borden said. "I have several hundred more in my possession.

"It's one thing to put together a business that earns an honest buck by serving its customers. It's another to get rich by ruining other people's lives."

Deke started to run toward Borden, but realized that he'd never get through the crowd. In addition, he saw security guard Max Heinrich pushing through the crowd toward Borden.

"This country was founded on free enterprise, but it was also founded with the slogan, In God We Trust. Is this an approach God would approve of? Well, I believe that this form of business comes from another source."

Deke smiled as he knew that Max would not make the same mistake twice. Borden would be dead within seconds.

* * *

His knees were shaking, his voice was quivering, but Harris knew he had a captive audience. At last, he had the ears of at least a hundred reporters. Harris played two testimonies that Katya had thought to record over the phone in those first two crazy days at home. Then he told the reporters what he knew was going on with Universal. The portable sound system that Michelle had helped him prepare helped him speak over all competition.

Harris watched the reaction of those around him. Even though they were caught off guard by the surprise, he knew they were listening. Then Harris saw him across the crowd, standing in the doorway of a trailer.

Harris watched him and realized that his words were having their intended effect. Deke was sweating big time. Then Harris saw his expression change, and knew that someone was behind him.

Harris felt, rather than saw, the automatic pistol come up from the security guard behind him and point toward his head. Instinctively, he ducked. At that instant, Harris heard a boom and felt the rush of the bullet whizzing past his head. Harris grabbed the guard's extended arm and pushed it skyward. Another couple of bullets whizzed into the air. Harris heard screaming. As he wrestled the guard, who Harris realized was the man who had grabbed him on the rooftop and had visited his church. Harris turned his head and saw that the first bullet had hit one of the reporters, whose white shirt was rapidly staining red. The reporter lay on the ground. Harris wanted to do something to help him, but was on the wrong end of a losing wrestling match with a 300-pound blonde gorilla.

Even though Harris knew that only seconds had passed, time seemed to slow down, and it stretched into long minutes. Time was not on his side, and he prayed inwardly.

"*Relax*," a voice inside him said. "*Slow down*." Harris looked down and saw that his free hand still held the microphone. Instinctively, he raised it and clubbed the guard across the bridge of the nose. Blood spurted forth from his nose, and he fell backwards.

"*Don't run*," the voice told Harris. "*Relax. Don't run*." Free of the guard, Harris looked down and realized that he held the automatic pistol that had shot the reporter. Harris looked up at the crowd around the fallen reporter, and they screamed. Panic ensued. The crowd of people moved like a living wall, pushing toward the temporary fence around the enclosure—and away from Harris.

He knew that they saw him as a crazy man with a gun. He knew that if he ran it would only support their conclusion. And so, instead of being rational, or following the advice that God's voice gave him inside his head, Harris did the instinctive thing. He ran.

The crowd moved like a single, living creature, and pushed the fence down within seconds. The reporters and cameramen ran into the middle of California Street, then in all directions. Harris paused for a second, then seeing armed security guards coming at him from three sides, he ran as well.

The sound of pistols being fired and bullets whizzing past did nothing to slow down the panic that the crowd felt, and Harris was one with them. He did have the presence of mind to know that he didn't want to be on an empty street with guards shooting at him from behind. Thus Harris decided to run across the street and into the abandoned office building.

* * *

"Yes!" Deke said, as he watched Borden cross the street. "Yes! It couldn't have been scripted better," he said. "Wide-eyed radical minister disrupts second presentation, kills an innocent bystander—a reporter no less—and disappears into an abandoned building that just happens to be scheduled for demolition.

"Nothing like getting good news coverage—and getting rid of a headache at the same time," Deke said to Whiting. "We'll wait for him to get completely inside, then go ahead and blow the building."

"What about your security guards?" Whiting asked. "You want me to call them back?"

"No," Deke said. "He might change directions."

Deke watched Borden's running figure as it disappeared across the street and into the entrance of the old building. He counted to ten, then switched on Whiting's radio.

"Tell them to go ahead with the demolition," Deke said.

"But men are inside," he heard the voice from the radio say.

"Do it," he said into the radio. "Do it *now*, or it's the last thing you'll ever do."

A second's pause was followed by a muffled boom, followed by another and another as he realized that demolitions in the building's foundation were going off. He watched as the building seemed to hesitate and hang in mid-air. Then it started to slide to the ground in slow motion, the outside edges going first, but followed quickly by the middle of the building. It reminded him of a large animal being shot and collapsing to the ground.

A tremendous roar filled the air as the building rolled to the ground. People who had been totally overwhelmed by panic stopped in their tracks to watch the immense structure collapse. The roar echoed down California Street, followed by a full minute of silence. Everyone stood in awe of the dust and rubble that just seconds before had been a building.

"We lost four men," Whiting whispered finally, overcome with awe.

"We'll hire new ones," Deke said, unemotionally. He had been standing in the doorway watching the collapse of the building. Now he stepped into the trailer and pulled the door closed behind him.

"The police are on their way, I'm sure," Deke said. "Notify them that four of our best men chased an insane killer into the building just before it collapsed. And of course, the collapse was an accident."

"Of course," Whiting said, uncomfortable with Deke's businesslike approach to the loss of his men. "What about the reporter?"

"I'm sure someone has already called for an ambulance," he said. "Make sure you call too so that we have it on public record. We wouldn't want to appear insensitive.

"How many security agents do we have left?"

Whiting looked at his roster. "Ten," he said.

"Send them into the rubble to check for his body," Deke said.

"Yeah, I know. No body, no death," Whiting said, lifting his phone receiver.

* * *

Harris had been frightened on the rooftop when he had realized that two guards were about to throw him off. But he had never given in to total, unbridled panic like he did there on California Street. Rational thought totally left him until he entered the doorless entryway of the old office building. Then as he realized that he had once again failed to follow God's direction, he became discouraged.

Harris ran into the lobby area of the old building, then around the elevator bay to a side entrance. He could hear the steps of the security guards who were right behind him. But knowing that he had once again failed God, he suddenly felt as if it didn't matter whether he lived or died.

"*Run,*" the voice said. "*Run as fast as you can.*"

There are many things Harris couldn't do at all, and several things he did, but didn't do well. That's where he got the nickname of *petrushka*, or Pinocchio, from Katya. But if there was one thing he knew he could do, it was run.

Harris bolted out the side entrance into an alleyway opposite Sansome Street, then turned left. He had taken two steps into the alley when he heard a muffled booming noise. There was a rumble, followed by the feeling that the sky was falling. The ground around Harris shook and he looked up. Loose bricks from the building fell like rain. And he saw that the whole building was following it.

As fast as Harris was running, he put on a burst of speed and turned right into another alleyway. This one was so small that a dumpster turned sideways partially obscured the entrance. He ran past the dumpster seconds before several tons of bricks fell on it. He didn't take time to see what happened to it. He knew that the metal container was flattened, just as he would have been if he'd jumped into it, as he'd first considered doing.

By the time the entire building had collapsed, Harris was two blocks away, running west down an alleyway between California and Sacramento streets.

* * *

"OK, we have 12 patrol cars outside, and two choppers on the way," Whiting told Deke. "Our own men are looking for a body. So far, only pieces."

"Keep searching," Deke said. "This guy has more lives than David Hasselhoff."

"OK, we got something coming in," Whiting said. "Son of a...." Deke stepped over to the control panel to see a video image apparently being fed through from one of the choppers. It showed a shot from the air of someone running at breakneck speed down an alley. Dust trailed behind him like the contrail on a jet.

"That's him," Deke said. "That's him! Where is he?"

"Chopper says he's headed west in an alley just north of California. Headed toward Chinatown."

"OK, get our men out of the building and after him. Get the patrol units headed toward him. Get the choppers on him. And tell them all, shoot to kill!"

Whiting looked up at Deke. "I can't tell the police that."

"He just killed five people. He's headed toward a tourist area. Shoot to kill! I don't want him alive to tell his story anymore. *I want him dead!*"

Deke watched in silence as the pursuit continued.

* * *

For several blocks Harris felt alone, yet knew he wasn't. He heard sirens on California to his left and Sacramento on his right. After about half a mile, he saw a police helicopter appear above his head. His suspicions were correct, and now that the chopper told them where he was, Harris knew it was only a matter of time.

"Should I stop running, God?" Immediately Harris realized that Universal would want him dead. Whether he went to prison or not was irrelevant. Harris had to stay alive to speak out against Universal. And, of course, he wanted to stay alive just to stay alive. He needed to find a way to surrender without getting shot.

In the meantime, the tall financial skyscrapers around him gave way to signs in Chinese. He was in Chinatown, and knew that tourists both gave him more chances to hide, and made the police more determined to stop him. Harris looked to his left as he passed another alley leading out to California, and saw that a patrol car was keeping abreast of him on the main street. Harris knew he had only minutes left to come up with a plan.

He came out onto Kearny Street and saw the police rounding the corner from California, headed his direction. Harris knew they expected him to turn right, away from their visible presence. But he knew other cops were coming from Sacramento Street. So Harris ran straight across the busy boulevard, with cars screeching and honking in both directions. Harris didn't hesitate but ran across the crowded sidewalk and up the steps to Old St. Mary's Cathedral there. At least thirty tourists were on the steps. He ran into the crowd, knowing that any cop trying to take a shot would be hard pressed to shoot at him without hitting anyone else.

Patrol cars screeched behind him, jockeying into position, but Harris didn't take the time to look at them. He pushed through the crowd and ran into the church. Inside, the Catholic priest was talking to someone in the lobby.

"I surrender," Harris said to him, puffing, interrupting them and holding up his hands. "I surrender, but I want to make sure they don't shoot me."

The priest's eyes opened wide as he looked at Harris' face, streaked with sweat and dust from the falling building, and then looked out at the dozen police cars parked haphazardly on the street outside with officers standing behind them, guns drawn.

"I surrender, I surrender," Harris whispered.

The priest paused, then nodded slowly.

"Son, you are in God's care here," he said.

Harris nodded his head and tried to smile, while gasping for air. "That's what I'm hoping for."

11 REPERCUSSIONS

"Meddows here," the news editor barked into his portable phone. The closer he got to deadline, the briefer—and more impatient—he tended to be on the phone. Right now, deadline was thirty minutes away, and his sentences rarely added up to more than five consecutive words.

"Hey Paul, this is Michelle. Did you see my story?" Michelle Kinkaid was charging in her silver Mazda Miata through the San Francisco evening traffic like she was a veteran cabbie. She turned onto Embarcadero and knew that she had just a few blocks to go.

"Yeah, I saw it," Meddows said. "Exciting stuff. But we can't lead with that."

"Yes, we can," Michelle said, downshifting into second gear and roaring past another bus. "Tell me one reason why we can't, other than the people involved have political connections. Would you have done this with Watergate?"

"Not fair, Michelle. Watergate was big. Huge."

"Paul," she said, switching her cell phone to her left hand and rolling down her window with her right to flash her badge at the parking attendant. "This is just as big. If you took the time to read the support material I gave you, you'd know that everything is supported factually by numerous sources, everything is checked and double checked; everything is verified."

Meddows exhaled sharply enough that Michelle could hear it through the phone.

"No," he said finally.

"Paul, *yes*." Michelle said, angling across two parking spaces, pulling her hand brake, turning off the key and palming them while jumping from her car, all within the space of two seconds.

"Michelle, I'm the news editor."

"Then act like it," she barked back. "For goodness sake, grow some *huevos!*" She hit the elevator button and waited, her toe tapping impatiently.

Meddows jerked upright, suddenly alert to the conversation. "Of all the news outlets on the west coast, we're the only paper crazy enough to say that today's terrorist attack was caused by the corporation that was also the victim? We'll be laughed at in every newsroom in the country."

"We may be laughed at, but it's the truth," Michelle said, charging out of the elevator door. "Isn't that what we signed on for? The Truth?"

"Well, somewhere back in my college days, I remember hearing about something called the Truth, with a capital T, but frankly, right now, I'm mostly concerned about keeping my job and making my next mortgage payment."

"Paul," Michelle sighed, then pushed through the glass doors into Meddows office. "You know I'm right." She looked at the harried news editor, tie askew, and for a second felt sorry for him. But only for a second.

Paul Meddows looked at her for a long, silent moment, the phone still in his hand. She was his most aggressive, intelligent and conscientious reporter, and he'd died inside when he'd been forced to take her off of investigative reporting.

"You know, when I look at you I see a heckova news editor in the making," he said, dropping the receiver back into its cradle. "Course, if we both get fired, it'll be that much harder for you to get that promotion you deserve." He grinned at her, then shook his head.

"Truth, justice and the American way," he muttered to her. "Isn't that what it's about?"

"I think that's from Superman, but yeah. Something like that."

He shook his head again.

"OK, front page, bottom."

"Lead, with a banner head," she responded.

He glared at her. "You really don't know when to say no, do you?" Pause. "OK, lead."

"And nobody touches my quotes," she shouted over her shoulder as she ran out the door, her cell phone still in hand.

"Keep pushing and you'll see what an unemployment line looks like," he barked back at the empty air.

* * *

"Ed," Deke said to the phone while standing in the darkness of his otherwise empty office. "After that fiasco today I need you to put some serious thought into an electronic security system for the new tower. Something foolproof. Something that not even that maniac—or someone like him—can get through.

Pause. "No, don't talk to Homeland Security, the FBI or any of those cracker heads. You I can trust, so I want to put it all on your shoulders. We need to be absolutely sure that we can have privacy and protection when the tower goes up. I'm counting on you, Ed. I always count on you, and you always come through for me. Thanks."

Deke hung up and slumped over his desk.

"Things are not going well," the voice in the darkness said.

125

Deke stood facing his desk, his head bowed, deep in thought. Suddenly, he took both arms and swept papers, books and lamp off the desk and onto the floor. His head was throbbing, his heart was pounding, and his mind was filled with hatred.

"He still lives," the voice said, a statement of fact rather than a question. Deke nodded, then turned to face the one being he feared.

"Yes, my Lord, he's still alive," Deke said quietly. "Despite all our efforts, he's alive and in the custody of the police as we speak."

"I understand," Baal said. "It is not all your fault, my servant. My minions have attacked his church and his loved one, but we have learned that he has spiritual protection. It is difficult to gain an advantage over someone who is protected by his God."

Deke stared at the floor. "Then what do we do?"

"Our strategy must adapt to the present circumstances. He gains his strength from his dependence on his God. We must work together to break that dependence. Once we have broken that, his spiritual protection will be weakened and he will be vulnerable."

"I see," Deke said quietly.

"In the meantime, he is imprisoned, and out of our way. My followers grow in numbers, and I gain strength. We will continue to grow, and he will be unable to stop us. But you must make sure that he has no opportunity to speak the truth. We must keep him away from the public eye at all costs."

"Which means making sure he stays in prison. That," Deke said. "I can do. After all, I haven't been cultivating all these political connections for nothing. Time to call in chips."

"Very good," Baal said. "I would also advise you to do something about his wife."

"Consider it done," Deke said.

* * *

126

Harris had gotten his share of speeding tickets in his day, mostly when he was in college and trying to avoid Washington state's finest while heading home to Boise for the weekend. But he didn't think he ever appreciated the police as much as he did that day as he was thrown to the sidewalk and handcuffed, then pushed into the back of a patrol car amid a sea of blue uniforms. Harris had this bad feeling that there was someone out there ready to shoot him if they got the chance. San Francisco's cops made that impossible by acting as his personal bodyguards.

Actually, they didn't realize they were doing Harris a favor by arresting him. They looked at him as if Harris had just assassinated the President or something. Harris responded politely, just glad to be alive.

A dozen police cars surrounded them, sirens blaring, as they headed for the main police headquarters. Again, Harris was pulled from the squad car amid a sea of blue uniforms and literally carried into the station. They went through the booking process and then Harris was taken to a small holding cell with a glass wall that he knew probably had a few cops behind it as well.

For a long while, he sat in the empty room, just Harris, a chair and a lone wooden table. Harris knew that they would come in to interrogate him soon enough. Harris was actually looking forward to talking to someone, and had nothing whatsoever to hide. As he sat there, Harris realized that getting to court may have been God's intent after all. Harris' case had become pretty high profile, and his day in court would offer him the platform to give another testimony.

Finally, a suited man came through the doorway. Harris expected him to be a cop, but this guy was too nicely dressed to be a detective. Harris wondered if he was from the district attorney's office.

"Hi, I'm Harris Borden," he said, smiling and holding out his hand. He reached as far as he could, but he was shackled to the chair, so that was limited. "You'll find that I'm willing to cooperate and will tell you anything you need to know."

The middle-aged man didn't smile, nor did he take Harris' hand. He sat down across from him and opened a briefcase with a fat envelope in it. He shoved the envelope over toward Harris, who opened it and looked inside. It was full of $1,000 bills. Harris gasped.

"That's $50,000. Here's the deal," the well-dressed man said, matter of factly. "We pay you off, we drop the charges, and you disappear. There's enough money there for you and your missus to disappear forever. Take her back to Russia. You could get fairly well established with a nest egg like that."

Harris stared at the money and then at the unsmiling man seated across from him. The man didn't look like he wanted to be here.

"I assume you're from Universal?" Harris said slowly.

"You assume correct." He stared at Harris without batting an eye. This guy didn't like him, not one bit.

"Look, Reverend Borden," the man said. "This is the carrot. Don't wait until we get to the stick to work things out. This is the last good deal you'll get."

Harris narrowed his eyes and looked the man up and down. Finally the whole thing struck Harris as intensely funny. He started to chuckle.

"You find me amusing?" the man asked, irritated.

Harris shook his head. "An hour ago, you guys were determined to kill me. Now you want me to take your money and disappear? Forget that everything happened? I have a hard time believing that you'll let me just walk away."

The man shrugged. "It's either that or wait for us to put you away in prison for good."

"Put me away? I didn't do anything illegal!" Harris pulled against the shackles.

"That's not the way the media sees it. They're calling you a terrorist. And I can guarantee that the judge and a jury of your peers will see that as well."

Harris looked at him in silence. Universal Finance had a lot of pull; that was very clear. But he took solace in the fact that at least he'd get a chance to tell his side of the story from the witness stand.

"This offer won't be good for long," the man said, suddenly bored with his company. "Better take it while you can."

Harris picked up the fat envelope the man had handed him and slid it back across the table.

"No thanks. I'll see what happens in court."

The man picked up the envelope and put it in his folder, then stood. Without another word, he walked out the door and disappeared.

Harris didn't see much action after that. Two detectives came into the room to see him about half an hour later. They seemed disappointed that he was so willing to talk; Harris guessed they were looking forward to prying the information out of him. After Harris told his story a couple of times, they yawned and called the officer outside. He escorted Harris to a cell where Harris was left alone.

He never saw a lawyer.

* * *

Greg Phipps looked around him. Half the congregation was sleeping; the other half was struggling to stay awake. He had sat through some boring, droning preachers before in his long life. Dr. Frank Hollis was right up there among the top ones.

He had worried that the church was going to explode when they got the news about Pastor Borden's arrest. There was a steady low rumble in the congregation as they gathered for church service. Greg worried that Dr. Hollis would take this opportunity to try to make some sort of statement condemning Harris. Instead he had completely ignored the events that had transpired, and apparently just wanted to preach. For someone who loved to hear himself preach, Greg thought, Frank sure did a bad job of it.

"….which leads us to the issue at hand," Dr. Hollis said, gaining Greg's attention and waking a few of the sleeping saints in the congregation. "One of our own has determined that he is receiving messages from God that call for him to not only embarrass his congregation in the public eye, but break the laws of man and kill innocent bystanders."

Guess I spoke too soon, Greg thought to himself, sitting upright in his seat. *Here it comes.*

"I feel it falls upon us as a congregation to make a public statement, condemning our former pastor for his actions, and separating us from him as much as possible."

Jules Russell stood and interrupted Hollis. "Excuse me, Dr. Hollis, but when was it decided that Harris Borden is no longer recognized as church pastor? That's a matter for the church board, and as we haven't met yet…."

"Technically, that's true," Hollis said. "But it's pretty apparent that his behavior makes Borden unfit to be the pastor here."

"Unfit!" said Moira Washington, speaking from her seat. "No one has convicted him of any wrongdoing. No one has shown any evidence that he's done anything."

"That man has been a problem for years," someone in the back said. "I say we distance ourselves from him so we don't get painted with the same brush."

Frank Hollis held up his hands. "Brothers and sisters, please. I thought it was apparent to everyone that Harris Borden was an embarrassment and should be removed as pastor. Apparently I was being hasty."

Greg Phipps stood slowly, and others turned to look at him, to see what he would say.

"I agree, Dr. Hollis, that you might have been a bit hasty. I believe this bears discussion at our next board meeting. In the meantime, he's still our pastor. Let's leave it at that."

Hollis locked eyes with Phipps for a long moment, then cleared his throat, looking down. "Uh, ok, we'll take up that discussion at our next board meeting on Sunday the thirteenth." Hollis ended the service with closing prayer, but his words were hollow.

Greg could see that the spiritual battle the church was already in would soon manifest itself as a battle of wills. He braced himself to assume a church leadership role again.

"God, give me strength," he whispered.

* * *

It was several days before Harris got a chance to see Katya. The last time he had seen her was outside the enclosure, right before Harris had opened his mouth and brought the vengeance of Universal Finance down on himself. After the short meeting with the detectives, Harris was moved to the County Jail for holding, where he spent close to a week in a cell by himself. They brought him his meals three times a day, but Harris didn't have any visitors beyond that. That surprised him at first, because the label "terrorist" had suggested to him that he would be interrogated by the FBI and probably Homeland Security. So far, he hadn't seen either group. Harris didn't know whether they were disinterested, or Universal had already developed massive political clout, enough to keep him isolated from anyone who might have a chance to hear his story and decide that he wasn't the madman that Universal painted him to be.

In the meantime, Katya was well versed in bureaucracy, having grown up in Russia, and she spent the entire week trying to get in to see Harris. He didn't know if it was something in particular she said, or that the San

Francisco Police just got tired of hearing her whine, beg and threaten them, but on Wednesday of the next week, she finally was successful.

That morning, about 11 a.m., a guard finally came into his holding cell and told him to come. Harris followed him through several locked doors to what he presumed was a meeting room. A guard stood at either end of the room, with security cameras in three locations watching his every move. The room was divided by a large plexiglass wall, with booths and chairs set up along the wall. It was only when Harris was directed toward the middle chair that he saw that it stood directly across from Katya.

His heart went to his throat. Harris quickly sat down and lifted the phone receiver to his left. Katya was already crying before he spoke a word.

"Hello, my sweet," Harris whispered. He put his right hand to the plexiglass, trying to reach her somehow.

She didn't say anything, but smiled through her tears.

"As you can see, I'm still alive," Harris joked. "I've been treated well, although I haven't seen a lawyer yet."

"Well, we will have to see what we can do," she said finally.

"Talk to Nils Andrusen," Harris said. "I'm sure he'll be willing to help out."

"I will get you some assistance, somehow," she said.

"Well, the police are supposed to supply me with a court-appointed lawyer if I can't afford one, but considering how much influence Deke has shown to have here, I don't think I'd better trust their choice of a lawyer."

"Harris," Katya said suddenly. He paused and looked at her.

"I am pregnant."

He looked at Katya for a long moment, not sure if he'd heard her correctly. Then he saw her teary face break into a faint smile. She nodded. It was true.

"Yes! I'm going to be a father!" Harris shouted, then remembered where he was.

"Quiet on three, or we'll send you back to your cell," the guard in the corner said to him. Harris hunched his shoulders and grinned, putting his finger up to his lips.

"Katya, that's….that's the most wonderful news in the world," Harris said, his face split by the largest grin he'd had in weeks. And then he realized something that took that smile away.

"What is it?" Katya said, when she saw his expression change. "Are you not happy?"

"I'm ecstatic," Harris said to her, smiling faintly. "Really I am."

"But what?" she asked.

Harris looked at her, at the inmates on either side of him, at the two guards, then at the security cameras that watched his every move.

"Katya….darling, I'm really happy, really I am. But I'm realizing that I'm not safe here. Universal controls everything. And…you…and the baby aren't safe here either. Neither of you will be safe until this is all over with."

Katya looked at him with a cloud coming over her face.

"And as long as I know you're in danger, they'll have control over me. I can't allow that. If I'm to do this task set before me, I can't allow them any source of power in my life."

Katya stared at him for a long minute. "What will we do, then?" she asked.

Harris shook his head, then looked around him again. Control over his life had become a harsh illusion. All he could do was continue on the path set before him. That and make sure those he loved were safe.

"Go home," Harris whispered. "You'll be safe at home."

"Home?" she repeated, her eyebrows raised. "To Nevada?"

Harris shook his head. "No, *home*. To your family. Universal has no influence there."

Harris hesitated to say "home to Russia" aloud, but she finally understood. He knew that she'd resist going, and she did.

"I must stand by my husband," she said, her bottom lip sticking out. "I will stay."

"Chickpea, if you love me, if you want to help me, this is how you can," he said, desperate. "I need you to do this."

She stared at him, and tears rolled down her face. Russian bubbled from her lips rapidly, and Harris knew that she was talking to herself, trying to make sense of what he was saying. Finally, she stopped talking and bowed her head. She nodded silently.

"Go quickly," Harris said. "Do it for me." He was crying now.

"*Ya tebya lublu*," Harris whispered, then hung up the phone and walked back toward his cell.

12 BEHIND WALLS

It was terribly painful to send Katya away, but after Harris did it, he knew he'd done the right thing. The further he got into this mess, the more power Harris realized that Universal had, and the more they could use Katya and his expected child against him.

It also seemed fitting that Katya was finally going to be with her mother and father. Harris felt he could survive anything knowing that she and their baby were safe and happy. Harris knew Katya's parents, and knew that they'd both understand and would be warm and protective to his only family.

Harris also found that he was able to focus on the coming trial with Katya and his life outside jail out of his mind. True to her word, Katya was able to convince Andrussen to send an attorney to help him out, although he made it clear that he didn't sanction his actions.

One morning, Harris was escorted over to a secondary meeting room. It was a lot more private, with a table and chairs where he could talk in seclusion with his counsel. The lawyer turned out to be a 60ish man named Sydney Houtt out of Reno, who looked a bit frumpy and unassuming, but who Harris learned was pretty sharp. Once again,

Harris told his story—all of it, no holds barred. He figured that if the attorney had any chance of helping him, he needed to know everything, even if Harris hadn't felt comfortable sharing parts of the story with the Andrussen and the others before. He also told Sydney his strategy of wanting to present his story in open court for the public and the media to hear. Sydney just shook his head at that point, but didn't tell Harris he couldn't do it.

After the preliminary visit, Harris met with Sydney a couple of more times. The third time, he came in, his face pretty grim.

"I don't want you to get your hopes up," he told Harris. "The legal team for Universal has an unlimited budget, and that Kenneth Deke really, *really* doesn't like you."

"I don't think I'm being unrealistic," Harris told him. "I know that with the previous contact I had, and their immense political influence, I might have to serve some time. I just want you to see what you can do to minimize it. And, more importantly, I want my day in court."

"That's the part about not getting your hopes up," the attorney said. "I have my suspicions about this judge, and I'm afraid she's going to close the sessions to the press and the public."

"Can she do that?"

"She can, with cause. Universal has filed with the Department of Homeland Security as a Vital Infrastructure. On top of that, you're considered a terrorist. Put the two of them together, and they can claim that the case will endanger national security."

Harris looked at him, disbelieving for a long second. Then he burst out laughing. Harris roared for a long minute, then noticed that Stanley wasn't laughing. If anything, he had a sad look on his face.

"You've got to be kidding," Harris said to him. "Me? A threat to national security?"

"Believe me, they're very serious. I'll do my best to keep it open, but I can't make any promises."

A week later, the two came before Superior Court Judge Harriet Weinberger. The woman looked like she hadn't smiled in twenty years. Harris stood next to Stanley, dressed in a suit he used to preach in. He looked around the audience, and wished that Katya was there to support him. He also prayed that she was safe. Then he saw that Greg Phipps sat in the back row. Greg winked at Harris, and he felt that he wasn't alone.

When all was said and done, Harris was charged with one count of first-degree and four counts of second-degree murder. He was held without bail until the trial. The prosecutor petitioned for a closed hearing due to concerns over national security. That petition was granted, despite Stanley's strenuous objections, and the date for trial was set for three months from then.

Harris realized then, that all the cards were stacked against him, and that Universal was dealing those cards. Not only would he not get a fair trial, he wouldn't get a chance to speak his peace in front of the media and the public.

"Remember, I didn't promise you anything," Stanley said after the judge banged her gavel.

"I don't have anything to blame you for. What now?" Harris asked Stanley.

"Now we either wait the three months till trial, or we make a deal. You wanted to get your day in court in front of the cameras. That's not going to happen. I advise you to deal."

Harris thought about it a long time. *I was innocent. Why should I have to make a deal?* he thought. And then he thought some more. And some more.

* * *

"Michelle, a guy named Greg Phipps is on line two."

Michelle put down the books she was packing and picked up the phone. She punched the button for line two.

"This is Michelle Kinkaid."

"Michelle, my name is Greg Phipps. I'm a friend of Harris Borden."

"What can I do for you, Mr. Phipps?"

"I read your article when the incident with Universal happened, and thought it was the most balanced article that I saw. Thank you for that."

Michelle smiled to herself. "Well, counting your phone call today, that is exactly one person who's said they've liked it. It's not unusual to hear the name 'terrorist lover' muttered by the people I pass by, and I've actually gotten a couple of death threats."

"Really?" Greg's voice went up in surprise. "Well, I'm sorry about that."

"S'Okay," Michelle said. "I guess I couldn't consider myself a serious journalist unless that happened sometime. I'm just glad it happened while writing about someone I consider innocent."

"Well, have you kept up with what's going on?"

Michelle shook her head. "They closed all the proceedings. No information in or out."

"You know who's behind that, don't you."

"Universal, of course."

"And...you know who's behind Universal."

Pause. "Yes...but I don't want to say so on this phone."

Greg chuckled. "I just wanted to make sure we're both reading from the same page."

"We are, but I don't think it'll do you much good. You see, my news editor and I were both fired this morning. I was in the process of clearing out my desk when you called."

Pause. "I'm so sorry," Greg said. "If there's anything I can do...."

"Well, if you know of anyone looking for an investigative reporter for hire, look me up. In the meantime, you'll be able to keep up with my personal campaign against Universal on my blog."

"Blog?"

"Weblog. My website. Look my name up on Google and you can't miss it."

"Hmm," Greg said. "I'm not real familiar with the Internet. I guess I need to get online more."

"Guess so," Michelle said. "It gives us undesirable—and unemployed—journalists a voice even when the big boys want to keep us quiet. Well, got to go."

"God bless you, Michelle. Keep your courage up."

"God bless you, too, Greg. Since He's the One who got us into this, we deserve at least one blessing from Him."

* * *

Harris thought and prayed about what he should do with the case for a week. As a pastor, he had told people many times that God always answers prayer. He just didn't always answer in the way you would like. And sometimes He just said wait.

After such clear, visual responses to his prayers, Harris found himself needing some clear answers to help with his decision, and getting none. He wanted to shout, "Lord, just tell me yes or no!" But he knew that shouting might make him feel he was communicating better than he already was. If God was going to answer him, Harris knew deep down, He was going to do it on His own time, in His own way.

And thus Harris came to the next meeting with his attorney without the clear direction from God he was looking for. Harris truly felt alone. And so he based his decision on the facts and decided to make a deal. It sounded reasonable to him. They dropped the five murder charges, which would have put him in prison for life without possibility of parole. If Harris pleaded no contest to first-degree manslaughter, he could possibly get out in two years.

Sidney thought it was fair. Harris honestly felt anything short of letting him walk free and officially declared innocent was unfair, but he didn't think it was likely. So a week later, he stood once again before the little frowning judge, hoping that she was in a good mood that day, however she measured "good mood."

Sidney didn't give him any indication of what was going to happen. He was helpful, but didn't want to establish any kind of personal relationship with Harris. Thus Harris constantly got the feeling from him that in the end, he was on his own.

Judge Weinberger sat in front at her desk, shuffling her papers as Harris stood with Sidney on one side of the courtroom, and the prosecuting team hired by Universal on the other side. Finally, she looked up.

"It is my understanding that the defense and the prosecution have come to an out-of-court settlement?" she said.

"Yes, your honor," the lead attorney of the prosecution said. "We've dropped the first- and second-degree murder charges and are charging the defendant with first-degree manslaughter."

"That is a sizeable reduction in charges, prosecution," Weinberger said. "How does the defense plead in this case?"

"No contest, your honor," Sidney said. Harris felt his heart go into his throat.

She then turned toward Harris. "Are you in agreement with that?"

He nodded quickly. "Yes, your honor."

Judge Weinberger sighed and shuffled some papers around on her desk. "I know that the purpose of settling out of court is accepting a lesser sentence in exchange for lightening the loads of our court system and saving us all a lot of time.

"But I, for one, feel that allowing someone accused of *terrorism*"— she added emphasis to the last word—"to walk with a lighter sentence set a dangerous precedent. Therefore I am inclined to hand down the maximum sentence I am allowed to for this particular charge. Harris Borden, I sentence you to 25 years in the California State Prison at San Dimas."

Harris' head buzzed. Sidney must have known what he was going through. He leaned over and whispered in Harris' ear. "It's not as bad as it sounds. You'll be eligible for parole in two years, and I'll appeal the sentence. I'll keep in touch. It's not the end of the world."

Harris stared at Sidney's face as they walked him back to his cell, in preparation for moving him to his new home, San Dimas Prison, one of the toughest maximum security prisons in the United States. Regardless of what Sidney said, Harris felt as if his life was over.

* * *

"Aeroflot Flight 9336 to St. Petersburg is now boarding. Please make sure you have all your possessions with you and your boarding pass available."

Katya couldn't remember the last time she'd been in Moscow. She had visited St. Petersburg just before Harris and she had gotten married, and now she was looking forward to seeing old friends that she hadn't seen in many years. Harris' plight never left her mind for more than a few seconds, but she knew that there wasn't much she could do for him other than ease his worry about her and the baby.

She got in line and headed for the boarding gate. Lines here in Russia didn't seem to be as long as the line she got in in San Francisco. Perhaps summer was the wrong time to be here. But she'd been here in winter, and now that she'd lived in Nevada, she much preferred summer heat to winter cold.

She'd just given her boarding pass to the attendant at the door and stepped through the entrance when her stomach rolled. She'd been concerned about traveling while pregnant—she had a history of motion sickness—but the trip on United Airlines from San Francisco had been uneventful. Now it was all catching up with her.

At first she thought she'd tough it out and use the restroom on the plane, then quickly realized that she wouldn't make it.

"*Izvinite*, I am feeling unwell," she told the attendant. "I need to use the restroom."

The attendant didn't hear her, as she was busy trying to translate for an American elderly couple boarding the plane. Katya couldn't wait to tell her again, and pushed her way out of the entrance and ran for the restroom. She made it just in time to throw the stall door open and lean over the toilet. *So this is morning sickness*, she thought. *It's still not too much of a price to pay.*

After 20 minutes, she was about to change her mind. Every time she thought she was done in the restroom, her stomach would send her back to lean over the toilet. Finally, it was over. White faced, she staggered back to the gate. One attendant stood behind the desk, typing frantically on the computer.

"Excuse me," she said to the attendant in Russian. "Did I hold things up?"

Without looking up, the attendant answered her. "Are you family?"

"Family? No, I got sick and had to get off the plane while we were boarding—."

The attendant looked up suddenly, and recognized Katya.

"Your name?"

"Ekaterina Borden, uh, Dubrovika." She paused when she remembered that she was traveling under her maiden name.

The attendant looked at her for an instant, then shouted over Katya's shoulder for two security guards, who came and attempted to whisk her away.

"What... what is going on?" Katya asked.

"We are taking you to security," the attendant said. "Your plane just crashed."

13 DAYS OF PAIN

As Harris was processed and moved from San Francisco County Jail to San Dimas Maximum Security Prison in the next few days, he had two revelations. First, that prison is one of the best examples of hell to be found on earth. He found that you have an eternity to think about the mistakes you've made in your life; you're constantly surrounded by fear, hatred and violence, and your freedom of choice is taken away from you.

Second, he learned that although everyone who's in prison claims to be innocent, some of them probably are. And even though prison life is hell on earth, in this hell you can actually find some compassionate people. Mind you, the vast majority of the inmates there want to hurt you in one way or another, or want to take advantage of you. But even in the first few days of madness, Harris was able to find a friend.

Rico was up on armed robbery charges, but one couldn't tell it by looking at him. Once he got past the scars and the tattoos, past the cigarette smoke that encircled him constantly, Harris found an intensely devout Catholic Christian whose first priority in life was serving God and taking care of his wife and his three children.

Harris went through processing in San Dimas Prison, frightened out of his wits. He'd heard so many stories about how horrible it was that he was afraid to trust anyone. And within the first few days there, he saw evidence that it was horrible. His third day there, Harris saw an inmate killed over a bar of soap. But Rico took him on as his personal responsibility and tried to explain everything.

Another thing that frightened Harris was the fact that he'd been watched from the moment he joined the general population of the prison. He'd made it a point to keep in shape and ran every day. He was relatively young. But Harris was immediately intimidated by the massive, muscular men of all colors who watched him as if he were just another new selection on the menu. Harris knew what they wanted, but he also knew he wasn't interested. He kept believing that he wouldn't be in prison forever, and had no intention of taking AIDS with him when he left.

The fifth day after he arrived, Harris was sitting with Rico in the cafeteria trying to be as inconspicuous as possible. He found it pretty difficult, considering he was one of the few white faces around, and that he looked like he just stepped out of a college recruiting poster. Rico had taught Harris to sit with one leg in the aisle so he could stand and get out of the way quickly if something went down. They were watching a massive black man named Ali who was the prison leader of the Crips gang. He'd made some comments to Harris as he walked across the room. Suddenly Ali was slammed against the wall, and a makeshift knife called a *shiv* appeared from nowhere. Before they knew it, Ali was dead, with blood flowing freely. Harris looked at the man who did it. He had a shaved head, a vicious scar down the left side of his face, and he looked like he could eat nails for breakfast and hubcaps for lunch.

"That's Sorenson," breathed Rico.

"Wonder what the fight was about," Harris whispered.

"They were fighting over you," Rico replied quietly.

As if in response to Harris' question, Sorenson turned and looked in his direction. He grinned and winked at him. From that point on, Harris made sure he stayed as far away from Sorenson as he could.

Harris was assigned to work in the machine shop, which he thought was very strange. Harris was terrible around machines and had never worked in such a shop in his entire life. It had taken a couple of days for his paperwork to be processed, so it was almost a week before they sent him over there. In the meantime, he spent his time either in his cell reading his Bible or in the exercise yard with Rico or walking alone. Harris had been sent to San Dimas on Thursday. On the next Wednesday morning, he went to the machine shop as they ordered. He'd been there about half an hour when a guard came and asked for Harris to follow him to the warden's office.

Harris expected to see an elderly man appear as the warden. Instead, he was surprised to see that Warden Shultz was a woman in her late 40s. As he thought about it, however, it made sense. She probably had a master's degree in administration and saw prisoners only a few times a day. Most daily contact was between prisoners and guards, and as Harris was quickly learning, between the prisoners themselves.

"Harris Borden, Inmate Number 12254-788?" she asked, shuffling some papers in front of her. Harris couldn't tell if it was a question or a statement, but he nodded anyway.

"Speak up!" the guard said, jabbing him in the ribs with his stick.

"Yes, ma'am," Harris said loudly.

"You're one of the higher profile prisoners to come through here in the past year," she said, without looking up. "You'll find that your notoriety in the world outside doesn't count for much in here."

"No, ma'am," Harris said.

"I've been in contact with Universal Finance, the company that you attacked, and have assured them that you won't be in contact with anyone from the media. Nor will you cause any problems here in the prison."

She shuffled papers on her desk again, and Harris thought that was his cue to go. Then she pulled up a letter.

"Oh, yes, this came for you several days ago," she said. Harris started to reach for it, but she opened it up and looked at it. It had apparently already been opened, and she looked at it as if she were reminding herself of an undesirable task to be done.

"Your wife—Katya is it?—was killed last week in Russia when the plane she was on crashed upon takeoff." She said the words matter-of-factly, and for a long moment Harris wasn't sure he understood what she'd said.

She looked up at him as if waiting for a response. "Did you understand? Your wife is dead."

Harris stared at her blankly. The words didn't make sense to him. Finally, as if hearing her through a long tunnel, he saw her give the letter to a guard and tell him to take Harris back to his cell for the rest of the day. The guard gave Harris the letter, who stumbled behind him all the way back to his cell.

When Harris was back on his cot in the cell, he read and reread the letter. It was from the U.S. State Department, and had been sent to his church, where in turn it had been sent to San Dimas Prison. The letter said that all persons on board were lost, that there was a fire, and that they were still in the process of sorting through the wreckage and bodies for identification. The letter used the terms *presumed dead*, but if she was on board, what else could she be? Harris stared at the letter for a long time, then turned toward the wall and sobbed. Eventually, he fell asleep.

In the morning, he was roused by the guard as if it were just another day, but he knew it wasn't. How could he go on? His reason for living was gone.

147

Harris stumbled through his morning duties; dressing, breakfast, brushing his teeth, and then walking down to the machine shop. He mechanically followed the instruction they gave him as he worked that day on a drill press. He stopped for lunch as everyone else did; then back to work at 1 p.m. At 5 p.m. they were all herded out the doors of the machine shop and to the showers.

Harris was still lost in thought at the showers, wondering what his life held for him, wondering if he wanted to live or die, when he noticed that the showers had emptied around him. Even the guard had disappeared. Alarm bells went off in his head. Harris shut off the shower and stepped toward his towel, when Sorenson appeared from the lockers with three other white men. They were massive and tattooed, dressed only in towels, their muscles rippling as they approached him. Sorenson had a shiv in his big fist, and held it in front of him as if he were offering it to Harris, blade first.

"Time to have a little fun," he said. Harris have never heard him speak, and was surprised that he had an English accent. "You're going to dance to our tune, from here on out, or you're going to get a little tickle." He jabbed with his shiv, and Harris remembered how he had used it against Ali.

"I'm not afraid of you," Harris said quietly to the man a head taller than himself. And surprisingly, he wasn't. He had been through so much danger already, and had lost the only person with any meaning to him. Death was just another pathway he could take.

"Ooh, listen to the little blighter," Sorenson said. "He thinks he's the big man because he blew up a building and killed some people. Well, did you do it face to face, like this?" The other three men spread out across the slick shower floor. Sorenson stood in front of Harris, still cradling the shiv in his hand.

"You're mistaken," Harris said, carefully. "I didn't kill anyone."

"Too bad," he said. "I was kinda hoping I could have my way with a terrorist." His face broke into a grin, and the two men nearest to Harris grabbed his upper arms, pulling them apart and rendering him helpless. They threw him against the shower wall and his head hit the showerhead. Their arms came loose from his wet skin and Harris pushed against the wall to steady himself and keep from falling.

"Hold the monkey," Sorenson barked. The two men grabbed Harris again and shoved his head down and into the wall again. Harris knew what was supposed to come next, but he refused to go down without a fight. He couldn't see Sorenson, but he knew he was close. He jerked his leg up and kicked behind him, catching Sorenson in the stomach. The leverage from the kick helped Harris pull away again from the two men who held his arms, but just as he pulled away, the fourth man gave him a sharp kick that caught him in the rib Harris had broken. Pain shot through his whole body, and he collapsed to the floor.

Then each of the four took turns kicking Harris. They stopped, and Harris got to his hands and knees. Sorenson approached Harris again from the rear, leaning close and whispering in his ear, "I'm gonna like this more than you will." Harris responded by quickly turning his head and biting down on Sorenson's ear. His rage took over. Harris bit as hard as he could until his teeth went all the way through. He tasted Sorenson's blood in his mouth, and realized that he wasn't just defending himself, but striking out at Sorenson for the death of Katya.

Sorenson pulled away and screamed in pain, holding onto the side of his face. Harris responded by spitting out the piece of ear he had in his mouth.

"I...am...not...afraid...of...you!" Harris shouted from bloody lips. Then he screamed at the top of his lungs. Someone was bound to hear them, and if they didn't, well, Harris wouldn't go quietly into that good night.

Sorenson's eyes went wild, and he looked at Harris. Before Harris realized what was happening, Sorenson grabbed Harris' scalp with his left hand, then took his right with the shiv and ran it across Harris' throat. Harris felt the blade slash through his skin, and felt the blood flow down his throat. Harris knew that he was going to die.

He collapsed on the tile floor, a growing pool of blood billowing from his throat. Harris heard Sorenson and the others run from the shower room. He lay there, helpless, staring at the shower heads.

* * *

Elijah Brown propped himself up on one elbow on his cot and watched them bring the new patient in on a stretcher. The doc had spent close to two hours working on this inmate, even though the general attitude around here was live and let live, or more accurately, live and let die. This one refused to die, even after he'd lost an incredible amount of blood. He'd been brought into the infirmary from the showers, and when the doctor realized he wasn't dead yet, he decided to improve his chances. He pumped some fluids into him, including plasma and finally, whole blood. After stopping the blood flow from his neck wound, he sewed it up as best as he could. Even with the bandages on it, it still looked like a nasty, vicious wound.

"OK, taking odds on the new guy," Miguel in the corner said. Miguel was there with a ruptured appendix. He'd been there a solid week, and was nursing the service as long as he could. Better to be bored and flat on your back in the infirmary than mingling in the general population and have a chance of becoming someone's anger management session.

"Two to one he doesn't last the night," Miguel continued.

"I'll take that, Miguel," Max, one of the orderlies said. "I saw how tough he was in the treatment room. Twice we thought he was gone, but he pulled himself up by his toenails. I give him a week."

"Hey, isn't that the new guy from East Block?" Miguel asked. "I think he bumps bunks with Rico Montes."

"He's going to sleep for a couple of days," Elijah said. "When he wakes up, we'll send for Rico and see if he can talk."

"If he wakes up," Miguel said. "I have my doubts."

"I don't," Elijah said. He didn't say more than that, but he'd seen many men in various stages of death, and he knew that determination played a *huge* part in whether they survived or not. This one was determined, he could tell.

Over the next two days, Elijah watched the new man carefully. He finally awoke on the third day, and Elijah sent for Rico. Elijah was there being treated for blood poisoning in his leg, but he wanted to see how this turned out, so he did what he could to make his symptoms linger. He cut back on his antibiotics, just enough to keep the coloration in his leg vein. Finally Rico appeared and went over to the new guy.

"Hey Harris, I thought you were going to stay away from that *pendejo*," Rico said. He looked at Miguel and explained with one word: "Sorenson."

Miguel nodded. "If he's smart, he'll simply say that he slipped on a bar of soap."

"Doesn't look like he's going to be saying much of anything for a while," Rico said. "You almost got a Columbian necktie, amigo. You're one lucky dude."

Harris looked up at Rico and blinked.

"Looks like you don't have much of a vocabulary these days," Rico said. "Gonna be funny having a preacher who can't talk and has to listen."

"Preacher, huh?" Miguel said. "Maybe he can help us out with church services. We need all the help we can get."

"Like Rico says, I don't think he'll be able to do much but listen for a long while," Elijah said.

Rico stayed for a few more minutes, then told Harris goodbye. Elijah continued to watch Harris. For that whole day, Harris lay on his back either staring at the lights above them or sleeping. Elijah knew that it would take a long while before he'd be able to do anything other than that. He would be patient, though, because he had a feeling about this one.

* * *

After Harris heard about Katya's death, the only solution he had to dealing with the news was to keep busy. He'd looked forward to doing something with his hands in the machine shop, and when he was in his cell, he buried himself in his personal Bible studies. Now he could do neither. Harris had no strength to hold his Bible, nor did he have a way to ask for one. He simply lay and looked at the ceiling, forced to confront his thoughts and the reality of his life behind bars.

It seemed like an eternity since he'd first prayed that God would use him. Harris' life had spiraled downward since that night. He felt like he'd failed to follow God's instruction, and that his actions had allowed Universal to run free, while leading to Katya's death. For a long time after he awakened, Harris wasn't sure if he was glad that he'd lived. It was easy to speak in ignorance and ask for God to trust you with a mighty task. It was another thing to actually do what God asked you, regardless of who was pointing a gun at you or ready to throw you from a skyscraper. Harris had tried to pray to God both before and after he'd arrived at the prison, but felt that his prayers were bouncing off the ceiling. For the first time in his entire life, he felt completely, entirely alone.

Had God given up on Harris since he'd demonstrated he couldn't follow directions? Logically, he knew that God would never give up on him. But the silence that surrounded him told him otherwise. Harris thought about it for a long time, and couldn't come up with an answer he was comfortable with.

So he turned his thoughts toward Katya. Harris missed her, oh, how he missed that girl. He could smell her fragrance when he thought of her. He remembered watching her angry, knowing that she could go from angry to loving as fast as he could say, "I'm sorry." And he remembered holding her, knowing that their loving embrace had resulted in a new life. Harris knew that she carried his son. He couldn't have explained how he knew it was a boy; he just did. And as he thought of the child that wouldn't be, he remembered her lullaby and as he thought of her singing it, his lips began to form the words. No sound came from his tortured vocal cords, but his lips moved as if he were singing with her.

"*Bai, bai, bai, bai,*
Báyu, Detusku mayú!
Bai, bai, bai, bai,
Báyu, Detusku, mayú!
Shta na górki, na goryé,
O visyénnei, o poryé,
Ptíchki Bozhiye payút,
F tyómnam lyési gnyózda vyut."

* * *

Elijah Brown watched the new guy—Rico said he was a preacher called Harris Borden—as he finally started moving his lips. His previous occupation had led him to learn how to lip read, and since he was bored, he tried to figure out what Harris was saying. After a while, he realized that he was singing. A few seconds later, he recognized several of the words as Russian, a language he hadn't heard in years. He got excited, both at the possibility of communicating in his mother language, and of the possibilities that the new inmate presented.

"*Shta na górki, na goryé,*

O visyénnei, o poryé,

Ptíchki Bozhíye payút,

F tyómnam lyési gnyózda vyut."

He remembered the words from an old Russian folk song, a children's song. His mother had sung it to him years before in another time, another place…another life.

He stood beside his bed and hobbled slowly to Harris' bedside. As he approached him, the preacher looked up at him, not sure what he was going to do.

Elijah leaned forward and whispered to Harris. "*Govoroyu russki?*" he asked. *Do you speak Russian?*

"*Da,*" Harris mouthed. "*Da.*"

Elijah Brown grinned and patted Harris on the shoulder. "*Khorosho,*" he said. "Excellent."

He then hobbled back to his cot. It was time for him to get well and back into circulation. The preacher changed everything. He would be released in a few weeks. In the meantime, Elijah had work to do—lots of work to do.

14 ALLIANCE WITH A TRAITOR

Elijah Brown was out of the infirmary in two days, thanks to his renewed use of antibiotics for his leg infection. When he was discharged, he immediately went to the prison library.

"Hey, Donner," he said to the elderly inmate who was in charge there. Donner Smith gave Elijah access to the library whenever he wanted because, well, Elijah was Elijah. He had the skills and knowledge to do things that other inmates could only dream of. Donner didn't know what Elijah's background was, and he'd been around long enough to know not to ask. One doesn't bite the hand of a gift horse, especially in San Dimas Prison.

Elijah headed past the rows of books stored there, most of which had never been checked out by inmates. That small percentage of inmates who did read leaned toward potboiler novels and other paperbacks, while Elijah's tastes were more substantive. As part of the arrangement he'd made with Donner, Elijah added a few important titles to the books that were on the wish list for the library. All of the books here were donated, but sometimes a church group or friends or family of inmates would ask what books were needed. No one else had specific tastes; thus, Elijah usually got his books ordered relatively quickly.

But Elijah wasn't interested in books today. He walked quickly to the rear of the library, where a bank of four computers sat back to back. Inmates were allowed to access the Internet, under very strict supervision. All sites visited were controlled, and all e-mail going in and out was screened. But those screening hadn't counted on the skills that Elijah possessed.

Elijah hit the power button on the computer and immediately hit F1 to go into the bios feature of the computer. He changed the configuration quickly, then went out of it as he'd done a hundred times before. A few minutes hacking, and he was into the California state prison records system.

He looked up Harris Borden, and within minutes got an objective look at Borden's past: his family situation, his employment as a pastor, and the two events with Universal that led to his imprisonment.

"Interesting," he murmured as he read further.

When he was done, he changed some of the orders for Borden. First of all, Borden's injury slated him to be transferred to a prison medical facility. Elijah couldn't let that happen; there was too much chance that he'd lose track of Borden if he left San Dimas. He'd have to stay at the infirmary here. So he typed a few words and made it so.

Then he saw that Borden was assigned to work at the machine shop. He typed in a few select words and had Borden transferred to work here in the library. That would not only make it easier to keep an eye on him, it would allow Borden to have access to books and other things that Elijah needed for his education. Finally, he changed his cell assignment. Rico was a good enough guy, and he knew he could trust him with Borden, but with Harris' situation, he needed more protection that Rico could or was willing to give.

He added a few more flourishes and finishing touches, and then shut off the computer. Now the hard part came—he had to be patient and wait for Harris Borden to heal. But patience had never been a problem for Elijah Brown. It was what kept him alive up to this point.

* * *

Sometimes God allows you to learn things in your own way, in your own time. Other times, he forces you into a situation where you're confronted by reality and have no choice but to take time and learn.

If it were up to Harris, he wouldn't have chosen going to prison to learn humility. He wouldn't have asked to lose his wife, the bright light in his life. He definitely wouldn't have asked to have his throat cut, coming way too close to death and losing his ability to speak. But God, in His infinite wisdom, had a plan for him. That's what the rational side of his brain kept trying to tell Harris, scrambling for some reason for the downward spiral his life had taken in the past few weeks. He reminded himself time and again of the words that The Messenger had told him up front: "With great responsibility sometime comes great pain and sorrow." Well, at least he was honest with Harris. That's what the rational voice in his head kept saying.

Meanwhile, the emotional side screamed: "God, what are you doing to me? What do you want from me? I can't take it any more!" Harris no longer wondered where he was going or what task was before him. Instead he wondered whether he'd survive—not only physically, but mentally and spiritually. Little did he realize it at that point, but that was one of the beginning stages of the refining process that God had for Harris.

One morning he woke up, dreaming of his past life, a smile on his lips. Harris opened his eyes and once again realized that he was in prison, unable to speak, with people seeking to kill him. The smile faded. Then a sentence came into his head, one that didn't make sense at the time: *It's not what you do; it's who you are.*

Harris pondered the statement, wondering what it all meant. The doctor came in to change his bandages, and Harris found that finally he could clear his throat.

"Good," the doctor said as Harris sat on the side of the cot. "Good! It will be still quite a while before you can speak again, if ever. In the meantime, see if you can whisper."

Harris moved his lips, but nothing came out. He reminded himself that one had to exhale to gain any sound, so he purposely exhaled through the vocal cords, and was rewarded with a stabbing pain in his throat. A raspy sound escaped for an instant before he stopped.

"Still a lot of healing going on there," the doctor said. "Keep trying and you will get some sound eventually. In the meantime, we'll keep you here for observation. We don't want any infection."

The doctor brought Harris a mirror and he took his first look at the wound. A jagged line ran from just below his left ear down at an angle to past his adam's apple. It was a miracle that his jugular hadn't been cut, and that other valuable parts of his throat were still able to heal. The edges of the cut were sutured together, but the area around the cut was still very red, tinged yellow with the betadine ointment they had used at the time of his attack. The "accident"—as they were now calling it—had been more than a week before, and Harris hadn't been shaved in that time. Harris realized that with his new scar he'd probably need to get used to a full beard.

After the doctor left, Harris decided to look around. It was the first time he'd really sat up in more than a week, and he was still pretty wobbly, but he was determined to do something more than lie on his cot and look at the ceiling lights. He wandered around the almost empty ward room. Miguel was gone, as was the other guy who'd been there for a leg infection. In the first days of fading in and out of consciousness, Harris barely took notice of them. Later, the only entertainment he had was to listen to them banter back and forth. Miguel was a talker, often to himself, as the other guy didn't talk much at all. Now Harris was alone with the exception of an elderly man who lay on a cot against the far wall.

Harris walked slowly over to him. He was asleep, so Harris just stood and looked at him for a long time. His gaunt frame, as well as the medications that were left by his bedside, told Harris that he was fighting cancer—and losing. Harris had been at the bedside of a couple of his church members over the years who had died of cancer. He'd done what he could to comfort them and ease their minds as they struggled with this terrible disease. Harris had found that in many cases his ministry consisted of listening to them and praying for them.

Well, I can't preach and I can't speak words of encouragement, Harris thought, *but I can still listen and pray*. He picked up an old Bible that lay on the bedside and sat down next to the old man. Harris held the Bible between his hands and bowed his head.

Harris wasn't at the stage where he could pray for himself. He still struggled with a massive feeling of failure at the last incident with Universal. But he could pray for this man. Harris didn't know his name, but God did. Harris didn't know how he felt about God, but he knew that God loved him. And so he prayed.

After a while Harris raised his head and looked up. In the doorway stood a man that looked vaguely familiar. The man had thrown a ratty suit coat over a rumpled shirt and jeans. In his hands he held a bunch of flowers. He stared at Harris, then at the old man. Harris quickly realized that he was here to see the inmate, and Harris stood up as quickly as he could. Harris bowed to the man and backed up, stumbling back to his cot. He watched from a distance as the young man took the seat Harris had occupied and sat watching the man. It became obvious after a short time that the young man was the dying man's son. A while later Harris realized where he'd seen the young man before. He'd sat on the stage with Kenneth Deke when Harris had almost been thrown from the rooftop.

* * *

When he realized that the man was from Universal, a feeling of panic hit him and Harris wondered if the man knew who he was. When it became evident that he didn't, Harris relaxed. Suddenly the idea of growing a beard became more attractive to him, and he decided to let his hair grow long as well. Harris had always kept his hair stylishly short, but everything he could do to distance himself from the pastor Harris Borden was before prison would help him stay alive.

Harris was in the infirmary for about five weeks. He continued to work on his voice, and after about two painful weeks he was able to rattle out a throaty whisper. He would probably never sing again, but at least it was something. There was also some doubt about his ability to preach—of course, there'd always been doubts about his preaching—but time would tell if he'd have the voice to address a crowd again.

With his whisper returned to him, Harris took it upon himself to serve as chaplain to those who came through the infirmary. Most were very receptive to his advances. The official chaplain—a Catholic priest—was elderly, and failing health meant that he wasn't around very much. The inmates welcomed his whispered prayers and words of comfort, very likely more because he was a prisoner just like them. Harris also spent a lot of time with the dying inmate, whose name he learned was Gordon Whiting.

Gordon knew he was dying. He'd been raised going to church, but had left it years before. Now, with his days numbered, he desperately sought answers. Harris worked with him as much as he could. Some days Harris saw peace come over him; other days Harris had to leave him with a troubled look on his face. Harris knew it would eventually come down to one thing.

"I know what's in your heart," Harris whispered. "God knows what's in your heart. When you're ready to make things right with God, let me know. I'll help you."

Gordon struggled with pride—as everyone does—and with a feeling of unworthiness—which Harris could very much relate to. Harris knew that Gordon would have to master those feelings and surrender completely to God before the end. He was still struggling when Harris was discharged.

Harris didn't know what would happen to him when he left, but knew that God had a plan for him. Harris had had a long struggle accepting God's plan so far, and continued to struggle with the loss of Katya, but was slowly resigning himself to his circumstances. Harris had no clue where he'd go from here, but decided to accept God's plan for him. The day that Harris was discharged, he thought about that statement that he'd been told: "It's not what you do, it's who you are," and wondered if he'd do anything else in God's plan.

A guard came to escort Harris out of the infirmary, and he was taken to a new cell. *What happened to Rico?* Harris wondered, but of course, didn't ask anything. Instead, he was met by a short, stocky man with graying hair who looked familiar.

The man sat on the edge of his cot until the guard left and then looked at Harris sharply, as if sizing him up. He stood up beside Harris, and slowly straightened up. The short man became taller, and it became evident that he and Harris were the same height. He'd purposely slumped over to make himself shorter.

The old man stood inches away from Harris. "*Udivitelnyi,*" he muttered to himself. He stared at Harris' face as if examining him in detail before he spoke again.

"*Govoroyu russki?*" he asked.

Harris shrugged. "*Da*, a little."

"You will learn more as time goes on," he said in English. "But is important that we be able to communicate in the language of the *Rodina* if my plan is to succeed."

"Allow me to introduce myself," the man said, switching back to Russian. He launched into a story that Harris had a difficult time following, but patched it together as Harris improved his Russian and spent more time with him.

"My name is Mikhail Ivanov Gorovko. That is the name I was born with. I am known here as Elijah Brown, and for my purposes here, that is who I am.

"I have a colorful and tragic past, which you will get to know as time permits. Suffice it to say that I worked for the government of the Soviet Union in what you might call a special capacity. I was stationed here in the United States for many years, until I was discovered by the Americans. Your brothers here gave me the option of—poof!—disappearing in a way that is permanent, or working for them. I chose to stay alive and work for them."

He shrugged. "I have learned over the years that when you get to a certain point in government, they are all pretty much the same. Anyway, for many years I continued to work for both sides. Sometimes they would have different needs and that would be good. Sometimes they would have the same needs and I would have to choose who to give the right information to and who to disappoint.

"Then there came a day when the Soviet Union was no more," he said, his teeth bared in a feral grin. "With the old regime gone, I knew that it would be only a matter of time before the two agencies that used to be mortal enemies started comparing notes. I got my first clue when an old friend of mine tried to kill me. That is when I decided to disappear."

He inhaled slowly and let it out in a whoosh. He smiled in a forced way, then shrugged. "If there is one thing I know how to be, it is invisible. And what agent in their right mind would hide in a prison?" He laughed. "I am sure they think I am dead, but someday I will make a wrong step and they will know that I am still very much alive."

Harris stared at the man in disbelief. "A secret agent?" he whispered. "A spy?"

He shrugged again. "I have been called lots of things through the years. Those are two of the terms I have heard. But now I am simply, Elijah Brown, inmate 472283-122."

Harris still stared at him. He grinned, then chuckled, realizing all the mental gymnastics Harris was going through. He was having a hard time digesting it all. Harris somehow knew he would wait until the younger man was ready to take the next bite.

"Where do I fit in this?" Harris whispered. "Why am I here?"

"I see you as—a hobby," he shrugged. "I saw something special in the way you survived that knife attack. A lesser man would have died on that shower floor. I need someone who is intelligent and somewhat educated. You have a college degree. And I am happy that you and I are the same height. And when I realized that you spoke Russian—well, *neyzeli.*"

"Someday soon I will ask you to do a favor for me," he said quietly, staring through the bars into the open area beyond. "I have searched for the right person to do this task, and you are he, *kamarad.*"

Harris narrowed his eyes in suspicion. "And what do I get in return?"

Elijah chuckled and slapped Harris on the shoulder. "Why, you get to go back to school, my friend." Then he grew serious. "But this school is intended to save your life."

* * *

After the startling introduction, Elijah turned out to be a pretty relaxed, easygoing guy. Harris found himself becoming more and more comfortable around him. Eventually Harris realized that the old man could assume and drop personalities as easily as Harris changed his shirt. Later Harris saw him as a high-strung, demanding tutor; then another time as a serious, somber judge of Harris' abilities. Overall, he found Elijah Brown to be the most complicated, mysterious, and provocative man he'd ever met.

"The first thing we must do," Elijah told Harris, "is have you tell me your story. I have seen your records, but I need to hear the truth from you. Do not attempt to hold anything back. I will know."

And so Harris spent several hours that first day telling Elijah Brown the story of his calling. Elijah listened intently, his eyebrows going up once or twice as Harris talked about the angel and the vision of Mount Carmel. These were details that the records did not include, and he absorbed them like a sponge. At the end, Elijah stood in front of Harris, surveying him with one eyebrow raised.

"And so, now, you are on a mission from God, eh?" he said, a slight smile on his lips.

"Well, that's not the way I would put it," Harris whispered, thinking how the phrase reminded him of a popular movie from the 80s. "I made God an offer, and he took me up on it."

"When I was in Soviet Union, it was not permitted to talk or think about God. The Party was our god. But after I left the *Rodina*...." His voice trailed off.

"So what conclusion have you come to?" Harris asked him.

"I am still looking for evidence," he said. "But the question is there, just the same."

"If you're looking for evidence of God, you may be looking for a long time," Harris whispered to him. "My relationship with God is based on faith, not evidence."

"And yet he has sent His Messenger to talk to you," he said. "I have not had such a visit."

Harris shrugged. "Perhaps it'll still happen."

"Perhaps." Elijah shrugged, then grinned. "Come, time for school." He took Harris' arm and led him over to a small table in the cell. A chessboard was set up on it. "Do you play?"

Harris nodded. He hadn't played chess since high school, but was pretty good back then. He remembered that there wasn't another student in school that could beat him, and eventually he stopped playing simply because no one would play him.

"We will set this up this way," Elijah said, turning the white pieces in Harris' direction. "I will give myself a small handicap." He reached onto the board and took all of his pieces off but three pawns, a knight and the king.

Harris looked at the board and shook his head. "It's going to be a short game."

"Perhaps," Elijah said. "But appearances are often misleading."

It was a short game. Within fifteen minutes he had Harris checkmated. Harris stared at the board for a long moment.

"Heh heh, you play well," Elijah said. "Again!"

* * *

The next morning after breakfast, Elijah took Harris to the library and introduced him to Donner Smith, the burned-out inmate who ran the service. Donner shook Harris' hand, then left for his rounds of pushing a cart filled with paperbacks to those inmates who were denied access to the exercise yard.

"Here is your first homework," Elijah told Harris, taking him to a back bookcase and loading him up with books. Harris looked at the titles: *The Campaigns of Napoleon*, a couple of books by Clausewitz on war strategy, and *The Art of War* by Sun Tsu. Harris looked at Elijah.

"You will find that whether it is physical or spiritual in nature, whether it involves thousands or only two men, war is war," he said sagely. "And remember, there will be a quiz afterward." Elijah chuckled at his own joke.

Elijah continued to play chess against Harris, as much as possible. Sometimes they played as many as four and five games per day. However, often the games would only last a few minutes. Frustrated, Harris found a book on chess strategy and started memorizing some of the defenses that were listed there. Elijah laughed at Harris when he realized what he was doing. "A stationary defense will never last," he said. "You must learn to anticipate and improvise." Then Elijah went on to slaughter him.

Slowly, Harris started to get better. As Harris improved, Elijah added pieces to his side of the board. After a long time—months, in fact—Harris realized that they were finally starting with all of their pieces intact. From that point on, Elijah began pressuring Harris to speed up his moves.

"Faster," Elijah told him, impatiently. "You move like an old lady!" When Harris didn't move faster, he would kick him under the table. One day Harris lost his temper after being kicked for the third time. Harris flashed him a look of anger, and Elijah burst out laughing.

"*Kamarad*, it is only a game," Elijah chuckled, then grew serious. "Or is it?"

After a couple of weeks, Harris finished the books on war and strategy that Elijah told him to read.

"What did you learn?" When Elijah was not satisfied with Harris' answer, he told Harris to read them again.

Occasionally, Harris caught flashes of genius behind what Elijah was doing. But most of the time he was totally confused by Elijah's actions and the demands he made on Harris. Harris welcomed his companionship—for weeks Elijah never left his side—and Harris was amazed at the respect that other inmates gave Elijah. Even Sorensen didn't come near Harris. But on the other hand, Elijah became more and more demanding, and Harris looked for an opportunity to do something other than read books and play chess.

His opportunity for some diversity came when Rico approached him in the library. "Our chaplain has stopped coming," he explained. "And we need someone who can lead out in our church services on Sunday morning. Can you do it?"

Harris almost laughed at him. He whispered back. "You want me to preach in sign language?"

Rico shook his head. "We can always have someone else preach, or we can do something else, like just study the Bible. More than anything, we need someone who'll organize and coordinate it."

And so it was agreed that he'd lead out in church services, such as they were. Occasionally they got someone to come in and preach, but most of the time they sat in a circle, and Harris led the group in a Bible study. Apparently the prison had been unsuccessful in getting a permanent replacement for the old priest, and had agreed to let a prisoner lead out; a rare situation. Harris' lack of voice made it necessary for the rest of them to participate more, with Harris interjecting a comment only when they seemed to be going in the wrong direction.

He felt like a pastor again, more or less. From the Bible services, a few of the men started to ask questions about salvation, and he began personal Bible studies. At Elijah's insistence, Harris had them come into the library or his cell for the studies. Elijah was never far away. And often Harris caught him listening as they studied.

One of the inmates he studied with was Gordon Whiting. He was truly searching, and knew that his time was short. He soaked up the Gospel like a sponge, and it was Harris' pleasure to finally lead him to Christ. They asked the doctors if it would be possible to have him baptized, but the doctors and the warden both said no. Harris told Gordon that they'd continue to work on the request. In the meantime, Harris told him that his salvation was assured; baptism or no.

* * *

Harris had been there about a year when he had the dream. He was finally free, walking down a familiar street in San Francisco. He looked up at the buildings and recognized most of them. But one was new. A glowing green building stood on the site where the old office building had been destroyed. This one was dazzling; just looking at it made one's mouth drop open. It dominated the San Francisco skyline, and as Harris looked at it, it seemed as if the other buildings leaned toward it as if bowing down.

Harris walked past the building and into an alleyway; the same alley that he had run down when he was escaping the falling building. Once again he saw the dumpster that had been flattened by the falling bricks.

Inside, Harris heard a voice say. He walked over to the dumpster and lifted the lid. In the bottom of the dumpster was a small package wrapped in brown paper. Harris reached for the package....

And he woke up.

15 THE ART OF WAR

"Ready for your quiz?" Elijah asked gleefully in Russian, and Harris sullenly nodded. His Russian was getting better after a year of Elijah's tutoring, but Harris had read the selected books he had picked out four times. Each time he finished, Elijah asked the same questions, and Harris had yet to give him a satisfactory answer.

"What did you learn from these books?"

Harris looked at him in silence for a long minute. *What did he want to know?* He'd almost memorized the books, but Harris assumed there was some magical answer that he'd not yet come up with. He spoke hesitantly, carefully, his voice having graduated from a whisper to a gravelly rasp.

"Napoleon based his whole strategy on having more troops at a given spot than the opposition," Harris began. "What he considered the strategic point in the line. It didn't matter if he was outnumbered as long as he had more force to bear on the strategic point."

"Ding!" Elijah said, gleefully. "One point for the *zaychik*. And Clausewitz?"

"Clausewitz believed that a soldier with high morale was worth three without it."

"Bravo!" he said. "And what does that say about the mind?"

"Mental preparedness and focus is crucial in any battle."

"How crucial?"

Harris frowned and thought. "More than physical strength or force?"

Elijah nodded. "You are almost there." His excitement began to show, and he leaned forward. "And what about Sun Tsu?"

"He said that the smart commander does not engage the enemy until the battle is already won."

"Do you understand what that means?"

Harris looked at the wall for a moment, and then nodded. "It's like chess. You play it in your head before you play it on the board. The player who just reacts to the opposition will lose. You have to make the other player play your game. And it doesn't matter how many chess pieces you have at the end, or even how many you started with, as long as you mate his king."

"Congratulations, *zaychik*," Elijah said, slapping him on the shoulder. "You have passed first grade."

"Wow. I'm thrilled," Harris said without energy.

"Now it is time to move on to other grades," Elijah said. Harris watched as he took the chessboard and turned it over. Six lines were written in Russian on the bottom:

Rule #1: Violence is the last resort of the incompetent.

Rule #2: The brain is the only weapon a person needs.

Rule #3: In combat, the one who wins is the one with more force at the decisive point.

Rule #4: Speed is more important than strength.

Rule #5: Know your enemy well enough to anticipate his next move.

Rule #6: The smart commander avoids battle until it has already been won.

Elijah let Harris stare at the rules for a while before saying anything. "Some of these you have figured out for yourself. Others you will learn as you continue your training. You have learned to walk. Now you will learn to *run!*"

With that last word, he reached over and slapped Harris across the face. It stung. Harris looked at him in shock. Elijah did nothing for a second, then slapped him again. Again Harris stared at him. After a pause, Elijah's arm began to move. Harris caught it in midair before it hit his face. Harris' face stung, but he sensed that there was a method to Elijah's madness.

"Why'd you slap me?" Harris asked him.

"To gain your attention," Elijah said. "If you had not stopped me, I would have done it again. How did you stop me?"

"I knew what you were going to do," Harris said. "I acted on your behavior."

"*Aha,*" he said. "You knew what I would do because you saw what I did before."

"No, I *felt* what you did before. I experienced it."

"Exactly," he said. "If you had seen me slap someone else, would you have reacted as quickly?"

"Probably not," Harris said.

"Likely not," he said. "You will learn to watch, observe and anticipate the actions of others. Knowing what they will do next will allow you to respond with the right action."

* * *

That was the beginning of what Elijah Brown referred to as Harris' "second-grade training." Whereas everything up to that point had been mental, he focused mostly on physical activity. He had Harris start lifting weights, and pushed him to run again in the exercise yard. He had Harris jump rope and do push ups and chin ups.

Harris expected at some point that he would teach him to box, but somehow Elijah knew that Harris would not be interested in that. He made one reference to "learning 126 ways to kill a man," but he said it in such a way that Harris wasn't sure whether he was kidding or not.

Elijah focused on agility and balance, telling Harris that they were more important in street combat than strength and power. He explained that power was simply the ability to focus on one point, once again using Napoleon's example. He worked with Harris on learning to anticipate, how to avoid getting hit, and how to turn the strength and momentum of attackers against themselves when avoidance was not possible.

The most amazing thing he taught Harris, however, was how to be invisible. When Elijah first told him that he was going to teach him this skill, Harris thought he was kidding.

"Watch," he said. Elijah pointed at a small alarm clock in the corner of their cell. Harris looked at it, puzzled, then looked back at him. Elijah wasn't there. Harris turned and looked behind him, but he wasn't there either. Harris turned completely around, but he didn't see Elijah in the cell at all. Then Harris heard him chuckle. He tapped Harris on the shoulder, and Harris was startled to see him standing behind Harris and to one side.

"That is an old ninjitsu trick," he explained. "Simply put, a man cannot look in all places as once. If you can anticipate where he will look, you simply move to where he will not be looking."

Harris wasn't sure he understood, so Elijah showed him. He gave Harris a mirror, then disappeared again. He crouched behind Harris as he stood. As Harris turned slowly to his left, Elijah moved silently to his right. As Harris turned the other direction, Elijah anticipated the move and stayed in Harris' blind spot.

"*Neyzeli*," Harris rasped.

"Learn to move like that, and you graduate from second grade," Elijah told him.

* * *

George Tillay worried about the area of Oakland that his girlfriend, Rochelle, lived in. She was important to him, and he not only wanted to keep her safe, he wanted to make a statement to her. Normally, most women cringed at the thought of having a gun in the home. But after last night, when she called him crying and telling him of being robbed at knifepoint in a grocery store parking lot, he knew that she might be more receptive to having one around.

He wanted her to have something small, but with enough firepower to scare off any would-be attackers. He was thinking of a snub-nosed .38 Police Special. And it would have to be relatively inexpensive. People assumed that when you worked in high-rise construction you were well-paid. For the most part, that was true, but until George could get into the labor union, he was classified as unskilled labor, regardless of his abilities. With union membership, he would get the wages he deserved.

He stopped by a small pawn shop on his way to work. A-1 Pawn wasn't flashy, but pawn shops rarely were. He looked at the guns they had displayed there for a while before he saw the little Colt Cobra in the Plexiglas case.

"How much is that one?" he asked.

* * *

It took Harris three more months of physical training and practice before he mastered the moves that Elijah had shown him. During that time, he continued to speed up the chess sessions. As Harris was getting better, Elijah began to remove pieces from his side of the chess board. Amazingly, he learned that in many ways it was easier to play with fewer pieces. Harris learned to anticipate his moves and eventually won every game against him, even when he only gave Harris a knight, three pawns, and a king.

"So that's second grade," Harris said, as Elijah clapped him on the back after successfully avoiding him in a game of *Where Did Harris Go?* "What does third grade hold for me?"

"You will not remain an inmate in here forever, despite what the warden believes." Elijah looked at him, puzzled. "I did not tell you, because there were other priorities. The warden has no intention of letting you leave this place."

It had been a long while since Harris had thought of Universal and Kenneth Deke. Now the old specter of why Harris was here arose again. With it, vicious black feelings began to rise in him. Harris turned away from Elijah, for a moment lost to his rage.

"As I said," Elijah said more loudly, regaining his attention. "You will not be in here forever. I have plans for you. And, I believe God has plans for you too."

Harris looked at him blankly, the fire still in his heart. "God has forgotten me."

Elijah stared at him. "Perhaps. Perhaps not." He sighed. "In any case, I believe that when you enter the world again, you will rediscover your corporate friends. I must make it possible for them to not rediscover you."

With Harris' curiosity piqued, Elijah chuckled to himself.

"The world is a complicated place, and you have made many powerful enemies. If it were possible, they would be watching you right now. They will be waiting when you leave. I will teach you how to be invisible to them, just as you have learned to be invisible in this cell."

Elijah went on to teach Harris how society works, and the technology that keeps track of each and every one of us. He showed Harris, through dress, posture and location in the room, how some people seem very obvious in a crowd while others remain unseen. He explained how security cameras were rigged, and how to avoid being seen on them, confuse them, or disconnect them in a way that no one would know they were nonfunctional. Most importantly, he taught Harris how to stay "off the grid," as he called it. With society relying on technology more and more, it was difficult to keep private things private for most people, but Elijah disagreed.

"I have powerful people looking for me to this very day," Elijah said. "I have chosen to live here for now, because it is easy to remain invisible in plain sight here. One can stay invisible in pretty much any location—if he does not make mistakes—but it is easier in some places than in others."

* * *

It had been a long time since Greg Phipps had visited a prison. The last time he had been in one was in 1989, in Thailand, when he was trying to help a fellow missionary who had been imprisoned because he'd come into conflict with an important general. The encounter hadn't been either successful or pretty, and Greg had avoided prisons ever since.

Today's visit was, once again, at the request of a friend. He waited patiently in the visiting room with the Plexiglas window, not sure what to expect. Harris had been gone for nearly two years now. He missed Harris, just as he missed Katya. The young couple had made their mistakes, but they'd added energy and enthusiasm to an otherwise unenthusiastic church.

He was surprised when a long-haired, bearded inmate stepped up to the chair opposite him and threw himself down. It took a long minute for Greg to recognize his pastoral friend. He'd filled out his slender frame with huge slabs of muscle. He sported a tattoo on the back of each hand. One on his right read: "Hebrews 10:31." The other read: "Exodus 3:14." His hair, now black, hung down over his eyes, and his full beard ran down his throat, divided at one point by an angry red scar that ran from his left ear to the center of his throat. But what frightened Greg most was the look in his eyes. Gone was the innocence, the sly sense of humor, the casual friendliness that had made Harris who he was as a pastor. Greg looked into the face of a man who'd been hardened by nearly two years in prison, rubbing shoulders with mass murderers. Harris looked at him with the eyes of a predator.

"Hello, Greg," Harris rasped, after picking up the phone receiver. Greg was startled by the voice that came from Harris' mouth. His heart suddenly went out to the young man.

"I'm so sorry," Greg said quietly. "I…I…."

"Don't be," Harris said. "God is having His way with me. It's all part of His plan."

"Is it?" Greg asked, suddenly defensive. "Do you really believe God put you here?"

Harris smirked. "Did God put Joseph in prison? Maybe. Maybe not. But he used him there. I don't have the same assurance. God has forgotten me."

Greg shook his head. "Harris, you can't say that."

"Why can't I?" he shot back. "What evidence do I have that God even cares anymore?"

"You're still alive," Greg offered.

"Yeah, there's that," Harris said, not impressed. "Despite all their efforts, I'm still here. But Katya isn't. And my baby isn't."

Greg looked at him. He wanted to reassure him that God hadn't forsaken him, that in fact, Katya's body had never been found in the wreckage. But Greg was here for another reason.

"Don't give up hope," he said. "Sometimes it's all we have."

Harris looked down and shook his head sadly. Greg wanted to cry.

"This life is all I have now," Harris said.

"Speaking of which, I finally got permission from the warden to come in and perform the baptism of your friend Gordon—."

"He's dead," Harris said, interrupting him. "Died last night."

Greg found himself without words, until Harris spoke up again. "How's my church?"

Greg smiled when he heard Harris use the word *my* to describe the church.

"Good," he said. "I agreed to take over as acting pastor until our new one arrives next month. The church board wanted to vote to keep you officially as pastor, but we didn't know how long you'd be in prison."

Harris nodded. "I understand. Someone has to lead the flock. Where's Frank Hollis?"

"Gone. He and his family decided to move to Reno. They were frustrated when the church refused to vote a letter of reprimand against you."

Harris smiled at that, and Greg was glad.

"You look good when you smile," he said. "You look more your old self."

"I haven't had much to smile about lately," Harris said, and Greg believed him.

"It's been tough on the church, these past two years," Greg continued. "The conference brought in one pastor, but he wasn't strong, and didn't last more than a year. Harris—," Greg leaned forward against the Plexiglas. "We've been under attack by Satan's forces, sometimes brutally, ever since you left."

Harris stared at him. Greg could tell that he hadn't realized how much his actions would affect others.

"Now it's my turn to be sorry," Harris said.

"Don't be," Greg said. "We were happily drowning in apathy. The attacks have forced church members to choose for one side or the other. We've learned to lean on each other, and more importantly, depend on God. Prayer meeting's never been so popular." He chuckled.

A wisp of a smile came over Harris' face. "Maybe we should have done it sooner then."

"Maybe."

The discussion slowed to a stop, and Greg once again found himself looking at Harris, not know what to say. He could see the bitterness in Harris' eyes, even as he dropped them to stare at the floor. He sensed that Harris was trying hard to hang on to his walk with God, but that prison and Katya's death were uniting to grind him down into a fine powder.

"Harris," Greg said, finally. "You'll get out of here. I know it."

Harris' eyes came up, but his face still looked down. "How can you be so sure? They've tried again and again to kill me. They'll never stop trying. And even if they did..." He sat up and ran his index finger over his throat where the blade had slashed him. "I could never go back to the life I had."

"You've asked God to use you for something special," Greg said, intensity coming into his voice. "You're his champion. You *will* get out of here. When you do, you need to know for sure whether you're ready to champion His cause for Him, do what He asks, whatever it is. You're not here because God put you here. You're here because somewhere along the line you depended on yourself rather than on Him."

"Yes," Harris said quietly, lost in thought. "I know."

"You need to depend on God's timing to get out. You need to learn to depend on Him for everything. This is the Refiner's fire. He's making you into a weapon of His work. God hasn't forgotten you," Greg said. "He never forgets His children. And He would never, never forget a Champion. He's not done with you yet, Harris."

Harris looked up from his reverie. "And what if I never get out of here?"

"Just remember: It's not important what you do. It's who you are."

Harris stared at Greg. "Yeah, I heard that somewhere."

16 CONDEMNED TO DIE

After that, life in prison continued on unabated. Harris found that it was helpful to have a focus. He enjoyed conducting Bible studies with fellow inmates. He enjoyed his job at the library. He even enjoyed the rigorous training that Elijah continued to put him through. But prison was still hell. Harris constantly had to watch his back when he was in the general population, even more so when Elijah wasn't with him, which was becoming more and more common as his training continued. Harris had the skills, but hadn't been forced into using them. He hoped he never would, but knew that was unlikely.

And as much as he had feared being attacked, now he feared what he would do if he were attacked. Despite the gentle side of his personality that Harris desperately tried to hold onto, a violent side was coming out as well. The rage that occasionally engulfed him when he thought of Katya's death threatened to swallow Harris whole. One incident made that evident to Harris and the rest of the prison as well.

They were in the shower, an occasion when Harris used great caution. A visitation day was coming up, where conjugal visits—private time with the spouses—was hinted at. Several other inmates were talking and joking about looking forward to seeing their wives.

"Hey, Harris, you got a wife?" someone asked casually. Harris didn't respond, and someone joked. "He's too tough to have a wife."

Harris responded by slamming the bathroom tile beside the shower with his fist. The hard tile shattered under the impact. The talking stopped suddenly and everyone left the showers without saying another word.

Harris felt ashamed of his reaction, but Elijah told him later that that action probably kept others from challenging him needlessly.

In addition to interaction with inmates and guards, strange things began happening around the prison, and Harris wondered if they happened because he was there. Inmates were attacked in their cells, when they were alone, and there was no way that a guard or another inmate could have attacked them. For the most part, these were inmates whom Harris had talked to about Jesus, but who had laughed at the possibility of Bible studies. Harris worried that his being there was endangering others, just as it had put his church on the outside in danger.

Elijah started talking about teaching Harris offensive skills. Harris could defend himself to the point of delaying the attack now. The problem was that unless he used some way of immobilizing the attacker, he would eventually get through Harris' defenses and injure or kill him.

"Look," Harris said finally. "I have real problems with learning how to kill someone, or even how to injure them permanently. It's not only against my beliefs and training as a pastor. I'm afraid I'll strike out in anger and regret it later."

"Rage is a problem," Elijah agreed. "One that you'll need to confront, and very soon." He thought for a long moment before his eyes lit up. "Would you have a problem with me teaching you how to subdue an opponent temporarily? I know several ways to do that."

Harris agreed, and Elijah taught Harris several martial arts techniques for immobilizing the enemy, as well as a few ninjitsu weapons simple enough to make, yet that could stop a bull elephant in its tracks.

"The only problem with these tactics is that they're temporary," he warned Harris, shaking his head. "When the attacker awakes, or is otherwise mobile again, he or she will come after you."

Harris nodded. "OK, I accept that fact. What happens after that is on my head."

Elijah shrugged. "It's your life…as long as it lasts."

* * *

Two years after the incident in San Francisco and his subsequent arrest, Harris Borden was up for parole. Michelle Kinkaid joined Greg Phipps in attending the parole board hearing to try to speak in Harris' behalf.

Michelle had been doing various freelance assignments throughout the Bay Area, and was working with a friend doing website design, but she really wished she could get another job on a newspaper staff. Not only did she love the pace and lifestyle of being a newspaper reporter, she felt that she was making a contribution to society. Her falling out with the *Herald* had not only hurt her pocketbook, but her ego and her credibility with her family as well. Her Sacramento family, which consisted of a heart surgeon father, two lawyers and a pediatrician as siblings, and a mother who was running for state senator, had a hard enough time with her choosing a career in journalism. Now that she wasn't holding down a steady job, they really looked down their pointy noses at her.

But Michelle knew that she'd done the right thing in pushing through the story about Borden. The man was innocent, and she'd do everything she could to get him out of prison. She did her homework on the case before she went to San Dimas Prison. What she wasn't prepared for was how prison had changed Harris Borden.

The quiet, pleasant, slender pastor was now a hulking, brooding, angry man. He tried to present himself as respectable before the board, but she could see the rage seething beneath the surface of Harris. She knew that usually a parole board looked for a candidate to admit that he'd done wrong, and that he wasn't a danger to society, but it was obvious from the start that neither of those points would come up in an interview with Harris. She looked at his long hair and dark, full beard, and wondered why he hadn't bothered to shave.

The board asked if anyone there was willing to speak on Harris' behalf, and Greg Phipps got up and spoke, followed by Michelle. Both of them said that this was a man of God, and that he was led by his burden to help people in distress. Michelle added her eyewitness account of what had happened two years ago on the day he'd been arrested. But after their accounts, it was pretty evident that the board had no intention of letting Harris Borden back into the world.

"If Harris Borden is an innocent man, why didn't he go to trial? That would have come out in public court," the chair of the board said at the end. "Our job is to determine if he's been rehabilitated, and at this point, we don't see evidence of that."

Michelle looked at Harris sitting across the room from her, his arms and legs in shackles, his scar a red roadmap across his throat. He hadn't raised his voice during the entire interview. She was shocked to learn that he couldn't now. His rattling rasp had scared her when she'd first heard it. She looked at him and thought, *he's a walking demonstration about how wrong our prison system is.* And then Harris raised his eyes and looked at her. She saw his unemotional look, even as they were announcing that his parole had been denied, and wondered what was going on inside his dark mind.

* * *

Elijah had warned Harris not to get his hopes up with the parole board, and so he hadn't. When the verdict was announced, Harris knew that the decision had been made long before he'd opened his mouth in his own defense. There were no surprises here. He was surprised, however, when the guards who were leading him back to his cell, hands and feet shackled, led him instead upstairs to the warden's office.

Warden Shultz hadn't changed in the two years since Harris had last seen her. He knew he had, though. Harris entered the doorway with a guard standing on either side of him. There, to his surprise, sat the warden at her desk. Seated across from her was a person Harris immediately recognized. Were it possible, he looked richer than that day in San Francisco when Harris saw him last.

"Harris Borden, I believe you know Kenneth Deke," Warden Shultz said, gesturing to Deke. Harris nodded curtly, and Deke stood to look at him, a faint smile on his lips. He apparently enjoyed where circumstances had taken each of them.

"It's amazing the difference two years makes, isn't it?" Deke said to Harris. "I'd shake your hand, Reverend, but I see you...well, you can't." He gestured at the shackles. "Tell me, I hear they're heavy. Are they?"

Harris didn't answer.

"I'd heard you were killed right after you got here," Deke said, looking him up and down. "But apparently the report was overly optimistic."

"Our man on the inside did a sloppy job," the warden said. "But we've corrected that mistake. He's begged for another chance, and he'll get it— soon." Harris looked at the warden and suddenly realized that the attack in the shower room wasn't a random act of prison violence. *Why hadn't Sorensen come after him again?*

Deke stepped closer to Harris, and his voice grew quiet. "You were a problem to me once. Once. Now you're just an afterthought." He stood tall, obviously wrapped up in his own importance. "Universal is now a lot more than just finance. We're into shipping, communications, petroleum, pharmaceuticals. Give us enough time and there won't be any area where we won't have considerable influence. Soon we'll be the most powerful force on earth."

He turned away, spun around, and then jumped into Harris' face. "What do you think of that? You thought you could stop us! There's no way you can stop us! Now, or ever!

He leered into Harris' face. "Even your precious wife didn't last long when we set our minds to it. You thought she'd be safe going home to Mother Russia. She would have been, if we hadn't known your plans every step of the way. The miracles of modern science! It can save a person's life…or give you the information necessary to end it."

The rage boiled inside Harris, and he wanted to put his fingers around Deke's throat. More than anyone, Deke was responsible for Katya's death. And then Harris realized that he was still just a puppet.

Harris looked at him, and realized he felt pity for the man. He had no concept of what life was about. His whole life was about power. But he didn't even know what real power was.

"You are just a pitiful yes-man that answers to a demon," Harris said quietly. "I just have four words for you."

He smiled broadly. "And those are?"

"*Mene, mene, tekel, upharsin.*" Deke looked at him blankly, and Harris realized that his Biblical reference was lost on him. "Look it up in Daniel 5. Someone else thought he was great, and you will suffer the same fate as him. You and your tin god."

The smile disappeared from Deke's face and it was replaced by rage. He reached inside his coat and pulled out a small automatic pistol. He pointed it at Harris' face.

"NO!" the warden shouted. "What are you doing with a gun in my prison?" she asked. "You can't shoot him here. There will be too many questions. Let us take care of it here. We've got our own ways of dealing with troublemakers. We'll take care of him."

Deke calmed down, and then looked at the small gun he held in his hand. He looked up at Harris, and turned it so he could see the automatic.

"See this?" he asked, suddenly calm again. "This is a Walther PPK. It's the same gun that James Bond used in his movies. In fact, this one was used on one of the shoots. It was also used to shoot a man later on." He flipped it casually back into safety position, then tucked it into his coat.

"I collect handguns," he said. "I have some pretty famous ones in my office. Sort of a hobby of mine. I even have a special assistant, Heidi Hilfinger, whose sole job is to find artifacts like this gun and buy them for me.

"I have the gun that shot Wild Bill Hickok, as well as the .32 revolver used when President McKinley was assassinated." He looked at Harris coolly. "Too bad you'll never see them."

He turned and looked at the warden. "You make sure he never sees daylight again."

"Trust me, Mr. Deke," she said. "As I stand here, I swear that as long as I live he'll never leave this prison."

* * *

"You were right, Elijah," Harris told him, back in our cell.

"Say it again," Elijah said, smiling broadly. "A little louder this time."

"You were right," Harris repeated. "The warden and Deke had all the cards stacked against me."

"Of course I was right, *zaychik*," Elijah said. "I am always right."

"So what do we do now?" Harris asked, switching to Russian.

"What do we do? We get you out of here, but only when the time is right." His smile faded, and once again he grew serious. "But first, you have one more task to perform before graduation. Call it your final exam."

"Which is?"

Elijah folded his hands and sat on the edge of the small table they had in their cell. He inhaled and looked at the ceiling. It was the first time Harris had seen him at a loss for words.

"*Zaychik,* I have had the pleasure of observing you very closely over the past two years," he began. "And what I see are two men, with greatly conflicting beliefs and goals.

"The first man is a man of God, a man of principle who has been called to speak out in the name of God against those who would do evil in the world. What is most important is that he obey the voice of God, to do the will of God. Only and always. *Nyet?*"

Harris nodded, understanding where he was coming from so far.

"The second is a man of rage, a man of passion, who has been forged by circumstances. This is a man who has lost the woman he loves, who has lost his sense of identity, even his sense of manhood. This is a man who will strike back and kill at the first opportunity. He is a man that is feared by many here, even as we speak. He has not acted yet, but it is only a matter of time before he reacts without thinking and kills someone."

Elijah stood and pointed his finger in Harris' face. "Both those men are inside you. But both cannot be allowed to stay there. The man of God will not tolerate the man of rage. And the man of rage has no time for God. Left together, they'll kill each other. You must decide which one will survive."

Harris stared at him. He had known the conflict existed inside of him for a long time. As usual, Elijah had put his finger right on the problem at hand. But what was he to do about it?

"Know also, *kamerad*, that this is not an academic exercise," Elijah said. "This is a very real conflict, not only a conflict of the soul, but of flesh and blood. And it is one you must deal with on a flesh-and-blood level."

He stared at Harris silently, his finger still pointing at his face.

"How?" Harris asked finally.

"You must challenge Sorenson," he said. "I have purposely left you without protection for the past few weeks, dangling you in the prison as if you were bait. Sorenson has been watching you. You can either delay the inevitable, and allow him to choose when you will be attacked...or you can take the initiative."

"The smart commander avoids battle until it has already been won," Harris breathed to himself.

"*Da*, rule six, but you cannot delay for long."

"But what about the first rule: Violence is the last resort of the incompetent?" Harris asked him.

"If you can think of another solution, use it!" he said.

Harris' mind spun with the new scenario that was laid before him, but Elijah grabbed his shoulders to once again gain his attention.

"When this is through," he said. "When this is over, then I will tell you of the favor I need you to do for me."

Harris nodded to him, still lost in thought about the challenge before him.

The next time Harris went to work at the library, he used the computer technique he had learned from Elijah over the past two years to enter the prison records. He spent several hours reading there before he knew that he had one more task before confronting Sorenson.

* * *

Sorenson was late coming from the machine shop. The foreman stopped him to criticize the quality of his work again. By the time he hit the showers, everyone was toweling off. He took his time, reveling in the fact that he had the whole place to himself. That was, until he started to hear voices.

"Sorenson," a voice rasped behind him. He turned quickly, not sure where it was coming from, and not sure who it was. No one was there.

"Sorenson," the voice came again. He turned and once again saw that no one was around. He knew that strange, evil things had been happening in the prison in the past weeks. People he knew had been attacked in their cells with no one else around. The thought of it made a chill run down his spine. He rinsed off quickly and shut off the water.

"OK, whoever it is out there, you're dead kippers," Sorenson said to the empty air around him. In response, he heard a laugh. It had a strangled edge to it, and Sorenson became less and less sure of himself. He hurried to his locker, toweled himself off, and pulled his pants on. He looked over at the shiv that he kept nearby, and started to pick it up.

"You don't need that," the voice rasped. "You're the big man here."

"Friggin' right I'm the big man here," Sorenson shouted back at the voice. "Show yourself and you'll see just how big I am."

In response, the fluorescent lights above the lockers started turning off, bank by bank, row by row. In less than a minute, only the lights above the shower area were on.

"It's only us," the raspy voice said. "Let's see what you have."

* * *

Elijah Brown had watched Harris prepare for the confrontation. He had confidence in his new pupil, but his curiosity was getting the better of him. When Harris had left for his rendezvous with Sorenson, Elijah had gone to the library. He hacked into the prison security system and watched Sorenson from the camera in the locker room. As things unwound, he decided to let others watch as well.

* * *

Rico was with a dozen other inmates watching Dr. Phil when suddenly the TV switched channels. Instead, they saw a familiar figure in the shower, looking around him.

"What's this?" someone shouted. "We're not pervs. We don't want to watch Sorenson get jiggy in the shower."

Rico watched and realized something unusual was happening when Sorenson looked around with a look of fear on his face.

"Wait, wait," Rico said, holding his hand up as someone went to switch the channel. "I think you guys are going to want to see this."

* * *

Sorenson took his shiv with him back to the shower area. If this bloke was going to show himself, then fine, they'd dance. He was ready.

"You ready to die, invisible man?" Sorenson shouted.

"In a minute," the voice rasped. "I just have one question before we begin."

"What's that?"

"How did you get that scar?" The voice was immediately behind him, and Sorenson whirled to see Harris Borden standing two feet away. This was not the long-haired wild man that had the prison scared. This one was clean-shaven, looking the same as the day they had last seen each other in here, save for the red scar that ran down Borden's throat.

Sorenson thrust the shiv toward Borden, but Borden stepped behind the tiled-covered wall dividing the showers from the lockers. Sorenson took three steps after Borden, turned the corner where Borden had gone, and saw nothing.

"You bit my ear off, you bloody sod!" Sorenson shouted after him.

"Not that scar, Sorenson. The one on the left side of your face."

"None of your bleedin' business," Sorenson said. "Show yourself!"

"I heard you got it when you were a child," Harris rasped. "I heard someone gave it to you." Sorenson continued to look around him, becoming more and more confused. "Who gave it to you, Sorenson?"

"A blighter who thought he was more of a man than me," Sorenson said. "A bully."

"It was your father, wasn't it?"

Sorenson stopped, shocked that such personal information came out after so long.

"I'll kill you!" he shouted suddenly, slashing at the darkness. "I'll cut your throat clean through this time. Come out where I can see you!"

* * *

"Sorenson's getting his!" someone shouted in the exercise yard, and the yard emptied. Everyone headed for a TV set where every eye was watching to see what would happen to this hated man. As was the case in every event of consequence in prison, bets were being placed. A few had seen Harris Borden reveal himself for an instant. Sorenson started off as the odds-on favorite, but as the others watched how Borden dealt with the braggart, the odds shifted to become more even.

"I heard that the preacher knows black magic," someone said. "He's put a voodoo curse on Sorenson."

"Nah," someone else said. "He's an assassin who actually works for the Mob. Sorenson is going to get hit."

And some, realizing where the event was occurring, headed directly for the locker room. Among those were a few from the Crips.

Sitting at the terminal in the library, Elijah Brown smiled and leaned back in his chair. Everything was going according to plan.

* * *

"It's not your fault," said the voice. "You were a victim. All of us are victims."

Frustrated, Sorenson began to strike out in all directions. He jabbed his shiv into the air. Unseen to him, the locker room began to fill with inmates and prison guards who watched his every move. Sorenson began to scream and spit at the unseen preacher who knew about his violent childhood. Finally, he grew tired and dropped his arm, beginning to sob. Others watched silently as the hulking bully fell to his knees, dropped his arms and began to cry.

"It's OK," Harris said, stepping from the shadows behind Sorenson. He tenderly put his hands on Sorenson's shoulders, and a softer side of Harris returned to him.

Watching from his console, Elijah looked at the transformation in Harris Borden and nodded. "Careful, *zaychik*," he muttered.

Sorenson turned to the waiting Harris. This time, Harris did not disappear. Harris stood, hands at his sides, apparently harmless. Elijah Brown knew he was far from it, as he suspected most of the crowd did, and probably Sorenson.

Sorenson flinched as if ready to defend himself, but Borden didn't move. Instead, he spoke calmly and quietly.

"You were a victim, Sorenson. It's not your fault."

Sorenson responded by swinging his clenched right fist, connecting with Harris' chin in a roundhouse. Harris was knocked back by the blow, but quickly stood again before Sorenson.

"You have a choice, Sorenson. You can choose to strike out—."

Sorenson's left connected with Harris' stomach. The crowd moaned as Harris doubled over, then once again righted himself. Sorenson stared at the stubborn pastor in front of him.

"—or you can choose to return evil with good." Harris stared at Sorenson, while reaching up and wiping blood from his chin.

Sorenson hesitated, then charged forward, shiv aimed at Harris' chest. Harris didn't flinch, but stood ramrod straight as the blade rushed toward him. It hit his chest and the metal blade shattered like glass hitting a stone wall. Sorenson stared at the broken blade for a long second, then collapsed on the floor, sobbing.

"*Muerte*. I've never seen anything like that," breathed Rico, who was standing in the crowd. Others gasped as well. Sorenson continued to sob, but his cries lessened, and within a minute was asleep.

"You will wake up later, remembering that you were a victim," Harris said. "It wasn't your fault, but you don't want others to be victims as well. Instead of hurting others, you will want to protect them. Remember this," he rasped at the prone form, and then looked up. It was only then that he realized that the battle was being watched. He stood over Sorenson, and saw that scores of others stood in the darkness observing silently.

"Can someone help me get him back to his cell?" Harris rasped. "He's awfully big."

"I'll give him what he needs." A dark figure rushed forward. Harris recognized it as one of the Crips, a follower of Ali, who had died in the cafeteria at the hands of Sorenson. The big black man charged Harris and Sorenson, a lead pipe in his hand.

Harris quickly reached across his chest with his right hand and popped the black man across the throat with the outer edge of it. The man clutched his throat and collapsed to his knees as if he had been hit with a bag of sand.

"As I was saying…." Harris said, but was interrupted. Guards, unseen up to this point, rushed forward and clubbed Harris. He fell to the floor, protecting his head. Six of them appeared, with two taking each of the three men who lay on the shower floor.

"Take them to the hole," Harris heard the warden's voice say.

17 THE FACE OF GOD

He had won, and yet he'd lost.

Even as the guards dragged Harris down the hallway, beating him as he went, he knew that his actions had made a statement that encouraged a lot of men in the prison. You didn't have to be a cruel, merciless killer to have dignity in this place. You didn't even have to hurt someone permanently. Harris heard cheering going on as word spread of his victory over Sorenson.

But Harris knew that he'd lost his battle with the guards, the warden and even Universal. The Hole was no-man's land. Once you entered the metal doors to The Hole, all bets were off. Men died there, and no one asked any questions. It consisted simply of a room with no windows, no furniture, and no source of light. The only contact with the outside world came once a day when food and water were handed in through a slot in the metal door and the slop bucket--his toilet—was taken out. Harris had heard horror stories of how men had lost their minds after two weeks in The Hole. As he heard the warden shout instructions, Harris realized that he'd be in there a month. In addition to problems of exposure—he would have nothing to keep him warm but the clothes on his back—he'd need to worry about sensory deprivation. No light and no sound but your own voice could easily drive a man insane.

Harris had other worries that for him were more serious. He realized that he would have no access to a Bible where he was going. For him, that was more frightening than the lack of human contact.

"Please, let me take a Bible with me," he begged the guards.

"You won't have any light to read by where you're going," one of them laughed.

"I don't care," Harris replied. "I'll give you anything I have for a Bible."

The guard in charge paused for a second as they stood outside the metal doors of The Hole. He finally nodded.

"OK, all of your clothes for a Bible. Take 'em off."

It was late September, and the air in the hallways was getting cold, but Harris didn't care. He gladly shed all his clothes, leaving them in a pile in the hall floor.

"My Bible," Harris said, holding his hands out.

"Inside," the guard said, shoving him in the door.

"You said I could have a Bible," Harris said a little louder, as they shoved him in the door and closed it behind him. He stood in the dark for a long moment before they slid open the slot at the foot of the door. A large flat metal tin—the slop bucket—was shoved through the entrance. He heard a ripping sound, and a single sheet torn from a Bible was thrown into the nasty interior of the bucket. The page floated down into the stinky mess inside the container, just touching it slightly before Harris snatched it up and pressed it to himself.

Harris wiped the page clean on his chest, the only thing he had to wipe it on. He didn't dare wipe it on the walls or floor, because he didn't know what was on them, and didn't want to lose any of the text on the page. Harris looked down. The guard hadn't completely pulled the slot closed at the base of the door, and a little light trickled into the room. He lay on the cold floor, shivering, facing the slot and its faint light, and read from the page they had left him. It was the first chapter of First Timothy. The light shone like a halo on several passages, and Harris knew it was a message intended specifically for him:

6   Wherein ye greatly rejoice, though now for a little while, if need be, ye have been put to grief in manifold trials,

7   that the proof of your faith, *being* more precious than gold that perisheth though it is proved by fire, may be found unto praise and glory and honor at the revelation of Jesus Christ:

8   Whom not having seen ye love; on whom, though now ye see him not, yet believing, ye rejoice greatly with joy unspeakable and full of glory:

9   receiving the end of your faith, *even* the salvation of *your* souls.

The words burned into his mind as he lay there thinking about them. A minute later he heard footsteps and the guard returned, slamming the slot completely shut. Harris was alone in the dark.

But he wasn't really alone. He knew that. And somehow Harris knew that after the physical challenge he'd endured, this was a greater spiritual challenge that was even more important. He had time—lots and lots of time—to think about his life, about the road that had led him to this place, about Katya, about what he considered important in his life. Harris had everything—even the clothes on his back—taken from him. All that he now owned was a scrap of paper with scripture on it, and his belief in God.

Within a day Harris was assailed by his own self doubt. He'd failed so many times, even after his own confidence and his words had sworn it would never happen. Even in the battle with Sorenson—when he had sworn not to use his own strength and skill to defend himself—he had ended up striking another inmate by sheer reflex. He'd depended on his own strength, and by doing so, failed to do what God asked. Harris had taken the glory away from Him, where it rightfully belonged. Harris wept and prayed. There were no alarm clocks, appointment books, cell phones or computers to interrupt him here. When Harris was done praying, all that remained was the darkness, four stone walls and a cold floor.

Then the spirits came. At first Harris thought he was hallucinating, something he associated with sensory deprivation. But soon he realized that these were truly evil spirits, allies of the demon Baal he'd declared war on. No wonder the guards and the warden didn't worry about killing him. The demons would either drive him insane or kill him with their own claws. Harris assumed that these were the same demons that had killed inmates in the past weeks.

The demons came in the form of whispered voices. They tried to scare him, they taunted him, and they appealed to his sense of self doubt. A couple of times Harris saw faces in the darkness as well. He prayed constantly, and eventually they lost their power and disappeared.

The only way of telling time in the darkness was knowing that once a day—at noon—they would open the slot to take his slop bucket and give him food and water. In the first ten days there were two occasions when the slot was not completely closed. On those times, Harris hastily took advantage of this oversight to read and reread the page of scripture they had given him. But each time the slot remained open for only a few minutes. Harris decided that some kind-hearted guard had intentionally left it open for him to have a little light. Later, another had passed by in the hallway and seen the oversight and closed it. Harris prayed and thanked God for the few minutes of light, which burst into the darkness as if directly from the sun.

He was determined to keep his hopes up, keep his spirits up; be strong. But the endless days and nights, the lack of human contact, and the total feeling of being alone finally got to him. Harris found himself sometime around the tenth day sobbing like a little baby. It was then that God came to him.

At first Harris heard a whisper, and it was much like the demons that had haunted him earlier. Then, as he listened, it became clearer. Harris had gone beyond worrying whether he was going to go insane. He welcomed any contact.

"Harris," the Voice whispered. Harris didn't answer at first, but sat huddled in the corner, rocking back and forth, trying to keep warm. The voice came again.

"Harris."

"Yes," Harris answered. In response, a soft glow began in the corner of the room and a warmth spread over his body. Harris stopped shivering for the first time in over a week.

"Harris, do you know Who I Am?"

Harris gulped. "Yes. You are the I Am. I would take my shoes off as Moses did, but as you see…." He looked down in shame at his naked, dirty body.

"That's all right, Harris. You are as you were created."

"I am here to serve You, Lord."

"Are you?" the Voice said. "Do you love Me, Harris?"

"Yes, Lord, I love you. That's why I've been persecuted."

"What have you done for me?"

"I have gone to prison for You, Lord."

"Many have been imprisoned in My Name. My servant Joseph went to prison. Daniel was thrown in a den of lions. Peter and Paul died in prison. Is that what you want?"

Harris wanted to say, *I want what you want.* Instead: "No, my Lord."

"What have you done for me, Harris?"

Harris stammered. "I…I spoke out against evil in front of a multitude of people."

"There have been many who have spoken out against evil. And many have died because of that. The faith has many martyrs. Is that what you want?"

"No, my Lord."

"What else have you done? What price have you paid?"

"I…I followed the path and had my wife and child taken from me."

"And the Father had His Son taken from Him, even when He was innocent of wrongdoing." There was a long silence. "Harris, do you love me?"

Harris realized that he hadn't done anything that thousands before had not done. He'd been caught up in the need to be strong, to be something special in the eyes of God and man. Now he realized that he was nothing special at all.

"Lord, there's something I don't understand."

"You wonder why I led you to Elijah Brown. You wonder why you needed to learn the things he had to teach you."

"Yes, Lord."

"Have you ever wondered why I allowed Moses to be trained as the prince of Egypt before I called him? Why did Paul learn the ways of the Sanhedrin and the Romans before I called him? Is there a place for the knowledge of men, or is the knowledge of God sufficient for His followers?"

Harris had no answer.

"Sometimes I use the knowledge of men for my purposes. Sometimes I allow men to gain worldly knowledge so that their choice between the World and God is clear.

"I am the I Am. I move as I see fit. You must learn, as do all, to trust me.

"Harris, do you love me?"

Harris bowed his head and cried. "Yes, my Lord. I love you with all my heart and soul."

"Then learn to trust Me. Will you learn to trust Me?"

"Yes, Lord."

"Then do what I ask. This is what I ask: Do not eat or drink in this room any more. Instead, trust in Me for your sustenance."

Harris had been ready to die for God. Would he be willing to go without food and water for another three weeks?

"I'll do as you ask, Lord." It was then that Harris realized something odd. The raspy sound had disappeared from his voice. He was talking with his old voice.

"You have healed me, Lord! Thank you!"

"Show me, Harris," He said. "Sing for me."

Harris opened his mouth and sang. The words came out sweet and clear:

"My Jesus, I love Thee, I know Thou art mine. For thee all the follies of sin I resign. My gracious redeemer, my savior, art thou. If ever I loved thee, my Jesus tis now."

Harris had accepted the fact that his voice would never be the same; that he'd never sing again. But to have his voice returned to him was a blessing he couldn't imagine. Tears ran from his eyes.

"Thank you, Lord," Harris said.

"You will receive another gift that will help you in your task. For you must know that the task before you is not over. In fact, it is just beginning.

"Also know that many things are not as they appear. You will experience great joy and great sorrow before the end. But know that you will not be alone. Trust in Me, and you will never be alone."

* * *

The presence of God remained with Harris for the coming days. He did as God commanded and didn't eat or drink for the rest of the time while he was in The Hole. Regular as clockwork, the food and water came through the slot, but Harris let it stay there at the entrance. And because he wasn't eating or drinking, the slop bucket didn't fill either. About five days after Harris stopped taking food and water, the slot stopped opening.

And God blessed him with light. A soft light glowed from the corner of the room, and Harris felt warmth as well. He was able to read and reread the page of scripture that had been given to him. The light gave him perspective as well. It was easy to lose touch with reality when all around you was blackness. But the soft light told him where things were, and how real and tangible the walls and the door and ceiling were.

Harris lost track of time when the slot stopped opening. But he'd thrown himself completely into the arms of God. Everything he had had been taken away from Harris, but then everything had come from God in the first place. Harris was simply, completely, living in and by the grace of God.

It was sometime after that that Harris slept and dreamed again of the Tower. It was a green translucent tower, rising from the San Francisco skyline. The rest of San Francisco seemed to move aside as if in deference for this tower. Harris walked through the empty streets below the tower. It was night. He walked behind the Tower and again found the dumpster. Again he looked in the bottom and found a small package wrapped in brown paper. Harris picked it up and saw the face of a person.

It was Kenneth Deke.

* * *

Harris was awakened from the dream by the sound of footsteps, followed by a metal scraping sound. It was followed by the sound of a key being turned and latches thrown on the door. Finally, the door pulled open, and light streamed inside, blinding him. Harris held his hand over his eyes to shade them from the outside light, and heard a gasp.

"He's alive," he heard a guard say. "Let's get him out of there."

"But how….?" Harris heard from another one, then they came into the cell and reached under his arms and picked him up off the stones. Still blinded, he stood limply in the hallway as they helped him into the blue prison fatigues that he normally wore. Harris was disoriented, and two guards helped him down the hallway toward his cell. It wasn't until he was almost all the way back to his cell that Harris realized that other prisoners were whispering around him, apparently shocked at something about him.

The guards used surprisingly tender care in taking Harris back into his cell and depositing him on his bunk. Harris lay there for a long time, just enjoying the feel of clothing on his body, a bunk under him, and a light bulb shining from the ceiling.

"*Zdravstvuj!*" he heard from the doorway. His eyes had finally adjusted, and Harris saw a young looking Elijah Brown standing in the entrance, his hands thrust outward as if to welcome him. "The whole prison thought you were dead, but I knew otherwise. No one can kill my *zaychik*."

Harris sat up and smiled weakly at him. "I'm a changed man, Elijah."

"Eh?" he asked. "That is not a surprise. Your confrontation with Sorenson will be told in the hallways for years to come, and now to survive this…well, *neyzeli*."

"God saved my life," Harris told him bluntly. He then related what had happened in The Hole.

"Well, I wondered how you could survive without food or water," he said, stroking his beard. "You know, of course, that after ten days they poisoned it so as to kill you. When you didn't take it any more, they assumed you were dead." As Elijah spoke, Harris realized that his beard and hair had grown out again, after shaving them for the battle with Sorenson.

"How long was I in there?" Harris asked.

Elijah grinned. "My friend, you have set a new prison record for The Hole." Then he grew very serious. "You were locked in there for 48 days."

Harris stared at him blankly. "*Neyzeli*," he breathed.

"Exactly," Elijah answered. He paused to look Harris up and down. "Well, you don't seem too much worse for wear."

"Nothing that a few pushups and a run around the track won't fix," Harris agreed. Then Elijah's eyes suddenly grew wide.

"Your voice!" he exclaimed. "It is healed!" He slapped Harris across the shoulder again. "Many are the miracles today. You must know the news."

"What news is that?"

"Ding, dong, the witch is dead." He grinned at Harris. Harris looked at Elijah for half a minute before he realized what he was saying.

"The warden?" Harris asked, incredulous.

Elijah nodded. "Two weeks after you went inside, she had a heart attack and collapsed on her office floor. She was already cold by the time they found her body."

Harris stared out the cell door. "She'd sworn that if I left here, it'd be over her dead body."

"Well, she got her wish," Elijah said. "The new warden is expected tomorrow. And I hear good things about him."

"Things?"

"Like he is fair and honest. That he can't be bought by anyone on the inside or outside."

"Maybe this is my chance to get another fair hearing," Harris said, but he was thinking, *if that is what God wills.*

"Maybe," he said. "Maybe not. Which brings me to the favor."

"Ah yes, the ever-elusive favor," Harris said to him. "I've waited for more than two years to hear what this favor is."

Elijah switched to Russian, and Harris knew that it was something very private, or important.

"It is time for me to disappear again," Elijah said. "I intentionally broadcast your battle with Sorenson throughout the prison, because I knew that word of it would get out to those who are seeking me." Elijah stood in front of Harris and drew his attention to his physique. Elijah had changed from the frumpy, overweight middle-aged man Harris had seen two years before into someone with the same physique as Harris. His hair and beard had grown and as Harris looked closer, he realized that he had taken the grey from his hair as well. *For someone who didn't look closely*, Harris thought, *he could be mistaken for me, and vice versa.*

"I need you to be me," Elijah said. "Tomorrow the warden will bring a pardon for me from the governor. I have arranged it. But when I leave here, it will actually be you leaving."

"Me? Why?"

"Because I will become someone else," Elijah said. "Elijah Brown is becoming dangerous for me. At the same time, when you leave here, Kenneth Deke and his evil empire will be looking for Harris Borden. Harris Borden must die. I will make sure that officially Harris Borden never lived beyond his time in The Hole."

Harris knew that Elijah, with his vast computer skills, could do just that. Harris would become Elijah Brown, and Elijah would become, well, someone else.

"Have you thought what your new name will be?" Harris asked.

Elijah shrugged. "It is probably best for you not to know my new identity, but I am debating between Brad Pitt and Pablo Picasso." He grinned at Harris through shark teeth.

Harris laughed and shook his head. "You're right. I don't need to know."

* * *

They switched uniforms and bunks that night. Elijah had made sure that he'd been seen enough in prison with his new muscular bulk that Harris could impersonate him when it came time. Harris covered the tattoos on his hands and the scar on his neck with makeup that Elijah kept. And Harris knew that he'd watched Elijah closely enough in the past two years to be able to impersonate him so well Elijah's own mother would embrace Harris as her long lost son. Besides, what inmate in their right mind would pass up a reprieve from the governor?

The metal lock on the door clanked early that morning, and two guards that Harris wasn't familiar with stepped in. Harris looked at them as they stared at a picture of Elijah.

"That's him," they said, pointing at Harris. "Elijah Brown, you've been pardoned by the governor. Come with us."

Harris climbed down from the bunk slowly as he knew Elijah would. Harris looked over at the sleeping form in the lower bunk. He knew that as soon as he left, Elijah would change his identity and his appearance once again, and leave the prison if he saw fit. Harris also knew that he'd never see his friend of the past two years again.

"*Dos vedanya, kamarad,*" Harris whispered. Then he turned to the two guards.

"I'm ready to go," Harris said in a loud, clear voice.

* * *

Foreman Bob Kreuger took another look around at the work area, and was relatively satisfied. Not all the floors were completed on the new building, but the "suits," as he called the professionals who occupied high rise executive suites like this one, would be able to move in on time. That was what his bosses wanted most of all.

He'd had to fire a couple of workers for not getting that concept though their thick heads, and a couple of guys—he thought of George Tillay—had been taken to the hospital when a scaffold collapsed. But for the most part, he had a pretty good crew to work with.

He continued to scan the room, until he saw a black lunch pail left in an inconspicuous place in the corner. He walked over to it and saw "Tillay" written on gray tape on the top. He'd have to get that to George, he thought. George would be back at work in a couple of weeks, and he made a mental note to do what he could to get him accepted as a member of the union. He took another step and inadvertently kicked a brown-wrapped package slightly larger than a brick. It looked like other scraps and bits of leftover trash in the room.

"Bill," he shouted to another worker. "Get one of the clean-up crew to police this area. Throw all this trash down the chute. They're supposed to lay carpet in here tomorrow."

Bill nodded. Fifteen minutes later, the brown package was thrown down the plastic chute along with leftover fiberglass insulation, screws and nails, bits of sheetrock, and other trash. They all traveled down the tube to a dumpster that stood in the alley behind the new Universal "Jade" Tower.

18 FISTS OR FAITH

A typical, fine San Francisco mist—more from fog than from rain—made the day gray. Harris looked up at the sign in English and Chinese that marked Bobby Chong's Whatnot Store and Pawn in Chinatown. Then he looked down at the claim check he got with Elijah's other stuff when they checked him out of San Dimas. Unless there was another Bobby Chong in Chinatown—which was very likely—something was waiting for him here.

Harris stepped in the door and out of the mist. A middle-aged Chinese-American man—Harris assumed Bobby himself—stood behind the counter.

"Yes?" he asked Harris in perfect, unaccented English. Harris responded by giving him the claim check.

"I believe you have something that belongs to me," Harris said.

"Name?"

"Elijah Brown," Harris said. The Asian man looked down at the ledger and shook his head. Harris frowned and thought.

"How about under the name Clausewitz?" Harris asked.

The short man behind the counter nodded quickly and disappeared behind a curtain. A minute later, he reappeared with a small suitcase. Inside it Harris found several objects he couldn't identify, some books in Russian, a wad of cash, several fake IDs, a couple of credit cards and a Glock nine-millimeter automatic pistol. Harris lifted the gun up, and a clip was stashed beneath it. He carefully replaced the gun. He stuffed the cash in his front pocket, closed the suitcase and nodded to the man.

"Twenty dollars," Bobby Chong said, all business.

Harris peeled a twenty off the wad in his pocket and paid the man.

He took the suitcase to Union Station and put it in a locker. Then Harris hopped on BART and took it down to the Civic Center exit, which was not too far from the City Planning Commission.

Harris pulled out another $20 and got a microfiche that showed the plans for the recently completed Universal Tower. He sat at a viewscreen at the Planning office and scanned it carefully. On several of the floors he made paper copies of what he saw.

Universal had been very open about their plans for the tower. It was obvious to Harris that the critical office area was the top six stories—floors 45 to 50. He was grateful for the information that was open to the public. Had they not decided to sell public stock, he doubted that he would have such easy access to the building plans. What he was worried about was what the plans didn't show him.

Harris asked at the front whether security systems had to be approved by the City Planning Commission.

"It depends," the woman at the counter said. "If it is part of the original plans submitted to the city, then yes. If it is added later, and does not affect the integrity of the building's construction, then no."

Harris knew that Universal wouldn't do without a state-of-the-art security system, so he got on the phone and called several security companies in San Francisco. The first two were clueless as to what Universal had done. Harris learned what he needed to know on the third.

"Pardon me," Harris said on the phone. "I've heard good things about the security system in the new Universal Tower. I wondered if your company was responsible for their system."

The guy on the other end of the line chuckled. "Don't I wish," he said. "They went around to all the security companies asking a lot of questions, but they did it all themselves. I've heard rumors, but most everyone has been kept in the dark as to what they actually have up there."

"Hmm," Harris responded.

"But we can do you some pretty good work anyway," he said.

"Thanks, but no." Harris hung up and mused. His options were running out.

Harris went down to Larkin Street and the main branch of the San Francisco Public Library. He wasn't in that much of a hurry, and was enjoying the fall weather, so he walked. Harris mused how one didn't realize how beautiful a city street can be until you're locked up behind walls for more than two years.

He found a computer in a somewhat secluded place on the second floor, and pulled up the Universal Finance main website. He hacked into the index, then their internal business directory. Within a few minutes he was into their mainframe, and looking for records of their security system. After half an hour, he knew that those plans were either more closely guarded than he could ever find, or the plans just weren't in there.

Harris looked at the ceiling and sighed.

"Trouble?" he heard a voice behind him say. Harris quickly hit a couple of keys and switched screens to the Yahoo main webpage.

Harris looked up to see one of the librarians, and smiled. He shook his head.

"No, just the usual frustrations."

She made a small laugh. "Yes, I've had those days before. Sorry."

Harris shrugged, and she kept walking down the aisle. He waited a minute until he was sure she was gone, and switched back to the Universal website.

"Time for Plan B," he said to himself. He looked at the directory for the executive staff, and tried to hack into Kenneth Deke's files. He couldn't get in. Then he took another approach. He looked at the list of secretaries, and found Deke's secretary listed. He had no problem hacking into her files, and from there into Deke's appointment book. Harris wrote himself into Deke's appointment book for 5 p.m. tomorrow under the name Elijah Brown.

Harris had one more stop to make that evening. It was getting dark and he was tired, but he caught a trolley car and rode back up to Chinatown. He'd noticed a chemist's shop just a couple of doors down from Bobby Chong's. Harris scribbled a list of items that he thought he'd need, stuff that Elijah had taught him about, and handed it to the chemist behind the counter. One couldn't find these things in a regular pharmacy, but he had a pretty good feeling he'd find them here.

The bearded old man looked like he'd been there for the Gold Rush. He looked at the list without saying a word, then took off his wire-rimmed glasses and cleaned them. He looked at it again for a long time, then looked up at Harris.

"You ninja?" he asked Harris, a faint smile on his lips.

Harris smiled back at him and shook his head.

"I'm nobody," Harris said.

* * *

Kenneth Deke was relaxed for the first time in two years. Of course, being relaxed for an executive of Deke's caliber wasn't real obvious to the average spectator. He still came in early and stayed late, still held power lunches and was on his cell phone more often than not. What it did mean was that, since Harris Borden was officially dead, he could go about building his empire without constantly looking over his shoulder. He was humming a little tune to himself, looking out the massive glass window of his new office, fingering one of his prized handguns, when a familiar voice came to him.

"You seem exceptionally pleased with yourself."

Deke turned and looked at the stone edifice in the far end of his mausoleum-like office. A dull red glow floated a foot above the altar there.

"I believe I have reason to be. The Jade Tower is practically finished, our stock is sky high, we have diversified in countless directions, and our biggest hindrance is gone. Am I wrong to be happy?"

"Harris Borden is alive," the voice said.

"No," Deke said, shaking his head. "They told me he died in prison. It's in the official records. You're just trying to scare me."

The voice roared. "*If I wanted to frighten you, do you think I would hesitate to do so?*"

Deke withdrew a step. "Forgive me, Master." He paused. "I just don't see how...."

"Forget your computers and your sources. Forget everything else but this. Harris Borden is alive, and he is on his way here."

Pause. "Here?" Deke said weakly.

"He is not only after you. He is after the cabal. He does not know that with our growth, other groups have sprung up. Perhaps he does not care. But I do know that he is after the cabal here—the original group. Perhaps he—and the One he serves—want to make a statement for the others to see. With the planned videoconferencing, any action he takes will be broadcast to our offices the world over."

Deke stared at the red glow for a long moment before responding. "Very well. You've never been wrong before. We'll be ready for him."

* * *

Compared to most of those senior executives at Universal, Ed Whiting lived a relatively clean-cut life. He had one addiction, however, that he refused to give up. While he and Deke were in college, long hours in the computer lab had led to his addiction to cappuccinos. Normally he had one of his assistants run to the Starbucks across the street from the Tower to get him one, but the endless hours of preparing for the cabal meeting had finally led to a great desire to get out and get some fresh air.

He'd paid for his cup and had turned to leave when he saw someone familiar sitting at a table facing the outside window. The long-haired bearded young man stared out the window in the direction of the Jade Tower. It had been a long time, and the circumstances and the clothing were different, but he recognized the eyes and the red scar that tracked down the side of his throat. He stood for a long while, debating on whether he should say anything, or possibly call security, before he decided to say something.

"I appreciate the time you spent with my father," Whiting said. Harris looked up at Whiting, startled at first. When he realized that Whiting wouldn't have him arrested, he relaxed.

"Your father was a good man," Harris said. "We had a lot of good talks about God and what heaven will be like."

"He was troubled for most of his life. There at the end, he was happier than I've ever seen him. I want to thank you for that."

Harris nodded. He gestured to the seat beside him. "Do you feel comfortable sitting down next to a convicted terrorist?"

Whiting shrugged. "I've been around criminals my whole life. The only thing that makes my life different now is that they wear expensive suits and buy and sell countries."

"You don't have to do what you do," Harris said. "There are alternatives."

"That's what my father tried to tell me. But I'm too far along to change now. God would never forgive me for what I've done."

Harris shook his head. "God will go out of His way to forgive you, if you ask Him."

"Right," Whiting said. "Well, I just wanted to tell you thanks, whatever happens."

"You're welcome," Harris said, smiling faintly and looking Whiting up and down.

"You know they're waiting for you," Whiting said. "They're going to kill you."

Harris looked across the street at the tower for a long time before responding. "Well, you know you can help my chances. Any possibility of letting me know a little bit about your security system?"

Whiting shook his head. "Not a chance. I will tell you this: your best chance of staying alive is in hopping the first plane out of here and disappearing in some faraway country."

Harris smiled back. "Well, I have my commitments too. We'll just have to see what happens."

* * *

Greg Phipps was putting on his coat, ready to step out his front door, when the phone rang.

"You're on your way to prayer meeting, aren't you?" the familiar voice asked. "Can I give you a prayer request?"

"Of course," Phipps said. "What is it?"

"Please ask the members there to pray for Harris Borden."

Phipps paused. "Harris Borden is dead."

"Not all things are as they seem, friend," the voice said. "Harris needs your prayers, now more than ever."

Could it be Harris? Phipps asked himself. *But the last time he had heard Harris he could barely talk. This one spoke like an orator.* "Fine, consider it done," Phipps said. "But tell me: who is this?"

"I'm nobody," the caller said, then hung up.

* * *

The radio in his motel room was tuned to a Christian radio station that presently featured the ramblings of a hellfire-style preacher. While his voice droned on, Harris finished shaving more than a month of whiskers from his face with soap, hot water, and a cheap safety razor. After visiting the Chinese chemist today, Harris had gone shopping at an electronics store. He bought one of those disposable cell phones that he remembered Michelle Kinkaid had shown him. Tomorrow the plan was to visit a good barber for a proper trim, as well as a store he'd seen today that sold some very nice suits. He didn't know if he'd be alive 24 hours from now. But if he was going to die, Harris wanted to look presentable when they found his body.

Too bad Katya isn't here to see the new me, Harris thought. She'd always liked the way he looked in a new suit.

"The new muscles don't hurt either," Harris said aloud. She'd have held onto him as if he were a rare collector's item. The thought made him smile, and miss her even more. He just wished he could do something about the scar.

He felt like a bullfighter getting ready for his final match. Perhaps it was good that Katya wasn't here to experience this. Harris wiped shaving cream from his face with a towel and left the bathroom sink. It would probably be a good idea to get a good night's sleep. Harris switched off the radio and picked up the Gideon's Bible left by the bedside.

Harris stared at the Bible, unopened in his lap, for a long time.

"God," Harris muttered. "Your ways are mysterious. But we're in this together—hellfire or high water."

He lay back on his bed, the light still on, and held the Bible to his chest.

* * *

"OK, most of you have been moved in for nearly two weeks," Deke said to the security officers standing around the conference room. Many were uncomfortable, since they were relatively new, and had never been in the presence of the company president, much less on the 45th floor; what most employees referred to as the "inner sanctum."

"A lot of what you see here today will be stating the obvious," Deke continued. "But we'll be also filling you in on some additions that only Ed and I know about that have come online in the past couple of days." He nodded at Whiting, who sat yawning in an overstuffed chair to one side. He gestured to Whiting, who reacted slowly.

"Uh, I pulled another all-nighter," Whiting said. "You know the particulars. Want to go ahead?"

Deke frowned at Whiting. It was unusual for anyone to say no to Deke, but if anyone had the juice to say no, it was Whiting. Deke turned back toward his security officers, and began letting them in on the changes. Whiting knew that within minutes, Deke was likely to forget the insult.

"OK, you should all be familiar with the general layout of the building by now. Offices and windows around the perimeter, elevator banks in rows on the east and west sides, with the atrium in the center.

"That's generally the same through all the building, with the exceptions of the ground floor, this floor—the 45th—and the 50th. The 50th, of course, has ballrooms A and B at the north and south side of the tower, and kitchen areas east and west." He pointed at the diagram spread out on the table between them.

"The main floor includes the lobby area along the south, banking offices on north, east and west sides, and security screening temporarily established between the entrance in the south and the lobby/atrium area."

"The 45th floor is split up by my office in the south, with the balcony area, the computer lab in the north, this conference room in the west, and security in the east. These are work areas we're all familiar with."

The others nodded and continued listening.

"After hours, general security measures include cameras throughout the building, regular rounds by security officers on all occupied floors, and electric eyes and lasers hooked to alarms in sensitive areas. In addition to this, we've added an additional level of security that should be new to all of you." He looked over at Whiting, who seemed impassive.

"In cases of extra alert, such as tonight, we've included a computerized lockdown system. If an intruder is detected in a sensitive area—say the computer lab, for example—the mainframe puts the entire building into lockdown mode. Steel doors sheeted with titanium will lock all exits to and from any level above the main floor. This can be overridden by only two people—Whiting and me. Having it this way will make sure that the building and the people in it are protected from any enemy—external or internal.

"One more item of notice, and this is very important," Deke said, looking at Whiting again. "When we go into lockdown mode, it's important that you avoid the hallways. Those will be painted by heat sensors. If anyone with any heat signature is detected, an additional security system will take them out."

The security officers looked at Deke blankly, and one raised his hand.

"Sir, I'm not sure I understand," he said. "What kind of security system? Take them out? Kill them, sir?"

"Yes, kill them," Deke said. "And as far as the particulars of the system, you don't need to know the details, and you don't *want* to know." He looked again at Whiting, who nodded knowingly. "Suffice it to say that Ed has taken advantage of some of the distinct attributes of this corporation to develop a fail-safe system. Only I'll be immune to the new system.

"Just make sure you don't get caught in the hallways if the alarm goes off."

Deke looked at the faces of the guards, all hand-picked by him. Some had law enforcement experience; all had military experience. He had confidence in them. But he had continually underestimated Harris Borden; he couldn't afford to do so again.

"We're likely to have an unwanted visitor tonight," Deke said, opening a green folder and pulling out copies of photos of Borden. "His name is Harris Borden. He has a history as a pastor, but don't let that fool you. This man is highly elusive, and on a mission from God, or so he thinks. We have highly reliable information that says he'll try to infiltrate our cabal meeting tonight and kill all or some of its attendees.

"Borden has visited us twice before. Both times he's appeared in the middle of public presentations and caused a public scene. Considering the level of security we have here tonight, we suspect that he'll attempt to get in by impersonating someone who is already on the invite list. We'll have security tight throughout the building, but we'll be especially tight in the ballrooms on the 50th floor.

"Let me make this clear: if you see him, shoot to kill. Don't hesitate. Do you read me?" Deke watched as the security officers nodded, and he dismissed them. He watched them leave, then turned to Whiting.

"They'll do their best, Kenny," Whiting said.

"They'd better," Deke said. "There won't be another chance—for Borden, or for me."

* * *

It felt great to be clean shaven, with a fresh haircut and wearing a new suit. Harris could almost pretend that he was on his way to a church meeting, rather than presumably to his death. He smiled when he thought back to the boring church service that marked the beginning of this insane adventure, and longed for just one more boring event like that in his crazy life.

It was early evening, and the traffic was beginning to head out of town. He saw white-collar workers coming out of the various buildings in the financial district as he walked down California Street. Harris could see the new building they called the Jade Tower. The afternoon sun made it reflect a greenish hue, and he imagined that as the night arrived, the light from their interior would make it glow a bright green. No wonder the newspapers referred to it as the new landmark of the San Francisco skyline.

Harris came to Sansome and turned left, walking past the tower and back behind it. His heart began to thud as he turned another corner, and, just as he'd seen it several times in his dreams, there was a dumpster.

Harris looked around to make sure no one was watching. He was prepared to dive into the dumpster if necessary to find the package he was sure waited for him there. But he hoped he could keep his suit clean, especially since his plan called for him to present himself in a professional way when he got to the tower. He lifted the lid of the dumpster on the right side and looked inside.

Apparently, it had been emptied just that morning, which relieved him. But that also made him worry that perhaps he'd missed the package. He went to the right side and lifted the lid there.

A long, wide, flat board had become jammed between the front and back of the dumpster. Harris reached down and jerked it free. Beneath the board, pressed against the bottom of the dumpster, was the package.

It was wrapped in brown paper, about the size of a toaster, and was a bit dusty, but surprisingly intact considering that it had been covered with other refuse just this morning. Harris reached into the dumpster and pulled it out.

He debated as to whether he should open the package or not, and decided to do it, more because whatever it was would look better than presented in a soiled, brown-paper package. Harris unwrapped the package, and looked at a well-used silver-plated snub-nosed revolver encased in Plexiglas, complete with bullets.

He was ready to confront Universal once again.

19 INVISIBLE

Harris felt completely calm as he stepped through the front doors of the Universal Tower. He thought back to that day more than two years ago when he entered the Pan-Pacific Hotel, and how frightened he was then. Time, experience, and a deeper relationship with God had changed all of that. Now Harris had committed himself to the task ahead, and knew how Japanese *kamakazi* pilots must have felt toward the end of World War II.

The massive building opened up before him. The entryway was at street level, with about 20 feet between the doors and a line of security checkpoints. Beyond that, the floor dropped into an atrium area with a ceiling that stretched 50 floors up. A full orchestra was playing in the waiting area below, and he could see live trees, rock formations and waterfalls beyond. Even some birds flew by in the cavernous atmosphere. Harris stood in a line behind several other people leading up to the security gate. He was glad he decided to wear the new pinstriped suit. Rather than standing out, it made him fit in with the crowd headed to the gala event he knew was just beginning upstairs.

The trick to being invisible is to become one with the environment, Elijah had told him in prison. That meant that in a place like this, you wanted to look like you just stepped out of a Fortune 500 executive suite. Harris looked at all the beautiful people in their gorgeous clothes, and felt pity for them. Great clothes couldn't make up for a corrupt soul.

He stepped up to the security desk. Three guards in uniform checked everyone coming in. "Do you have any metal on you that we should know about?" one of them asked.

"Just this," Harris said, pulling the Plexiglas case with the revolver inside out and laying it before the officer. His eyes opened wide when he saw the gun, then he looked up at Harris.

"I have an appointment with Mr. Deke at 5 p.m."

It impressed Harris that the officers were disciplined enough that they did not see the gun as an immediate threat, especially since he presented it voluntarily. Nevertheless, two of the officers left the table and circled around behind him. The third sat where he was and looked up at him suspiciously.

"Your name, please," he asked.

"Elijah Brown," Harris responded. "The appointment was made quite a while ago by a Ms. Heidi Hilfinger."

The guard's eyebrows came up, then he saw someone start to walk by.

"Ms. Hilfinger," he shouted to someone walking out the door. A tall blonde woman, barely in her twenties, turned and looked at him. The guard gestured at Harris, and she approached. She looked at Harris as if she was trying to remember him, but couldn't. Harris, in turn, had never seen her before in his life, but pretended that he had.

"This man says he has an appointment with Mr. Deke at 5 p.m. An Elijah Brown?"

Heidi's blank stare made Harris think he was lost. But then she looked down at the revolver, and a wave of recognition took over. Harris saw her lips move as she read the serial number on the side of the revolver's barrel.

"I brought it, just as you wanted," Harris said. "Sorry it took so long for us to connect."

220

She looked at the gun, then at the officer, a look of amazement on her face. "This is it. This is the actual gun Jack Ruby used to shoot Lee Harvey Oswald." She looked at the gun, then at Harris. She cleared her throat.

"Uh, Mr. Brown, this is just plain bad timing," she said, obviously torn between two duties. "We are having an important meeting here tonight. Any chance of us rescheduling for, say, tomorrow?"

Harris shook his head. "I have other obligations tomorrow. I understand if your client is not interested in the gun. But that's not a problem. I'm sure other clients will be interested—." Harris reached out as if to take the case and walk away.

"No!" she exclaimed. "Mr. Deke would fire me—or worse—if he knew that this gun got away. I'll work something out." She gestured for Harris to come past the security barricade and down the steps into the lobby area. They walked across the sunken floor, past the orchestra and the waterfall and palm trees to the elevator doors. Harris carried the gun in its case under his arm.

"I'll take you to Mr. Deke's office on the 45th floor," she turned to tell Harris. "I'll need to escort you up there—security is pretty tight—but I'll make sure you get there OK."

Harris smiled back at her. "I appreciate your special attention."

* * *

"He's here," the deep voice said behind Deke. Preoccupied with his speech scheduled for later tonight, Deke turned without understanding and looked in the direction of the voice. It took a moment before he realized who the voice referred to.

"Here?" Deke said finally. "That's impossible."

"He is in the building."

Deke nodded, then lifted the receiver on his desk phone and punched a button. "Borden's in the building. All guards in the hallways. No, we have guests still arriving, so we can't go to lockdown yet. But I want all eyes and ears open. The man must be stopped—at all costs."

Deke stepped out of his office and walked quickly down the hall to the security office. There were actually two security offices; on the main floor, where people were usually sent for interrogation and where officers were headquartered. The second, on the 45th floor, took the place of Whiting's "batcave" in the old building. From it, Deke could see practically every inch of the building's interior—and exterior. The only exceptions included sensitive areas of his own office.

He stepped into the darkened command center and quickly scanned the large wall of monitors. Critics called the Jade Tower a technological marvel, but few realized how dependent the Tower was on technology. Deke had gasped when Whiting had presented him with the price tag for his new security system, but now he was glad the monitors, lasers and heat sensors were all in place and activated.

The wall was a solid bank of 50 monitors. However, with over 1,000 security cameras throughout the building, each camera had to take its turn to be automatically rotated through a monitor. The Cray supercomputer also had programming that allowed it to focus in on suspicious activities and call them to the attention of the five officers who scanned the monitors for trouble.

"How do you know he's here?" asked the supervisor in charge.

"I know," Deke answered simply.

"Well, if he's here, we'll see him sooner or later," the super said.

Sooner than later, I hope, Deke thought.

A minute later, a security guard brought Deke the phone. It was Heidi.

"Sir, I was escorting a man up to your office—someone named Elijah Brown—he had, I swear it was the actual one, I couldn't believe it. But I looked at the serial numbers and double checked them myself...."

"Slow down, Heidi," Deke said. "What happened?"

"He got away from me, Sir. I turned around and he was gone. I think it's him."

"OK, thanks, Heidi."

"And sir," she continued. "He has a gun."

"Right," Deke said, hanging up. He turned to his security supervisor. "Remind me to kill that inept broad."

"There he is," an officer in the first seat said. "Hallway E-28, 14th floor."

"What would he be doing on the 14th floor?" the supervisor asked.

"Send three guards down to eliminate him," Deke said.

"Already on their way." As if on cue, one monitor showed elevator doors open and three armed men enter with guns drawn. They rushed down an empty hallway to the end, then looked around, confused.

"He's not here," they reported.

"There," an officer pointed at another monitor. "21st Floor, west wing."

"How could he get from the 14th to the 21st floor in less than a minute?" Deke asked. "Something is wrong here. Call Whiting in to check it out."

Deke turned to go, and heard someone else call out. "He's on the 50th floor!"

He hesitated, then turned to go. Let them chase ghosts. He had work to do.

* * *

Greg Phipps opened the door and let another elderly couple in the front door of the church. The sanctuary was filled to overflowing, with not only every church member there, but quite a few visitors as well. Last night's prayer meeting had been busy, but when he'd told the group of his phone call regarding Harris Borden, it had turned into a marathon prayer session. He'd gone home a couple of times to get a few hours' sleep and eat a couple of times, but every time he returned, the group praying was a little bigger.

He shook his head. He'd never seen anything like this. Correct that: he'd never seen anything like this in North America. In the mission field, twice he'd seen such a passionate outpouring by a congregation. Both times it had resulted in both a revival in the church and miracles in people's lives.

He continued to pray that another miracle—a big one—would happen in Harris Borden's life.

* * *

Kenneth Deke's cell phone chirped. He flipped it open and spoke, his eyes continuing to scan the crowd in Ballroom A on the 50th floor. The orchestra was going, people were laughing, and the champagne was flowing freely. Were it not for Borden, Deke would feel that everything was running smoothly.

"Deke here," he barked.

"Front door security," the voice said in the phone. "Everyone on the list is accounted for and sent upstairs."

"OK, we are going to lockdown mode in five minutes," Deke said. *Once everyone was in the room, with armed guards inside as well, there'd be no place for Borden to go. If he is inside, the guards will kill him and no one will complain. If he's outside, then Baal will take care of him.* He thought of the idea that Whiting had shared and Baal had agreed on, and the hair stood up on the nape of his neck. *Demons roaming the hallways of my tower. I'd hate to be Borden,* he thought, and was glad that he had a mutual understanding with Baal.

As he talked on the phone, he saw a man in a tuxedo with a scar on his neck. He realized that Borden could be in this very room. With this many people here, it would be relatively easy to avoid detection, while posing a grave security risk.

He watched the man wade through the crowd and disappear. Deke switched off his phone and followed the man.

* * *

It wasn't hard to evade Heidi. When she turned to push the elevator button, Harris took a step and disappeared in the crowd that ebbed and flowed in the lobby. By the time she had turned back to him, he was gone.

Harris also had no problems losing the three guards who thought they knew where he was. A few tricks with the security cameras had everyone confused. He chuckled to himself, imagining what pandemonium the control room must be in right now.

"Greetings, my friend," he heard beside him, and Harris almost jumped. Harris was on the 44th floor, standing in the hallway just behind the elevator bank. He turned to see The Messenger, as he'd appeared over Mount Carmel. He held a flaming sword and wore a breastplate and leggings of high-polished silver.

"Hi," Harris said, glad to see someone who was a definite ally. "Good to know I have help here."

"You just have to do what God asks, and your path will be clear," he said. "I, on the other hand, have a different task at hand. Remember the vision from Mount Carmel?"

Harris nodded, and for a second remembered the angels flying in combat around Mount Carmel as Elijah faced the priests of Baal. He suddenly felt more alone.

"You're taking on the demons," Harris responded.

He nodded. "We're vastly outnumbered, but your fellow Christians are praying for you. That will strengthen us for a while, enough for you to do the task you have to do. The demons are after you. We'll protect you. Just complete it as quickly as you can."

"Believe me, I don't want to hang around here any longer than I have to."

The Messenger flew down the hall, massive wings flapping, followed by row after row of bright warriors.

"Go get 'em, guys," Harris whispered.

One of the warriors turned and smiled at him, right before they each transformed into globes of flying flame.

* * *

Deke's cell phone chirped again. The man he'd followed had turned out to be a major stockholder, so he'd let him go. The ballroom was full, with some people out on the balconies as well. It was time to get serious.

Deke had called for the lockdown to begin, then realized that he'd left his script on the desk in his office. He hurried out the doors and rushed to the elevator bank in hopes of getting to his office and back to the ballroom before lockdown. After fighting the crowd for several minutes, he'd resorted to the stairwell, running down the five flights of stairs to his office. Just as he'd entered his office he heard the computerized voice announce: "Lockdown is now in effect," followed by the metallic clank of hundreds of deadbolts falling into place. He was now a prisoner in his own office.

Whiting was on the cell. "Is he here?" he asked.

"Yeah," Deke responded. "Where are you?"

"In the control center debugging stuff. You in the ballroom?"

"I was. I came back to the office to get my speech, and got caught by the lockdown. Is there anything you can do?"

"Kinda hard to get you from here to there in time for your speech, but let me see what I can do. I can probably free up this floor at least. I need to get back to computer central anyway. In the meantime, why not speak from your office?"

"What do you mean? I don't have cameras in my office."

"You do," Whiting said. "They're just deactivated. I can reactivate them from here, and you can do your speech sitting behind your desk. It'll look stately. Besides, the other sites will be seeing you on video anyway. You can argue that it puts everyone on the same level."

Deke thought about it. "All right, how long will it take to set up? I have my speech in ten minutes."

"I'll be ready in five," Whiting said, then hung up.

* * *

The noise level in the grand ballroom continued at a dull roar. All the tables were full, and many people were rubbing shoulders around the edges of the room as well as out on the balcony. Despite the misty rain, it was a great night to enjoy the San Francisco skyline and the city lights.

Suddenly the lights began to dim and a large screen dropped from the ceiling in one end of the room. A projection system turned on and the smiling face of Kenneth Deke appeared. The room burst into applause.

Deke nodded in response to their heartfelt gratitude. "Thank you, my friends. We have lots to be grateful for. It's been a fantastic year. I want to take this opportunity to thank—." His words were cut off as Deke glanced up at the opposite end of the room where he was, and a look of panic came over him.

The scene switched to the camera on the opposite side of the room. It showed Deke from a distance. In the foreground, walking slowly toward Deke, was a man in a blue pinstriped suit and a scar running down his neck. In his hand he held a revolver pointed at Deke.

Men gasped, women screamed, and one waiter dropped his tray of drinks. Every eye was on the drama unfolding in front of them.

* * *

This isn't happening, Deke thought. *How could he have gotten in here?*

"Hello again," Borden said quietly. "Remember me?" Deke said nothing, but watched the haunting figure, his nemesis, as Borden slowly approached him.

"The last time we met I believe you held the gun and I was the one that had nothing to say." Deke stared at the .38 that Borden held.

"You'll never get out of here," Deke breathed finally.

"Why would I want to get out of here?" Borden said. "It took me too much effort to get in."

"What do you want?" Deke asked. *That's a stupid question to ask*, he thought.

"Me? I don't *want* anything. What I want, you can't give me. What I'm here for is to deliver a message. And that is, your time is up. God has given you ample warning. Tonight is the night you die."

Deke wet his dry lips and looked down at the snub-nosed revolver that was pointed at him. That barrel looked awfully big.

* * *

"Hey, that's the Jack Ruby gun," Heidi said from the ballroom, looking up at Borden and Deke on the screen. "He'd better not pull the trigger. It'll lower the resale value significantly."

The people around her turned and looked at her as if she were insane.

"Well, it will!" she said.

* * *

"Any last words for your international audience?" Borden said, cocking the revolver, raising it to aim at Deke's face.

Deke suddenly realized that all the wealth and power he'd accumulated couldn't help him. He had important allies in government, in business, even in the military, but none of them could help him stay alive. And Deke realized he very much wanted to stay alive.

His knees began to shake as he stared at the gun. *Why hadn't Baal intervened?* He felt his knees collapse beneath him, and he knelt before Borden.

"I take it all back," he sobbed. "It's all been a sham. I've killed people, robbed millions, cheated, lied, swindled. I was wrong, and I would give up all the money, all the power in the world, just for one thing. I want to live!"

"What about Baal?"

"He gave me power, but where is he now? Is he keeping me alive? I renounce him if doing so will keep me alive. Don't shoot me!"

"You renounce Baal?"

"I spit on Baal. I regret the day that I began to worship him. I wish that I'd never heard of that demon!"

* * *

Time to go, God's voice told Harris. *Put the gun down.*

* * *

Harris held the gun at arm's length for a long minute, then uncocked the hammer and lay it down on the desk in front of Deke.

"That's all I wanted to hear," Harris said, smiling.

Deke realized what he had done. Roaring, he snatched up the revolver and thrust it at Borden, pulling the trigger. The gun clicked harmlessly. He looked at the gun, then pulled the hammer back and tried again. Click.

Borden shrugged. "I removed the firing pin. I never had much use for guns."

Deke turned and grabbed a Beretta automatic off the wall behind him. He slammed a clip into the handle and pulled the action back, chambering a round. *I know this one works.* He turned to fire at Borden, and faced an empty room.

At least it looked empty. Beyond, on the far wall, the dull red glow was growing, and a growling sound grew.

Deke would have to face the wrath of Baal.

20 REDEMPTION

As Harris had learned the hard way, God knows what He's doing. One doesn't always know why at the moment, which is the situation he was in at the time, but it always seemed to work out. Harris didn't know the logic of putting the gun down and walking away, but he was glad to get out of there.

In addition to having the pleasure of thrusting a gun into Deke's face, he sensed a second presence in the office with them. Harris had a good idea who or what it was, but it was one of those situations where he'd rather not think about it. All he knew was that whatever it was would probably be hopping mad when he left. And in that situation, Harris was ready to put distance between him and it. Let Deke deal with his own demons, pun intended.

Harris bolted out of Deke's office and through the secretary's office and waiting room into an empty hallway. He knew that Deke had been trying to get out of his office just before he interrupted him, and he assumed that someone—probably Whiting—was working on freeing up the locks on this level. Harris had Deke, his guards, and a legion of demons after him. The sooner Harris got gone, the better. The Messenger had told him that the demons would be coming after him, but that his forces would defend Harris when it became necessary. Harris paused to try to remember which way was out, and then ran north along the corridor.

He heard an unearthly roar behind him, from Deke's office. *Poor guy has his hands busy now.* Harris continued north, then paused as he realized that the next door to the right was the security office, their command center. As Harris stood looking at it, Ed Whiting came out the door. Harris started to fade into the shadows, then realized that Ed might be able to help him get out.

Whiting took a step out the door, then stopped in his tracks when he saw Harris. Whiting jerked his head, gesturing for Harris to follow him, and continued north down the hallway. Harris slipped past the security door and followed.

Whiting closed the door behind him as Harris followed him into his office. He had a small, unremarkable work area littered with empty Mt. Dew cans and cappuccino paper cups as well as computer printouts.

"Nice décor," Harris said.

Whiting shrugged. "Cleaning lady's day off, sorry." He looked at Harris, shaven and in a new suit. "I almost didn't recognize you."

"I gotta get out of here," Harris hissed at him.

"That you do," Whiting said. "The deadbolts for this floor have been retracted, but it will be another 45 minutes before the lockdown is completely over throughout the building. You can access the elevator, but it won't work. You'll have to hit the stairwell, but…."

Harris nodded. "I know about your demons. I have a plan for them."

Whiting looked at Harris, obviously impressed. "You *are* prepared."

"I'm on a mission from God." Harris winked at him.

"Right," Whiting said. "One more thing."

"Yes?"

He stared at Harris, suddenly very serious and near tears. "Is it too late for me? Can I still be saved?"

Harris smiled. "It's never too late. I'd talk more about it—."

"I understand."

"But I do think we have time for a prayer." Harris bowed his head and prayed with Ed Whiting. Harris led him in asking for forgiveness and letting Jesus into his heart. When Harris opened his eyes, Whiting was crying. Harris hugged him.

"Come with me," Harris said. "You know this place better than anyone."

Whiting shook his head. "Those demons would tear me apart. Besides, I still need to undo as much damage as I can." Whiting hit him open-handed on the shoulder, then slipped into the door that went to the main computer area.

Harris watched him for a long second, then slipped back out the door. Immediately, a hand of white light pushed him back against the wall. Harris looked out into the middle of a fierce sword-and-fist battle between white angels and red and black demons. The angels were holding their own, but the demons continued to swarm forward, trying to get past them. The Messenger's hand held Harris against the wall, as the battle continued. Then the tide surged down the hallway and the bright angels followed the demons, and he released Harris.

"The elevators don't work," The Messenger said, turning to Harris.

"I'll have to take the stairs," Harris told him. "Can you clear the way for me?"

The Messenger nodded. "We will do our best. It has been a long while since we've met these particular demons in open battle. They are fierce, and there are many of them, but we will prevail."

"Just hold them long enough for me to get clear," Harris said.

"Wait a few seconds, then follow," he said. The bright angel turned and flew down the hall and through the door of marked stairs. Harris counted to twenty, then followed him.

When Harris had been in The Hole, God had told him that He had another gift for Harris. He realized now that it was the ability to actually see both sides of a spiritual conflict. Harris had seen good and bad angels before—in The Messenger's memory of Mount Carmel and in his dream— but it had never been in real life. He wondered if seeing the actual evil that threatened man constantly was truly a gift.

Harris opened the door to the stairwell and looked down the lit hole. He could hear battle between angels going on beneath him. Harris whispered a prayer and took his first steps down the stairs.

* * *

Even before Kenneth Deke had asked Ed Whiting to develop the database and support software for Universal Finance, Whiting had a personal backup plan in mind should things go bad. Universal had made him rich, so rich that he never needed to look at another bill in his life. But he'd been constantly dogged by the belief that what they were doing was wrong. The credit card scam had ruined the lives of millions of people. Now Universal was expanding in a dozen different directions. Secretly, Whiting had wanted out, but he knew that one didn't simply walk away from a corporation that was owned by a demon like Baal.

When his father had died, he started thinking less about his own survival and more about what was right. He was amazed by how the assurance of salvation had changed his father. In the few days between his father's conversion and his death, Whiting had seen him become a totally different man. His father had abused him emotionally and physically as a child, and they'd never been close. After the conversion, he had the first meaningful, heartfelt conversation with his father that he could remember.

His visit with Borden earlier in Starbucks and then tonight had gradually made him realize that there were more important things in life than wealth and power—even than being alive. He knew he had no chance of staying alive anywhere in the world once he had double-crossed Baal, Deke and Universal. But he made the decision to do it anyway.

The Cray room was empty; it usually was this late at night. Whiting didn't have any life beyond these walls, so he was in here pretty much every evening. He stepped to the main terminal and entered his user name and password.

He slipped a mini-DVD from his shirt pocket. It was marked "Redemption" with a black laundry pen. He popped it into the drive and gave the command to copy to the main drive.

"Has Borden been in here?" a voice shouted from behind him. He turned and saw one of the security officers from the command center standing at the door. Startled by the interruption, Whiting didn't respond for a second. Then he simply pointed down the hall. The guard nodded and ran in that direction.

Whiting looked down at his shaking hands. Somewhere in their lives, all hard-core programmers brag about plans to do something this daring somewhere along the line. But a huge rift existed between talking and doing, Whiting now realized. He looked at the screen, with a cursor that blinked one word: *Confirm?* This was the point of no return.

He hit the Y button and pressed enter. Line after line of code scrolled across the screen from top to bottom. Whiting knew that within three minutes the entire supercomputer would be in total meltdown.

* * *

"Hold it right there," Harris heard behind him. He had one foot raised, ready to go down the stairwell. He'd been so focused on the demons that waited for him below that he hadn't considered human opposition.

"Turn around slowly," the man said. Harris turned. The security guard had been joined by a second coming in the doorway.

"What are you doing? Deke said to kill him," the newcomer said.

"I got it," the man in front said. He was being extremely careful and didn't take his eyes off Harris. "Now take your hands out of your pockets slowly and raise them."

He'd caught Harris with one hand in his outside coat pocket. Harris completed his turn and raised his hands. What he didn't know was that in Harris' hand was some of the exploding powder he had made at the chemist's shop in Chinatown. Harris suddenly threw the powder at their feet. The magnesium in the powder flashed, startling them and blinding them at the same time. The guard's gun went off, with the bullet flying past Harris. By the time they had recovered from the flash, Harris was gone.

He continued down the stairwell, the sound of guards above him and the sound of angelic battle going on below him. Harris stopped on the 41st floor and looked up the center of the stairwell to see how far behind his pursuers were. Suddenly the doors to that floor blew open. Someone had used Semtex to circumvent the lockdown. The blast threw him against the stairs and he lay there for a minute, stunned. The smoke cleared and Harris looked up to see a guard with a shotgun aimed at him. A few seconds later, the two guards from above joined him.

"Waste him," one of the guards from above said to the one holding the shotgun. In response, all lights in the stairwell and the hallway behind the guard went black.

Harris leaped to his feet in the darkness and wrestled with the guard for the shotgun. It went off, aimed at the ceiling. Harris pushed him down and ran past him onto the 41st floor.

* * *

All through the Jade Tower, power was systematically shut down. Further, backup generators did not function either. Lights went off throughout the building, the air conditioner shut down, the security cameras shut off, lasers and heat detectors switched off. But the deadbolts remained in place, and only Whiting knew how to unlock them. The only place where power still existed was in the Cray room where Ed Whiting sat at his console. He watched as a monitor signaled the death of the Jade Tower.

Whiting knew, however, that the obvious effects of the virus he'd uploaded to the Cray were not the most important. Power would eventually be restored, and those who worked here or were partying upstairs would go on their merry way. But much more significant was the destruction of the database containing the names, addresses and account information of millions of Universal Finance customers, as well as the software program Whiting himself had created for the corporation. Without that important piece of software, Universal Finance was worthless. The Tower was just a pretty face, the people who worked here were the hands and feet of Universal, but the software was the brains of the beast. Without it, Universal was a babbling idiot.

He sat back in his chair and waited for the real fireworks to start.

* * *

Heidi Hilfinger knew that something was happening, but wasn't sure what it was. She'd been with the crowd in the ballroom when the drama had unfolded between Mr. Deke and the man with the gun. She watched the guards talk constantly on their radios to each other. Despite officially being considered part of middle management and having an office on the 44th floor—not upper crust, but close—she had duties that didn't involve anyone other that Mr. Deke. She knew nothing of banking, management or political intrigue. Her job consisted of shopping around the world for rare artifacts, including handguns for Mr. Deke's collection. That's all she knew. And for once, she was glad for that.

A lot of nasty stuff was going on, that was for sure. What was funny was that after Mr. Deke's short presentation on camera, almost everyone went back to the drinking, dancing and dining. It was still early, but she could see some of the more senior members of the cabal acting very drunk. Twice the security had to run out to the balcony and rescue someone who had almost fallen off. This was going to be a very interesting, very unusual evening.

As if in response to that thought, suddenly the room went dark. The room had gotten close for her, so she stood near the air duct at the side wall. She realized that the air conditioning had shut down too. She waited for the auxiliary generator to kick in, but after 30 seconds realized that it was off as well. A dim light from the cityscape shone into the room from the doors that were opened to the two balconies, and people began to crowd toward the doors. Before long she realized that anyone on the balcony had a good chance of being forced off by the action of the crowd and falling to their deaths 50 floors below.

"Just breathe," she told herself, and waited for someone to speak up.

"Everyone just calm down," a security officer finally said from the stage. The mikes didn't work either, so it was good he had a strong voice.

"Security officers have flashlights, and we'll use these, but we need to reserve the batteries as much as we can. In the meantime, please stay calm."

Despite his words, a panic began to spread. People didn't like standing in the dark, especially when ventilation had been shut off. Even the open balcony doors didn't seem to air out the room. Heidi felt as if the oxygen was purposely being removed from the room.

A bright light appear on the other side of the room, and every eye turned that direction. An old man had pulled out his Zippo to light a cigar. Men and women were drawn to the flame like moths.

"Hey!" the man said. "Quit crowding!" But the crowd continued to press in the direction of the flame. Someone hit his arm. The lighter flew from his grasp, covering the room in darkness. A sigh of despair flooded the room. Five seconds later, a curtain on the other side of the old man burst into flame, with fire racing from floor to ceiling. The sigh became a scream.

"Fire! Fire!" the cry went out. The tide of humanity pushed the opposite direction now, toward the balconies again. Several people were pushed out the doors and out of sight. Heidi wondered if they were still on the balconies or had gone over the edge.

Security guards entered the ballroom with fire extinguishers, and pressed forward to put out the fire, but the crowd was thick and panicked. By the time they got to the site of the fire, it had spread to other curtains, tablecloths and a tapestry that covered half the wall. Heidi realized that within a few minutes the entire room would be engulfed in flames. She looked up at the fire sprinklers on the ceiling.

"Why haven't they gone off?" she asked out loud. She pulled out her cell phone and dialed Deke's number. It rang several times before going to voice mail. There was no help coming from outside.

Meanwhile she watched as the panicked crowd began pushing each other off of the balconies to their deaths.

21 THE WRATH OF GOD

"What in the name of heaven and earth are you doing?" Deke screamed at Whiting. Ed turned and looked at the executive standing in the door of the Cray room. *He looks smaller*, was Ed's first reaction. The red and blue light from the computer room illuminated Deke's already apoplectic face, with total blackness framing him from behind.

"Hi, Kenny," Whiting said calmly. "How's it going?"

"Going?" Deke responded at the top of his voice. "Going? The whole world is falling down around my ankles. Borden is loose again, the building is in a stranglehold with this lockdown of yours, and on top of that, I totally humiliated Baal on planet-wide TV."

"You shouldn't do that," Whiting said, his voice never rising. "He'll get mad."

"What are you on?" Deke said, slapping Whiting. "You smoking crack? We have a crisis here."

Whiting put his hand to his face and rubbed it. "Calm down, Kenny. As usual, I've solved the crisis."

Deke stared at him, and relief came to his face. "You did? Bless you, Ed. You always come through for me. I guess I shouldn't have panicked."

Whiting shrugged. "It's what I do." He turned back toward the monitor, and Deke watched over his shoulder.

"What are we looking at, Ed?"

Ed pointed at the charts on the oversized monitors. "This indicates that power is off throughout the building. That includes lights, ventilation, security cameras—everything but the lockdown system. That's still in place everywhere but on this level."

Deke blinked. "Oh-kay, so what's the plan?"

"Well, that's not all. This line," Whiting pointed again at the screen. "Shows that the Cray has been infected with a serious virus that is corrupting the hard drive. By now, everything on the main drive and the backup should be destroyed. And I mean totally destroyed—so bad that it can't be recovered."

Deke stared at him, not sure how to react.

Whiting smiled, realizing that Deke didn't understand him.

"Do you understand what I am saying, Kenny? I purposely destroyed all the account files, and all the management software for all of Universal Finance. We're out of business, buddy!" He chuckled and slapped Deke on the back.

"Fix it," Deke whispered.

"What?" Whiting said, leaning forward.

Deke pulled out his Beretta from the inside coat pocket and aimed it at Whiting's face.

"Fix it, I said! Fix it! Fix it!" He screamed at Whiting, the spittle flying from his mouth, his face twisted in rage. Whiting realized that he was losing it very quickly.

"Calm down, Kenny. Calm down. I can't fix it. But we can start over, and this time we'll do it right. Ethically. Without hurting families—."

Whiting's words were cut off as the Beretta fired three times into his face. Blood and bone spattered over the monitors behind him.

Kenneth Deke looked down at the still body of his friend. Everything they had done since they had been in college, they'd done together. Deke was the face of Universal, but Ed Whiting had been the brains. Deke felt as if a 100-ton freight train were charging toward him, and he couldn't move. It was only a matter of time before....

His thought was broken by a chirp from his cell phone. He looked down and saw that he had three calls from Heidi, as well as several from security in the ballroom. He called security first, but no one answered. Finally, he called Heidi.

"You've got to get us out of here!" Heidi screamed even before he said his name. "The whole place is on fire."

"Have you tried the fire extinguishers?" Deke asked. "What about the sprinklers?"

"The extinguishers were used first. Now they're empty." Deke heard her coughing, and screaming and crying behind her. "Nothing else works. Not the sprinklers, not the doors. Deke, people are jumping off the balconies. We're 50 stories up! They're jumping to their deaths rather than burn!"

"I'll get security up there to blast the doors open," Deke said calmly, but he had his doubts about what was possible.

"I called command central, but no one's there," she said, coughing again. Deke remembered that he had sent all of them after Harris Borden. "Besides, every door is dead bolted. I called the San Francisco Fire Department, and they said they were on their way, but they can't get through either.

"What idiot came up with this idea for a security system?" she asked. "These people are going to die."

"That idiot is dead," Deke said quietly, looking at Whiting's body, then thought, *and he's the only one who could have opened the doors.*

"Deke," she said, her voice much weaker now. "Deke, we're dying. We're dying."

Kenneth Deke listened without saying anything. Finally he shut his cell phone off and put it in his pocket. He had run out of things to say.

* * *

After the lights went off, Harris leaped past the guard with the shotgun and entered the office area of the 41st floor. Spending a month in The Hole had taught his eyes to see well in the dark.

He saw that this floor was where many of their entry-level accountants were located. Where he'd seen luxurious office suites higher up he now saw relatively plain cubicles around the outside perimeter of the floor. The interior consisted of a secretarial pool, with offices back to back and shoulder to shoulder through the main portion of the central room. Harris was glad that this floor consisted of open offices, since that meant that no interior doors would be dead-bolted here. Beyond that, he saw the open atrium in the center of the room. Smoke and ash drifted down from above, and he realized that something was burning. Harris imagined that he could hear people screaming somewhere in the distance.

His reverie was broken as a flashlight beam caught him standing by the atrium edge. He leaped just as a shotgun blast came past him. A few pellets hit his arm, and he gritted his teeth against the pain. Harris collapsed behind a potted palm and crawled toward a cubicle. The flashlight beams criss-crossed through the empty part of the room, and slowly crept his direction. He could hear the three guards talking.

"He's got no gun and there are three of us," one said. "This should be pretty simple."

"But did you see him *move*," the other said. "Like a friggin' ninja."

"Ninja or no, I—." Their words were interrupted by screaming. Harris saw a massive black shape grab one and throw him across the room. The demon smacked a second, even as the shotgun went off. The third leaped away from the demon and down into the atrium. Harris could hear him scream as he fell 41 stories to his death.

The demon stamped on the guard again for good measure, then turned toward Harris. It was immense, and perhaps the ugliest thing he'd ever seen. Harris knew it saw him, so he stood to face it.

"Lord, now would be a good time to come to my rescue," he breathed.

The demon charged Harris with incredible speed, and closed the distance between them in seconds. It reached for him…

…and instead, its claws closed on the form of The Messenger, who appeared through the floor beneath them. The brilliant angel soared upward through the giant demon, slashing it with a fiery sword from bottom to top. It screamed in agony, and jerked backward. Its form vanished, and The Messenger turned to Harris.

"He won't be back any time soon," he said, sheathing his sword.

"Thanks," Harris breathed. He looked up at the ash and smoke in the atrium. "There's a fire somewhere."

"God's wrath," The Messenger said, looking up. "That is what people call it, but it's actually just stupidity. The 50th floor is burning."

Harris blinked. "Isn't there anything you can do to save the people there?"

He shook his head. "They're living with the consequences of their actions. They've removed themselves from God's protection." He looked up again. "We won't intervene." The angel shook his head again, sadly, and Harris could see that he wished he could go up there and help. Finally, he turned back to Harris.

"We're almost free, but there's too much combat on the stairwell. You can't go down that way."

Harris looked at the elevator shaft. "Well, unless you know how to fix the elevators, I've run out of ideas."

The Messenger looked at Harris, then at the atrium. "I have one," he said.

Harris looked at him, then at the giant hole that led to a 41-story drop. *Oh, no*, he thought. *You just saw someone fall to their death that way seconds ago.* He looked back at The Messenger and wondered if his face was as white as he suspected it was. Next to small places, his worst fear was high places.

Harris took a deep breath. "You'll be at the bottom with a safety net or a bed of feathers, won't you?"

The Messenger smiled. "Trust me. I've been protecting people like you for a long time."

Harris had been reasonably calm through the entire visit to the Jade Tower. Now his pulse was beating quickly, and his heart was in his throat. Harris felt his knees knocking together as he stepped up onto the railing that surrounded the hole in the middle of the room. Below he could see people walking on the ground floor like ants.

Harris looked back at The Messenger, then nodded quickly.

"When you're ready to fall, just take a step forward."

Harris tried not to think, but have faith. *Catch me, Lord*, he prayed silently.

He took a step forward, and felt nothing but air beneath him.

* * *

Kenneth Deke had run out of options. The fire roared uncontrolled in the locked ballroom upstairs, with everyone dead or dying. The database and software that were the foundation of Universal Finance had been destroyed. And he had shot and killed his partner and only long-time friend for causing this disaster.

He stared out the window of his office at the San Francisco skyline. The continuing fog blurred the city lights, but it was still beautiful. He knew that he'd never see anything quite so beautiful again. He took the cell phone in his pocket and threw it on the floor. Everyone likely to call him on that device was dead by now.

He looked around at his immense, spectacular office. He'd planned it for a long time, putting concentrated thought into each and every detail. The handgun collection was one of the best in the world. The relics on the opposite wall were the envy of every museum of history. He had money beyond the dreams of many a billionaire. He had power, influence, prestige. And now it was over.

He'd always been a gambler. He'd learned of the power of Baal and the Brotherhood of the Altar from his father, who had belonged for many years and kept it secret. They had wanted to go into business, and Kenneth Deke had been willing to work with them to establish this corporation. He knew that Universal may have lost their credit card company, the foundation of their enterprises. But they had diversified and now were established in so many industries that the disaster he had witnessed tonight would never be repeated.

Nevertheless, someone would have to pay the price for tonight, and he knew it would be him. He reached into his top drawer and pulled out a pack of cigarettes. He put one in his mouth and lit it.

"Didn't you quit smoking years ago?" the deep voice said.

Deke shrugged. "I heard it was bad for your health. Now it doesn't seem to make much difference."

"I guess you know that I am disappointed."

"Disappointed is not the word I would have used, but yes." Deke inhaled and blew out the smoke. "Yep, this was one messed-up enterprise." He stared out the window.

"I will say that you're being very civil about the whole affair," Deke said. "I've heard stories."

"Those are just stories," the voice said. "They were made to scare children. You have been a good servant to me, so it only right that I be civil to you."

Deke turned and stared at the altar at the end of the room. He dropped his burning cigarette on the Persian rug below him and mashed it out with his foot.

"But I still have to pay for failure."

"That is true," Baal said.

"Do I want to know what you're going to do to me?" Deke asked.

"I doubt it."

Deke took another look around his office, then shrugged.

"Let's get it over with."

The last sound Kenneth Deke heard was his own screaming.

* * *

Harris wished he could remember the trip down. It would have been pretty cool to tell his grandchildren what it was like to fall 41 stories inside a building and survive. But the honest truth was that he passed out. Harris woke up on the ground floor, lying in a gigantic flower bed, with fire fighters running past him on their way up the stairwell.

"Take it slow!" Harris shouted behind them, but they ignored him. "It's a long way up to the 50th floor," he finished to himself. He looked down at himself, wondering how his new suit had fared after a long night of dodging bullets and demons. He was surprised to see that it was relatively unscathed, with the exception of his left arm, which had caught a couple of pellets from the shotgun blast.

Harris brushed himself off, stepped out of the planter, and walked slowly out the door. He wondered for a while if he was invisible, for no one even stopped to look at him. They were all concerned with the fire on the 50th floor. He felt sorry for those people in the ballroom, then shrugged. What The Messenger said was true. How can you expect mercy from God when you reject Him and all He stands for? He is a merciful God, but He also respects freedom of choice. They had made their choice, and now they were dying by it.

Harris walked out the entrance to the Jade Tower, glad that he'd never have to enter this edifice again. He walked into the mist and stood in the shadow of a neighboring building as he watched the 50th floor burn. He was wondering whether he should go try to find a late-night diner when he realized he wasn't alone.

"You look content with yourself," The Messenger said, this time taking the form of a middle-aged black woman, dressed in a long raincoat and holding an umbrella.

Harris looked at him. "Shouldn't I be? We won, didn't we? You did win in there, didn't you?"

The Messenger looked down. "We measure wins and losses differently than you do."

"Come on. Did the good guys win in there or not?"

He looked at Harris and nodded. "Yes. We won."

Harris chuckled and started to turn away. The Messenger grabbed his shoulder to get his attention. Harris looked back at him.

"You do understand that the war is far from over. Universal Finance is destroyed, Deke is gone, but there is more to be done. Universal has diversified and Baal is still active. In a short while he'll be more powerful than ever."

Harris stared at him, suddenly grim. "So what are you saying?"

The Messenger stared into his eyes.

"The war between good and evil won't be over until the Second Coming," he said. "There's a lot of work to be done. Baal is influencing powerful people. Lots of folks will suffer because of that.

"Once again, you get to choose. You can stop right now, knowing that you've done a great thing. No one will say that you're not strong in the Lord."

"Or I can continue down this path," Harris said, completing the thought.

"It's not an easy one," The Messenger said. "But you'll never have to travel it alone. The Mighty One is constantly looking for champions he can put in harm's way."

Harris thought about it for a long moment, and shrugged.

"If I say no, what life do I have to go back to? I'm still a wanted man. Katya is gone, my life as a pastor is gone, everything I cared about is gone."

"Appearances can be deceiving," The Messenger said.

Harris chuckled. "Yeah. I heard that somewhere."

He paused again. "OK, I'm still in."

"Until the end?"

"Until the very end."

The Messenger smiled and patted him on the shoulder, then disappeared.

Harris stood watching the fire for a while, trying to decide what to do. He had no one waiting for him, no one to tell that he was OK. And if he did tell them, did he endanger them? Harris was still wanted as a terrorist. He snorted. *Me? A terrorist?*

Then he had an idea. He reached into his inside coat pocket and pulled out the disposable cell phone he'd purchased yesterday. Harris had called Greg Phipps yesterday; he didn't dare try him again. But he wanted to send a message to someone he considered family.

He remembered that Katya's father carried a cell phone faithfully. Cells were easier to get than a land line in Russia. He was a pastor and Katya was calling him quite regularly. Harris thought for a long moment and remembered the number.

He typed in a text message that he thought he'd enjoy, added his international phone number, then pressed send. An international call would be expensive, but what did Harris care? He waited until it confirmed that the message was sent, then he broke the phone in half between his hands and threw both pieces into a street trash can.

Then he walked off into the night, solitary, but not alone.

* * *

The quiet of the morning in the home of Pastor Ivan Dubrovik in St. Petersburg, Russia, was broken by the shrill ring of the pastor's cell phone. He walked back into the kitchen where he'd left it in his coat pocket. He pulled it out, and looked at it for a long minute. Someone was sending him a text message. He'd never received one before.

Scratching his head, he pressed Read and the message scrawled out. The message was as puzzling as the fact that he'd received it.

"Katya," he shouted into the living room. "Katya, do you know anyone named Petrushka?"

Katya was sitting on the hardwood floor playing with 18-month-old Harris Junior. She looked up at her father, her face lost in thought. Then her eyes went wide. She grabbed the cell phone from her father and read:

It is a fearful thing to fall into the hands of the living God.

Hebrews 10:31—Petrushka.

EPILOGUE: A CALL FOR VENGEANCE

It was one of those moments when followers of the Great Satan knew better than to be before him. His wrath was legendary, and right now it was being poured out on Baal, the mighty one who himself had for thousands of years held humans and demons quaking in fear. For what seemed an eternity, bolts of pain had shot from the ether to connect with the demon. Now he cowered in a huddled mass before his master, who had the power to end his existence in an instant.

"I'm not going to kill you," Satan said, his wrath suddenly subsiding. "No, you did do some good. After all, the plan is still proceeding—although with a few adjustments." The Devil stood with a baseball bat in his hand, wielding it as if at any instant it might strike out in any direction. A faint smile crept onto his face, but then suddenly disappeared.

"I just can't imagine how you could let a human get the *best of you*." He emphasized the last three words with a smack of the baseball bat across the shoulders of the dark demon who lay prostrate before him. "*Again!*"

The four of them in the room were instantly transported in memory back to the embarrassment that had happened on Mt. Carmel. And all four of them had the same thought, though only one dared speak it.

"Could he be—the one?" Baal squeaked. "Elijah reborn?"

"Nonsense," the woman said. "He's just a wet-behind-the-ears pastor. I can prove it."

They all turned and looked at the woman/demon. Satan raised one eyebrow, paused, then nodded.

"Very well," he said. "Where power has come short, let lust take over. You have my permission to proceed with Phase Two."

The woman/demon nodded quickly at Satan and disappeared.

GLEN ROBINSON

Read on for a sneak peek at

THE HERETIC

BOOK 2 IN THE CHAMPION TRILOGY

Coming June 2013

EIGHT YEARS LATER

The sidewalk outside the Worthington Renaissance Hotel in Fort Worth was packed with reporters, each one jockeying for the best view of the breaking news. Michelle Kinkaid struggled to get a glimpse of anything newsworthy. Right now, she had a burly cameraman from Fox News and his sound guy between her and her story.

She saw a gap in the crowd and tried to squeeze through it to get in front, and immediately knew that she was a second too late. The Fox man with the boom mike shifted back and she felt herself shoved aside, losing balance and falling on her rear on the hard sidewalk. Her new digital camera swung around her neck, the weight jerking her head backwards. The Fox crew didn't even look back at her.

"Not like the old days, is it?" She heard a familiar voice, and turned from her position to see a stocky man in a faded Aerosmith T-shirt looking down at her. He smiled and reached down to help her up.

"Hello, Pudge," she said. "Yeah, we're both a long way from San Francisco."

She took his hand and pulled herself up.

"So, you're with AP now," he said, nodding toward her press badge. "Your adventures with the *Herald* didn't hold you back for too long."

"Long enough," she said. "Been freelancing for years until I could rebuild my portfolio and my rep. Associated Press here in Dallas finally decided to give me a shot. I'm the new assistant editor. Been in the office for six whole weeks now."

"And they trusted you enough to let you cover a Universal story," Pudge said, chuckling. "Well, they'll learn their mistake soon enough."

Michelle frowned at him. "It's news, Pudge. Legitimate news. And I can be just as objective as the next reporter." Michelle didn't remind him that AP had only a few domestic reporters and that she was covering this for herself.

"Right." Pudge looked forward at the camera crew he was babysitting as site producer. "Don't see much news coming out of here now. Feds have this all buttoned up pretty tight."

Michelle nodded. "Yeah, I got one crowd shot when they loaded the guy into the ambulance about 20 minutes ago. Since then, they've been pretty quiet."

"Rumor is that he's the only survivor. Not sure of what, though."

"Gunman? Don't think it was a bomb, otherwise they'd have the bomb squad here."

"Dunno." Pudge pointed at the glass doorway to the hotel. "Look, see that big guy? The one who looks like he's from Walker, Texas Ranger? That's the fed in charge. His name's Roy Bassett."

A tall, dark man in his late 40s with a Stetson hat stood talking intently with two other men in dark suits. He looked right at Michelle as he talked to them. As she locked eyes with him, a chill began to run through her.

"The dude knows you, Michelle," Pudge said. "What a break."

"Yeah," Michelle said. "Maybe."

Bassett paused for a second, then pointed directly at Michelle. The other two looked her direction, then motioned for her to come through the crowd.

Michelle looked at Pudge, grinned and shrugged.

"Remember me, darlin'." Pudge said to her as she disappeared through the crowd and into the hotel.

Michelle joined Bassett in the plush lobby of the luxury hotel. The room was buzzing with scores of police officers, FBI and crime scene investigators. Bassett grabbed her arm and walked her to the elevators.

"Michelle Kinkaid? You the reporter that used to be in San Francisco?"

Michelle nodded.

"The one who did all those stories on Universal Finance."

"Yeah, till I got canned."

"I presume that's why you're interested in this story." Bassett pushed the up button.

Michelle looked at him blankly. "I just heard on my police scanner that there was a multiple murder at the Worthington Hotel. My job is to cover all the Metroplex homicides for AP." The statement was a lie, albeit a small one. Usually the stories were covered by someone else, and she did the rewrite. But old habits are hard to break, and when she heard the call go out, she got off the freeway and joined the others clamoring for bits of information. Just like the old days.

"So you didn't know that this involved the Five."

Michelle looked at him blankly, and then it all clicked. Of course, she should have known. The Five was the nickname for the five men who were in charge of Universal Pharmaceuticals.

"Uh, no," she said, although she realized how unlikely a coincidence it seemed. She took one more look back at the crowd outside before she stepped into the elevator. "That explains a lot of things, though. I thought that was a pretty big news crowd for a simple murder."

Bassett shook his head. "Nothing simple about it. Look, I need information from you. And I've dealt with enough of you reporters to know that nothing comes free. So here's the deal: you get a peek at what's upstairs—no pictures, mind you—and in exchange you tell me everything you know about Universal."

"Deal," Michelle said without hesitation.

"And a pastor named Harris Borden," Bassett added.

Michelle looked at him and frowned. "Borden's dead. He died eight years ago."

The elevator door opened and Michelle was ushered into the presidential suite on the 12th floor. She paused at the doorway.

"Wow, someone was partying hearty," she muttered. She looked at the massive table set out with every conceivable delicacy. She then looked at the far end of the table and saw that a body lay on the floor, police investigators still busy taking pictures of it from all angles.

"Wasn't Borden behind the Jade Tower massacre?" Bassett said to her from the doorway.

Michelle looked back at him. "No," she said, shaking her head. "No, like I said, he died in prison. The guy at the Jade Tower was named Elijah Brown."

"Right," Bassett said. "Funny thing is, Borden and Brown were cell mates at San Dimas, and the description of this Elijah Brown sounds a lot like this pastor."

Michelle stared at Bassett for a long second. Borden was gone, dead. He had pursued Universal, more than she had ever been willing to pursue them. And he had died for his efforts.

"No," she said, after thinking about it for a moment. "Not possible."

Bassett stared at her, his dark eyes scanning her as if trying to read her mind. "OK, then I want you to pretend, just pretend, that you didn't know that Borden is dead. All things being equal, if you were me, who would you say is the likeliest suspect for this?" He strode quickly across the room and to the bedroom, motioning for her to follow. Michelle first saw the huge bed covered with a pile of bodies. Some were naked, others were dressed. All of them looked as if they had died in terrible agony.

"Not a drop of blood on them, no visible wounds, no obvious external trauma," Bassett said. "It was a great party for a while. But someone had a problem with them." He gestured to one wall that had four words in red that appeared to be written on it:

Mene, Mene, Tekel, Upharsin.

"That's Hebrew isn't it?" Bassett asked Michelle, who stood in shock in the doorway. She paused, then shook herself when she realized that Bassett had asked her a question.

"Yes, it's from the Book of Daniel, in the Old Testament," Michelle said. "Roughly translated, it means your number is up, and you aren't going to survive the night."

"That's what I thought," Bassett said. "You know, ma'am, after 35 years in crime work, I've seen a lot of things, some of them even with religious overtones. But this is the first time I've come across this particular passage of scripture in a homicide investigation. So I ask you again: all things being equal, knowing that Universal is involved, and knowing that there is a religious angle in all of this, who would be your first suspect?"

But he's dead, Michelle said to herself, staring silently at Bassett.

Or was he?

* * *

The leaded glass doors of The Buzz swung in and a young, black college student stepped in, a guitar case in his right hand. He paused for a second to let his eyes adjust to the gloom and looked around. He heard the latest hit from Tori Ash playing overhead, and the few diners who were there bobbed with the music whether they wanted to or not. Finally he saw the face he was looking for, seated in the corner booth. A broad smile split his face and his long legs carried him across the room in three strides.

The old man waiting for him rose to greet him. Smiling, he held out both hands and clasped the young man's.

"Dougie," he said affectionately, then pulled him into an embrace. "Good to see you."

"You too, Pastor Phipps," the young man said as they sat down in the booth. "And if you don't mind, I go by D.J. now."

Greg Phipps paused a second, then nodded. "D.J. it is. A young man gets out on his own in the world, he should have the right to decide what the world calls him."

D.J. looked down at that, his hand coming to his mouth. "Well, sometimes the world calls you what it wants whether you like it or not." Greg's eyebrow raised, and D.J. paused before waving his hand.

"It's nothing. It's just that some of the black kids feel I grew up in the wrong part of town. It leads to nicknames." He cleared his throat. "Not a big deal."

Greg chuckled. "Well, nicknames, that's another issue. I've had my share over the years. You should hear some of the names I got in the mission field." He paused. "On second thought, I probably don't think I should repeat them."

A young waitress wearing the distinctive TA circle earrings from the Tori Ash collection came to the table and asked for their order.

"Water for me," Greg said.

"I'll have a Sprite, please," D.J. said. She left.

"Anyway, it was good you were able to come by and see me, Pastor Phipps."

"Well, my meetings are in Roseville, so it's wasn't much of a stretch for me to come up here and see you." Pause. "How's your mom?"

D.J. shrugged. "Same as always. Holding her own. She moved into an apartment in Sacramento, and is working as a secretary downtown."

Greg smiled. "I'll make a point of seeing her before I head back to Nevada." He put his arm on Greg's shoulder. "But I had to come by and see our scholar first. You know, you're the first youth—first *person*—from our church to ever win a scholarship, much less a full scholarship.

"So what are you majoring in?"

"The essay I won the scholarship for was on the future of America, so they expected me to major in political science," D.J. said, fiddling with the Equal packets in the middle of the table.

The waitress returned, and D.J. dropped his straw into the iced Sprite.

"Expect you?"

"Well, I'm taking the classes, but I'm not sure that's what I want to do with my life." D.J. stared across the room at a young female student who stood talking to the waitress at the counter. "She's new," he muttered to himself. The blonde girl turned briefly as if she had heard him, and flashed a gorgeous smile. D.J. felt his face flush.

"D.J., college is the place where it's supposed to be safe to try new things out, to decide what you want to do with your life. Nothing is set in stone. Just make sure that you let God lead your life."

D.J. continued to stare at the girl, who had returned to talk to the waitress. Then he remembered that Greg was talking to him. He turned back to the retired pastor, who sat looking at him with an amused smile.

"College is also a place where you get to know others your age," Greg said. "Sometimes others that happen to be girls."

D.J. suddenly grew embarrassed, and looked at the floor. Greg chuckled.

"Look, D.J., I need to head out, but before I go, do you mind if I pray for us?"

"Sure, Pastor."

The two bowed their head while Greg prayed for D.J. and his mother. D.J. felt a little uncomfortable bowing his head in this very secular environment, especially among those who he saw in class every day. But he got a warm feeling—a feeling of home—being surrounded by the prayer of Pastor Phipps, his father figure.

Greg finished the prayer and stood to go. He hugged D.J.

"Remember to stay in touch, Dougie—I mean, D.J. And remember what I said, make sure that you let God lead your life."

Dougie nodded, and waved as Greg exited the coffee shop. He paused, then turned toward the waitress, who was cleaning glasses in the near-empty room.

"Pardon me," D.J. said. "That girl you were talking to. Who is she?"

* * *

The organist droned on while the chorister led the congregation into the third stanza of "Nearer, My God to Thee." Dr. Frank Hollis struggled to hide an ironic grin as he looked around the scattered crowd in the church. *Didn't they sing that as the Titanic went down? Appropriate.* He sat in the back row and looked across at two toddlers fighting over the last few Cheerios in a plastic bag on their mother's lap. Normally, he found solace in the predictable security of church service. Today it was annoying.

His cell phone vibrated. *Not as annoying as that cell phone.* That was the fourth time in the last 10 minutes it had rung. He looked at who it was without answering it. It was his business manager. *Not today, Dick.* He let it stop buzzing and tried to concentrate on the program up front. Some snotty-nosed kid was reading the scripture now.

They finished the scripture and stood for prayer. Frank was just sitting down when someone touched him on the arm. It was one of the ushers.

"There's an urgent call for you on the office phone, Dr. Hollis."

Frank stood and followed the usher into the lobby and through it to the pastor's office. *If that's Dick again, I will not be happy.*

"This is Dr. Hollis," he said into the phone.

"Frank, this is Dick Summersby." Frank started to speak, but didn't get a word in before Dick continued.

"I apologize for calling you at church, but I have news that will rock your world. Rock *our* world, partner."

"And that is?"

"Universal is out, Murcheson-Settle is in! After what happened two days ago in Texas with the Universal honchos, the CDC pulled the contract for the Hale's Disease serum and gave it to us. When the market opens on Monday, our stock is going to go *through the roof!*"

Frank paused as he tried to soak the news in. "So Dick...Dick...what's the bottom line here? What are we talking about?"

"The bottom line is, *Frankie-boy*, that you, your children, and your children's children will never, ever have to worry about paying your bills *ever* again!

Dick Summersby was still hooting loudly as Frank Hollis put the receiver down and walked out of the office. Pastor Leigh Brackett was already into his sermon for the morning, but Frank didn't hear a word he said.

He would have trouble hearing anyone's words today.

ABOUT THE AUTHOR

Glen Robinson is a university professor and the author of numerous books in both Christian suspense and science fiction. His best-known books are the Christian end-time novel *If Tomorrow Comes* and *Infinity's Reach*, the modern retelling of *Pilgrim's Progress*. This is his 13th book in print. He lives in north Texas.